"I thought about you, Darcie."

"What?"

"You should know that. I thought about you a lot. And it meant a lot to me, making love. Our first time."

Darcie's muscles jumped. Her right heel skidded on the worn flooring, and she sat down again, hard.

"I used to wake up," Zeke said, "and know I'd dreamt about you again. I could still smell you. It was like the scent and taste of you were inside a box, and I could keep it locked when I was awake, but when I slept it came free."

He faced her and she could see his desire clearly. "I still dream of you," he said softly.

Now she knew why she'd pushed him away. Why she hadn't listened to Jennifer's certainty that Zeke had fallen for her. Why she'd been afraid.

Because this was real.

Dear Reader,

This beautiful month of April we have six very special reads for you, starting with *Falling for the Boss* by Elizabeth Harbison, this month's installment in our FAMILY BUSINESS continuity. Watch what happens when two star-crossed high school sweethearts get a second chance—only this time they're on opposite sides of the boardroom table! Next, bestselling author RaeAnne Thayne pays us a wonderful and emotional visit in Special Edition with her new miniseries, THE COWBOYS OF COLD CREEK. In *Light the Stars*, the first book in the series, a frazzled single father is shocked to hear that his mother (not to mention babysitter) eloped—with a supposed scam artist. So what is he to do when said scam artist's lovely daughter turns up on his doorstep? Find out (and don't miss next month's book in this series, *Dancing in the Moonlight*). In Patricia McLinn's *What Are Friends For?*, the first in her SEASONS IN A SMALL TOWN duet, a female police officer is reunited—with the guy who got away. Maybe she'll be able to detain him this time....

Jessica Bird concludes her MOOREHOUSE LEGACY series with *From the First*, in which Alex Moorehouse finally might get the woman he could never stop wanting. Only problem is, she's a recent widow—and her late husband was Alex's best friend. In Karen Sandler's *Her Baby's Hero*, a couple looks for that happy ending even though the second time they meet, she's six months' pregnant with his twins! And in *The Last Cowboy* by Crystal Green, a woman desperate for motherhood learns that "the last cowboy will make you a mother." But real cowboys don't exist anymore...or do they?

So enjoy, and don't forget to come back next month. Everything will be in bloom....

Have fun.

Gail Chasan
Senior Editor

Please address questions and book requests to:
Silhouette Reader Service
U.S.: 3010 Walden Ave., P.O. Box 1325, Buffalo, NY 14269
Canadian: P.O. Box 609, Fort Erie, Ont. L2A 5X3

WHAT ARE FRIENDS FOR?

PATRICIA McLINN

SPECIAL EDITION®

Published by Silhouette Books

America's Publisher of Contemporary Romance

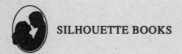

SILHOUETTE BOOKS

ISBN 0-373-24749-4

WHAT ARE FRIENDS FOR?

Copyright © 2006 by Patricia McLaughlin

Visit Silhouette Books at www.eHarlequin.com

Printed in U.S.A.

Books by Patricia McLinn

PATRICIA McLINN

finds great satisfaction in transferring the characters crowded in her head onto paper to be enjoyed by readers. "Writing," she says, "is the hardest work I'd never give up." Writing has brought her new experiences, places and friends—especially friends. After degrees from Northwestern University, newspaper jobs have taken her from Illinois to North Carolina to Washington, D.C. Patricia now lives in Virginia, in a house that grows piles of paper, books and dog hair at an alarming rate. The paper and books are her own fault, but the dog hair comes from a charismatic collie, who helps put things in perspective when neighborhood kids refer to Patricia as "the lady who lives in Riley's house." She would love to hear from readers at P.O. Box 7052, Arlington, VA 22207 or you can check out her Web site at www.PatriciaMcLinn.com.

This is dedicated to Lombard, Illinois, my hometown. To its people, past and present, who have been true friends. And to the Helen M. Plum Memorial Library, which has fostered many a reader over the years. Keep those lilacs blooming!

Chapter One

"You were about two words short of giving the whole thing away, you know that, Zeke?"

Without breaking stride Anton Zeekowsky looked down at Peter Quincy, his best friend and VP of public relations, as they followed a sunny corridor to his office.

"Sorry."

"Sorry? We've been preparing the launch of Z-Zap for nearly a year. A year—and you almost gave it away to that reporter. You're a loose cannon. God, I wish I could stash you on a deserted island for the next few weeks. I wonder if Elba's available."

What else could Zeke say, besides he was sorry? *I forgot?* He didn't think that would go over any better, though chances were good that Quince, who'd been his college roommate, knew that's exactly what had happened.

Zeke's mind had been on the future. Working on new

problems, new challenges. He simply forgot Z-Zap was still a secret. It seemed a long time ago that he'd had the idea that became Z-Zap. And, to be totally honest, he wasn't interested in the project anymore. It was done, solved, completed. No more challenge.

He especially wasn't interested in the launch. Which Quince also knew and also didn't want to hear.

"Can you slow down, Zeke? We already worked out today." Quince heaved a gusty breath as Zeke slowed his pace. "Next time I'm going to work for a boss who's not six-five."

Zeke chuckled. Quince was six foot himself, and besides, he'd always worked with him. Always would.

That thought triggered a vague memory. What was it his assistant had said about Quince? Something about Zeke paying attention to his VP for public relations' job satisfaction or he'd be without a VP for public relations. Brenda was often right about things like that, as she never let him forget, but Quince would never leave. Still…

"I am sorry about the interview," Zeke said.

"I know."

Quince had worked hard on the interview's setup, then had unceremoniously yanked Zeke away and passed the reporter over to Vanessa Irish, Zeke's partner. Vanessa was brilliant with organization and finances, not to mention a heck of a lot easier to look at, but for some reason reporters wanted to talk to him. All Zeke wanted to do was work on the next puzzle.

"If I screwed up and let it slip about Z-Zap, there'll be another launch for you to orchestrate. Isn't Z-Pix coming out…uh, soon?"

"October tenth, Zeke. October tenth." The way Quince said it, Zeke knew he'd been told before. Quince continued, "And there'll be more after that. So many that I'm exhausted.

I wish you had a hobby or something so you couldn't be so damned productive."

Quince sighed again, this one so deep and heartfelt, that Zeke was reminded of Brenda's warning.

Zeke frowned as they turned into his office suite. Brenda immediately stood and began spouting messages while she and Quince trailed him into his office.

"…and the last item is from your hometown—"

"Throw it out."

"But—"

"From his hometown? What is it?" Quince asked. His promotion antenna practically quivering, he took the paper from Brenda.

"An invitation—" she started.

"To yet another reunion," Zeke cut in. "Come on back to good old Drago High and relive those wonderful days when you were a geeky outsider ridiculed by the student body. No thanks."

"Doesn't your mother still live in Drago?" Quince asked absently.

"Yeah. I can't pry her away. At least not permanently. She'll visit, but just when I think I've persuaded her to move here, she announces it's time to go back."

"He always makes her come here for visits, never goes home to see her," Brenda volunteered.

"Thank you, Brenda," Zeke said with his best sarcasm. "You can go now."

She shrugged, but didn't budge.

"This isn't an invitation to a reunion." Quince said, studying the page.

"Then route it to the foundation."

"It's not hitting you up for a donation, either. They're inviting you to be Grand Marshal of the Drago Lilac Festival parade, head judge of the Drago Lilac Queen pageant and guest of honor at the Drago Lilac Festival dance. Got a few lilacs in Drago?"

That sweet, spicy scent. Spring of senior year, standing a block away from the parade route, well back from the crowds along the curb waving at the bands and clowns and floats. Something had drawn Zeke there, though he would *not* stand at the curb and gawk with the rest of them. He'd leaned against a tree, separate from the parade and the crowd.

And then came the float he'd been waiting for—the one with the Lilac Queen and her court. There were pale purple and white flowers everywhere—he thought he could smell them even from this distance. A flash of hair gleaming in the sun, faces smiling, hands waving. Then it was gone.

Abruptly, Zeke realized he hadn't answered Quince. Brenda was watching him with interest.

Quince was looking at the letter. "It's signed by Darcie Barrett— Do you know her?"

Zeke felt a tug at his mouth. Darcie, sitting across the chemistry lab table from him, grinning as she recited that poem—again—until he was about to go nuts.

"Darcie was a friend." The only person in Drago he'd ever thought of that way.

"Kept in touch?" Quince asked.

Zeke turned away, and picked up the mail Brenda had opened. "No. She left town, too. She must have let them use her name for this festival."

"How about Jennifer Truesdale?" Quince asked, shaking the letter. "She signed along with Darcie Barrett. It says they're co-chairs of—"

Zeke didn't look up. "You mean Jennifer Truesdale Stenner."

"It just says Jennifer Truesdale."

He snatched the paper from Quince. "Let me see that."

Quince let it go willingly. Zeke was aware of him moving

to the computer, bringing a large flat-panel screen on the wall to life, but his attention was on the paper.

There it was, printed in black on white: Jennifer Truesdale. No Stenner cluttering up the end.

Jennifer Truesdale had dumped Eric Stenner? *The* couple of Drago High had split up? She was available?

Anton Zeekowsky, founder and owner of a technology company that not only had weathered the dot-com bust but had come out of it stronger, couldn't form any other coherent thought. Zeke's brain short-circuited the way it had in high school at the mention of Jennifer Truesdale when a glimpse of her long blond hair and pouty lips could put him out of commission for days.

"So, where is Drago?" Quince demanded, looking at a map of Illinois on the wall screen.

"Southwest of Chicago," Zeke answered automatically. "West of Kankakee, east of Peoria."

"And this Jennifer Truesdale?"

"Nobody."

Brenda harrumphed, hands on hips. "No matter who she is, what you should be looking at is the other letter that came in the envelope. It's from your mother. Asking you—begging you—to accept the invitation and finally come home for a visit. How you can treat that sweet woman this way, I will never understand."

Before he could defend himself by reminding Brenda that he brought his mother here to visit as often as she would come, provided her with as many conveniences as she would accept and called twice weekly, Quince crowed from behind him.

Zeke turned and saw that Quince had zoomed in on the dot on the map that was Drago, Illinois.

"I think we just found your Elba, Zeke."

* * *

"Keep your hands up!"

"Officer—"

"Be quiet. Now, back up toward me. Slow...slow..."

Darcie Barrett eyed the figure inching backward across the parking lot of the long-closed D-Shop discount store. Broad shoulders tapered to narrow hips. A one-on-one tussle might be a struggle if this guy was in as good shape as he appeared to be. So she'd make sure it didn't come to that.

Especially since she really should have waited for backup.

The driver had responded promptly to her patrol car's flashing lights by pulling into the empty parking lot—the dark, empty parking lot. That might indicate this wasn't the armed and dangerous kidnapper, last seen driving a sporty red or orange import car, possibly headed west on Illinois Route 285. But if this *was* the car the APB had come in about...

Maybe this guy thought he could pull something. Or talk his way around her. All the while, a little girl could be terrified or hurt, and this could be the scumball who knew where. Maybe even in the car.

That thought had motivated Darcie to act quickly. She'd given the dispatcher her location and the plate to run—as soon as the computers came back up. And then she'd started the drill to get the guy out of his car and under her control. Slowly. Giving her backup time to get here, because she was no hero.

She stayed behind her open car door, both for protection and so she could give chase faster if he dove back into his car and tried to make a run for it.

"Okay. That's far enough. Get on the ground. Face down."

He looked over his shoulder, squinting hard against the glare of her headlights. The effort twisted his face into a grimace exaggerated by the harsh lights and drastic shadows. Why was he looking at her? Was he checking to see if she was alone?

"Officer, if you would—"

"On the ground! Now! Don't turn around!"

He'd started to turn more fully toward her. She sighted her gun on him.

Maybe he saw that from the corner of his eye, because he turned away from her and lowered himself to the ground without another word.

"Spread your legs and put your arms out straight."

He complied.

She heard a siren coming nearer. The sound dipped, meaning the car was going under the railroad viaduct at Main Street. Another three blocks.

She should wait. Just a couple more minutes.

What if that little girl didn't have a couple more minutes?

She eased out from behind the car door and moved quickly to his side, pulling out the cuffs as she put one knee to his back. He grunted.

"Hands behind your back—now!"

She slapped the cuffs on him—one, two—and checked them. Then she breathed. The siren cut off as her backup pulled in front of the suspect's car to box it in.

"Okay, get up." She tugged at the cuffs, then backed away so she could keep the gun on him without being so close he could knock it away. "On the car—no, face the car."

"Got him," Benny said from off to her left.

"I'm going to pat you down," she told the driver. "Do you have anything in your pockets I should know about? A gun? Anything sharp? A needle?"

"Officer, if you would tell me—"

"Do you have anything in—"

"No."

She patted the front jeans pockets over narrow hips, found nothing more than a key ring and nothing in the waistband.

Around to the back—a very firm back—where she pulled out a wallet and put it on the trunk. Down the legs and around the ankles. Nothing.

Darcie was starting to get a strange feeling about this man.

Another car came into the lot and stopped. The door opened and she could hear the radio squawking.

"Okay, turn around."

A part of her she'd thought had sunk into permanent hibernation noticed that the front was as good as the back. He was tall—a good six inches above her five-ten—and had the kind of face where even with part of it in deep shadow, you could see the bones had been put together well.

"Darcie!" Sarge called from the newly arrived car. "This isn't the guy. They got him and the kid at a motel out on I-55. The kid's okay."

Through the buzz of adrenaline and relief—*the kid was okay*—Darcie knew she needed to make an instant switch from tough, in-charge cop to charmingly apologetic public servant.

"I'm sorry for this, sir. There was a kidnapping this afternoon. A little girl and—"

"They finally got the computers back up and Corine ran that plate you gave her, Darcie," Sarge was saying.

"Darcie?" the no-longer-a-suspect repeated.

She continued her explanation, "The description of the suspect's car matched the—"

"It's a rental." Sarge called. "Rented to—"

"Darcie Barrett? It's me, Zeke—"

"—car you're driving," she finished.

"Zeekowsky," the non-suspect and Sarge ended together.

The voice was lower, the body was a whole different thing entirely, like a sapling that had turned into an oak. The face had filled out, too, though she now could recognize those strong bones as the stark ones she had first observed closely on her lab partner.

"Omigod! Zeke. How long has it been?"

Now if that wasn't the most inane thing she'd ever said. As if she wanted to bring that up at all, much less first thing. Besides, they both knew the last time they'd seen each other had been the day they'd graduated from high school. More accurately, the night.

Unless he'd forgotten.

"I don't know what to say," she added.

He chuckled—dry, assured, even a little wicked. Quite unlike the almost always serious guy who'd been her lab partner. "Well, I do—can you take these handcuffs off me?"

Oh, God. Oh, God!

She had put the Lilac Festival Grand Marshal, Chief Judge, Guest of Honor and potential savior of the Village of Drago in handcuffs.

Not a great start.

"Hey, Zeke! Welcome back to Drago," Benny said.

Right before her eyes, this new Zeke morphed into an echo of the high school Zeke—the Zeke who'd shut down when he had to deal with strangers.

"You wouldn't remember Benny," she said. "He'd graduated by the time we were in high school."

"Yeah, don't remember you at all, but Darce talked me into buying stock in Zeke-Tech when it went public."

'She talked all of us into it," said Sarge. "And she wouldn't let any of us sell. Even when it dipped along with the rest of the market, she was a bulldog chewing on our tails to hold on. With that stock split last year it's looking good to send my kids to college."

Sarge's long-windedness appeared to have given Zeke time to recover.

"I'm glad," he said. It wasn't eloquent but it sounded sincere, and when he shook hands with Benny and Sarge, he looked the other men in the eyes, and she could tell they were completely won over.

"Say, why don't you come down to the station and take a look at our setup," invited Sarge. "We got the best coffee in town, and doughnuts."

"No, thank you."

The abrupt refusal seemed to deflate the other two police officers, but not Darcie. After that year as lab partners, she knew that *No, thank you* was actually a big improvement on *No, that's wrong,* which was a step up from *You screwed that up. Again.*

Zeke knew tech like nobody's business. Tact? Forget it.

"Give the guy a break, Sarge. He's just gotten into town. He probably wants to get home, see his mom, get some rest."

"His mom's not at home. She's at bingo at St. Ambrose's. It's Monday."

"Oh, right." She was losing it if she'd forgotten bingo night. "And that means you can't get in the house, Zeke. Unless you have a key?"

"No. I'll go to St. Ambrose's."

"I wouldn't recommend it," Darcie said, talking over hoots from Benny and Sarge. "It could be worth your life if you interrupt."

"Couple years ago they had a fire alarm, and one woman whacked the fireman trying to get her out with her purse. Kept yelling she was one square away, one square away," Sarge said.

"I'll get some coffee at the café."

Darcie shook her head. "Closed on Mondays. Loris plays bingo, too."

"Crenna's, then."

"Closed down three, four years ago," Benny said.

"And Dairy Queen's not open for the season yet," Sarge added. "Like I said, best coffee's at the police station."

Zeke raised his hands in surrender.

"Why don't you and Benny go ahead, Sarge. I'll lead him back to the station," Darcie volunteered.

After more handshaking, the other officers departed, leaving her with Zeke in the gloomy parking lot.

He scanned her face, then glanced down at the uniform that identified her as one of Drago's finest. His brows lowered. "I never expected to see you like this. I guess this explains why your signature was on that letter."

What did being a Drago cop have to do with being co-chair with Jennifer of the town's biggest event?

"We better get going. If we don't show up at the station soon, there'll be another APB out, and this time it *will* be for you."

She turned toward her car and took two steps when his voice came from behind her. "Uh, Darcie?"

She pulled in one long breath through her mouth, then released it slowly through her nose as she faced him. "Yes."

"It's good to see you, Darcie."

"It's good to see you, too."

Now there was an understatement—considering what she hoped to get out of him during these next three weeks.

"We've been having trouble with the darned things for months," Sarge said around another doughnut, jerking his head toward the bank of computers that Corine, the night dispatcher, commanded.

Doughnut number two left Sarge four behind Zeke. There was one thing that hadn't changed about Zeke since high school.

Darcie's shift had ended ten minutes ago. She'd put away her equipment, signed in her squad car and taken care of other details. When she'd returned to the bull pen housed in the basement of Village Hall, Zeke hadn't budged. She could have waved breezily and walked away. The sole reason she hadn't was that she didn't want Sarge and Benny to mess up what she and Jennifer had planned.

"We've had experts out the wazoo crawling all over this system, but when we have a lot going on, like that APB tonight, it crashes. At the worst possible time."

"Something could be drawing power all the time, but you only notice when the system can't respond."

"Yeah, that makes sense," Sarge said, with a wise nod.

Corine snorted. "I told you that the first night it happened, Archibald." She was the only one who got away with calling him that. Corine had been with the department longer than he had. She'd been with the department longer than anybody. "I'm thinking it's a hacker. Maybe that Wellton kid. He's always getting packages delivered to him. Off the Internet," she added portentously.

Corine found anyone who ordered off the Internet inherently suspicious.

"A hacker?" Sarge scoffed. "You back on that? That guy from Chicago said no way. He said if there ever had been a hacker, he was long gone and that wouldn't still be affecting the system."

"Not necessarily," Zeke said.

"Hah!" Corine smirked.

Sarge gave her a half-hearted scowl before presenting Zeke with an expression of earnest interest.

"Really? No one would know better than the CEO of Zeke-Tech, that's for sure. I bet you know a couple hundred gigabytes more than that guy from Chicago. Say!" he said as if he'd just thought of the idea, when Darcie would bet her next six months' pay that he'd been maneuvering for this since the moment he'd realized who Zeke was back there in the

D-Shop parking lot. "Maybe you could look, see if you spot what's wrong."

"You are not going to ask the CEO of Zeke-Tech to fix our computers," Darcie said. "Do you have any idea what his time goes for? You'd have to cut your pension in half to pay for him just putting his hand on the mouse."

Sarge blanched. That's what she'd thought—he'd been angling for a freebie. The old opportunist was not going to try to weasel time out of Zeke when Darcie had much bigger plans.

"I, uh, thought—"

"And surely you weren't going to hit up Zeke for free work. Do you know how many requests he gets every week for donations, for assistance? An average of thirty-seven hundred—more than five hundred a day, including weekends." She shook her head, which required no acting. She'd also shaken her head when she'd read that statistic. A man hounded that much would have to build effective defenses. "We invited Zeke to come home as the honored guest of his hometown for the festival. We're not going to start after him for things. We're just glad he's home."

She might have overdone the home stuff. Zeke swiveled his chair to stare at her. Not quite the intent look he used to give her in the lab when he was in scientist-in-command mode. Nor the even more intent look the night before he left Drago...

No, definitely not that look.

This was more the way he had looked at her in the parking lot earlier tonight when he'd squinted his gray eyes against the lights. Like he was trying to bring her into sharp focus.

She'd just as soon he didn't succeed.

Sarge was falling over himself to absolutely deny what Darcie had caught him at when they were interrupted by a new arrival.

"Hello."

That's all it took. No one moved, as if caught in a spell.

The husky voice came from the stairway behind them. "I heard at the club that you'd arrived in town, Zeke. What a pleasure it is to have you back home in Drago."

Zeke rose and turned toward Jennifer Truesdale, who had stopped with one foot on the bottom step and the other a step above.

Darcie didn't need to turn her head to know what he would see—blond hair, smooth skin, big blue eyes and a figure that might be even better than it had been in high school.

So she watched Zeke's eyes. She saw them light up as if he'd spotted the promised land.

If they'd all been back in high school, Darcie could have hated Jennifer. Darcie had been everyone's buddy, Jennifer had been everyone's princess. No, make that queen— homecoming, prom and, of course, Lilac Queen.

In fact, Darcie *tried* to hate Jennifer when they were younger. But even then she'd seen an innate niceness in the most popular girl in town. In the past few years they'd become real friends. Darcie was one of the few who knew exactly how far Jennifer's life was from the golden image most people conjured when they looked at her.

So she couldn't even hate Jennifer for causing that dopey look on Zeke's face.

"Zeke, is it really you? I can hardly believe it! I mean, we've seen pictures, of course, with those articles in the business magazines, but you look amazing. Docsn't he look fabulous, Darcie?"

"Just great," she muttered. Not that it mattered. Zeke had forgotten her existence entirely.

Unfortunately Jennifer hadn't, giving her an assessing look. Oh, hell.

"I'm sure Darcie's filled you in on the festival schedule, Zeke, and—"

"Actually, we didn't get around to that," Darcie said, adding quickly to keep Zeke from mentioning drawn guns, frisking and handcuffs. "We'll get him a copy of the schedule in the morning and go over it then."

"Good idea." Jennifer slipped her coat off with the ease of a runway model, revealing a deep purple dress that shimmered subtly with every move. Its skirt widened before stopping above the knees, revealing slender calves above delicate feet shown off by strappy black heels. Darcie knew Jennifer had been at Drago Country Club tonight, but only because her boss had invited her. "We can adjust some of the times if they don't work for you, Zeke, because we want to make this fun for you."

Jennifer continued talking about the festival with low-key cheerfulness. Darcie suspected she'd be good at selling real estate—if anyone around Drago had the money to buy a new house.

Darcie's attention stuck on the picture Jennifer made standing there in that purple dress. Darcie knew the dress was more than a decade old, the wear hidden by taking in seams when Jennifer lost weight a few years ago on the going-through-a-bitch-of-a-divorce diet. Darcie had been with her when Jennifer paid six dollars for the shoes at a consignment store in Chicago.

Still, Darcie's on-duty shoes had never felt clunkier, her uniform more blandly utilitarian—and designed for men to boot—her hair more brown and her body... Oh, hell. She never had been in Jennifer's class.

"Ashley?" Jennifer interrupted herself,

At that single word, Darcie jolted out of her self-absorption. She twisted around to see Jennifer's twelve-year-old daughter coming down the stairs.

Ashley was adolescent gawky, but the promise of great beauty had earned her the solitary Junior Princess spot on this year's Lilac Festival court—an honor that had given Jennifer major headaches with her previously shy and well-behaved daughter.

"What are you doing here, Ashley?" Jennifer asked. "You're supposed to be at Cristina's."

Color flooded the girl's cheeks, her chin came up and her mouth set with the mulishness Jennifer had been sighing over to Darcie two days ago.

"I wanted to see if he—" her gaze touched Zeke, then bounced away, though she didn't meet her mother's eyes, either "—had really come."

"My sister sent her to find out," said a new voice. A voice crackling and popping between childhood and adulthood.

A stocky figure stood behind Ashley. From the way everyone else peered into the shadows, she wasn't alone in having overlooked thirteen-year-old Warren Wellton.

Now Darcie had a good idea what happened. Cristina Wellton, Warren's older sister, a contender for the title of Lilac Festival Queen and Ashley's hero at the moment, had wanted confirmation of Zeke's arrival, along with a scouting report. But Cristina knew, or feared, Jennifer would be on hand and it was against the rules for contestants to meet judges outside official events until the queen was chosen. So she'd sent Ashley as her proxy.

But how had any of these people known Zeke was in town, much less that he'd ended up at the police station?

"Hello, Warren," Jennifer said. "How did you get here? It's late and…"

"Mrs. Wellton drove us," Ashley said.

"But—" Jennifer started.

"It's okay, Mrs. Stenner. She's okay," Warren said, hesitantly coming down three stairs.

Benny and Sarge frowned at him, still outraged that last summer he'd broken into Benny's patrol car and somehow rigged the radio so it only received a hip-hop station. That had infuriated Benny. Sarge had laughed about it until the cost to replace the radio came out of his budget.

But Warren wasn't the lost cause her fellow cops thought he was, she was sure of it. Her heart twisted for him, because he had to assure people his mother was okay to drive, and, especially, because his mother wasn't always okay to drive.

"I hope my daughter didn't inconvenience your mom too much, or you," Jennifer said to the boy with a warm smile.

"It's just Warren," Ashley started in apparent disgust at her mother's concern for Warren's convenience.

Zeke interrupted. "My God, she's your daughter, Jennifer?"

Ashley preened a bit—something Darcie had never seen her do before. No doubt she'd interpreted Zeke's expression as amazement at her beauty.

Darcie wondered if Zeke's reaction instead resembled her own amazement that anybody their age could have a kid who was almost a teenager when Darcie didn't feel any older than that herself.

Zeke turned from Ashley to Jennifer, and Darcie knew it didn't matter why he was astonished. The bottom line was that he still looked at Jennifer with awe.

At some level, Darcie heard Jennifer confirming that yes, Ashley was her daughter. But her thoughts were otherwise occupied.

What had she expected? That everything had changed in the past sixteen years? Darcie was proud that she'd matured enough to see the good in Jennifer, to become her friend. But expecting Zeke to stop being gaga over Jennifer was foolish.

She'd known that in high school. On graduation night she'd known exactly how things stood—and she'd still jumped him.

"What's going on here?" The deep voice of the latest newcomer to the doorway at the top of the stairs—this place had never been so popular—boomed the demand through the bull pen.

Corine spun her chair back to the console, Warren shrank against the wall as much as his solid build would allow, Darcie wished she'd left on time and Sarge and Benny launched into overlapping, hurried and self-exculpatory explanations of the evening's events.

Chief Dutch Harnett had arrived.

Great, just what she needed. The hard-nosed outsider who'd taken over Drago's police department almost a year ago, and who showed no sign of being a big Darcie Barrett fan.

"So there was no sense," Sarge was saying, wrapping up his explanation, "in Zeke going home—"

"My mother's house," Zeke said under his breath.

"—since she'd be at bingo. So we brought him here to give him a cup a coffee and some doughnuts to relax after…" Sarge trailed off with an apologetic look at Darcie.

She stood at attention. "After I stopped his car as matching the APB." No need to explain that. Chief Harnett seemed to hear every scrap of radio traffic, no way would he have missed an APB. "And put him in handcuffs."

That drew a wide range of responses. Jennifer gasped. Ashley gaped. Warren laughed. Zeke said, "No big deal."

None of those reactions particularly surprised Darcie. The one that did was the chief's. His brows drew down in a scowl and his mouth was straight, but she could swear his eyes glinted with amusement.

He cleared his throat. "As long as there's no harm done and Mr. Zeekowsky doesn't want to file a complaint…"

"No. I'm glad Darcie was looking for the guy."

"Then, since bingo broke up nearly half an hour ago, I'd say it's time for Mr. Zeekowsky to go home—to his mother's house," the chief corrected, proving he'd heard Zeke earlier. "Barrett, accompany Mr. Zeekowsky."

"Why? His car runs fine, and he knows how to get there."

"Officer Barrett?" No twinkling this time in the chief's eyes.

"I'm off duty," she grumbled.

"There's no need," Zeke started.

"Officer Barrett will accompany you," the chief said without looking away from Darcie, "to ensure nothing further untoward happens."

Chapter Two

Darcie had had better shifts, she acknowledged as she trailed Zeke's car through Drago's quiet streets.

Putting handcuffs on one of the New Technology's best minds—or so said *Time* magazine—in the mistaken fear he might be a child kidnapper and molester was not the sort of thing that made it onto a list of career highlights. Add in that she had designs on this particular mind, along with its wallet, and this was not the best start.

All of which wouldn't have been so bad if that best mind and its wallet hadn't belonged to someone she hadn't seen since graduation night. Which wouldn't have been so bad if on that same night she hadn't given her virginity to the guy in the backseat of his parents' sedan.

Which still wouldn't have been so bad if he hadn't been wishing at the same time that he were losing *his* virginity to someone else.

The someone else who had walked into the police station looking even better than she usually did.

Now *that* was a bad shift.

Darcie parked at the curb in front of the tidy white frame house with green shutters and got out, but left the door open, looking over the top of her car at Zeke. He'd pulled into the driveway and gotten out of his snazzy rental.

"I'll say good night," she said.

"Wait a minute. I've got something for you."

Not waiting for an answer, he turned, flipped the front seat down and bent in.

She closed her car door softly so as not to disturb the neighborhood, and walked up the driveway.

Zeke's position pulled his jeans taut across his hard butt. Her palms tingled. She knew how hard because she'd felt it.

Oh, only in passing, and at the time it had been totally businesslike. But she'd taught herself to mentally record everything that happened during a stop like tonight's so she could replay details later, for reports and in court. The prosecutor loved her.

At this moment, however, she wished she had an erase button on her memory—especially her tactile memory—because the tape of a certain few minutes was replaying entirely without her permission.

His upper body was hidden from sight in the dimness of the car. Didn't matter. The tape zoomed in on the broadness of his shoulders, on the line of muscle under her hand as she'd brought his arms together to clap on the handcuffs and on the way the V of his arms echoed the shape of his torso.

He shifted and the porch light shaped and sculpted his butt almost as lovingly as— No. Think of something else. Like how he'd looked at Jennifer. Yeah, that was good.

She knew she couldn't blame Zeke. Despite all his brains,

he was a man, and they were programmed so perfection like Jennifer's short-circuited their wiring.

Zeke slid one knee onto the car seat, emphasizing the muscles in his other thigh. She'd felt their ropey solidness when she'd patted him for weapons and checked his pockets.

Oh, God, how sad was this? She was getting retro-actively turned on.

"How long is this going to take?" she asked.

"Keep your pants on."

No. He hadn't said that. He couldn't have said it. At least he couldn't have meant it. If he'd meant it *that* way, he would have said, *Take off your pants.*

He hadn't said *Take off your dress* graduation night. He hadn't had to. After they had turned the front seat of his parents' car into a hormonal sauna, all he'd had to say was, *We could get in the back.*

It wasn't even a question.

"Hey, you okay?"

She jumped at the warmth of a large hand cradling her elbow. He'd emerged from the car and she hadn't even noticed.

"What? Yeah. Fine. I'm fine." She stepped back from his touch. "Tired. It's been a long day."

"Okay. Well, I wanted to give you this."

She automatically took the thin square from him. "A CD?"

"Thought you might be interested."

"Uh-huh, sure. Thanks."

His expression closed then. Oh, yeah, she remembered that patented Zeke *Do Not Enter* expression, and she felt like a jerk for her lack of enthusiasm. She cleared her throat. "As I said, it's been a long day and a longer night, so—"

"Sorry if you get in trouble over stopping me."

"I'm always in trouble with Chief Harnett."

"Yeah? It was, uh, an interesting way to see you again."

She manufactured a grin. "Got right past the awkward part, right?"

He studied her before saying, "When I first heard your voice, I had this kind of—" he hesitated, as if searching for an unfamiliar word "—feeling."

Was that why he'd peered into the light toward her? "Why didn't you say something?"

"You didn't seem to be in a listening mode."

"If you'd said you were Zeke, I would have been."

"I couldn't know that until I knew you were you. And Drago was the last place I would have expected to find you."

Find her? Right. As if he'd ever looked.

"Why? Drago's my home. And yours."

His gaze shifted as if focused on a distant street lamp, his expression impossibly neutral, except for that old trick where his facial muscles seemed to turn as hard as the bones. Had she forgotten how quickly he could withdraw?

"It is not my home," was all he said.

"Okay. You have a new address. Fine. This is still your hometown. You can't change that. It's still where you were raised and went to school."

"Anton!"

In the instant before he turned toward the voice, his face softened—as much as that stony architecture ever softened. "Ma."

He took the two porch steps in one stride, and encircled the small woman who stood at the top. He towered over her so that all Darcie could see of her were her arms wrapped around him.

Darcie could have stepped back into the dimness quietly, and been in her car and pulling away from the curb before either of them noticed.

She'd done her duty, followed the chief's orders to deposit Zeke at the front door of his childhood home and saw son and mother reunited. The shift from hell was finally over. She needed to go home, curl up with a book, maybe have a glass of wine...

"Darcie? Ah, Darcie it is good to see you. You want tea?"

Too late. She'd been spotted. "No, thank you, Mrs. Z, not tonight."

"You know my mother?" Zeke kept an arm around his mother while he faced Darcie.

"Yes," she said as if it were a defiant declaration. "Mrs. Z is one of the most generous sup—"

"Oh! Anton!" His mother's quick squeaks got his attention. "Darcie came to help me when the car—I told you—hit the fence. I remembered her from your class."

Darcie had been surprised when Mrs. Zeekowsky had immediately called her by name. Although not as astonished as Zeke appeared to be now.

"How?" he asked, clearing up any doubt that he could have mentioned her to his mother back in high school.

Mrs. Z chuckled. And didn't answer directly. "Of course, I know Darcie. She's a good girl."

Darcie felt her cheeks heat, which was stupid. Mrs. Z didn't mean it that way, and even if she had... For heaven's sake, she was thirty-four years old and being a good girl hadn't been among her ambitions for a long, long time.

"It's great seeing you, Mrs. Z. Welcome home, Zeke."

She backed down the driveway while she spoke so she could give a final wave good-night and escape into her car.

But as she drove away, she couldn't escape the question: had she gotten out of there because she feared Mrs. Z might pick up on her thoughts about giving up her good girl status in the back of the Zeekowsky sedan all those years ago? Or because Zeke showed no sign that he remembered that event at all?

* * *

Zeke crossed his hands behind his head and stared at the ceiling.

How the hell had he ever slept in a bed this narrow?

Of course he'd been narrower, too, then. So narrow he hadn't had much trouble making love with Darcie in the back seat of his dad's old Pontiac.

His first time. Their first time, he'd realized afterward—and would have realized beforehand if he'd been thinking about it. But he hadn't been thinking. Not with his head, anyway.

Funny. All these years, and yet when he'd heard a voice ordering him to get out of his car with his hands up, his first reaction had been *That's Darcie.* When she'd come closer, something else he couldn't pin down had made him even more certain. But he'd told himself it couldn't be. Darcie, a cop? In Drago?

She looked good.

Even in the harsh glare of the headlights, after she'd discovered who he was and stepped forward, she'd looked real good. It had been a jolt not to see her long hair at first, but he'd been relieved when they got to Village Hall to see she had it pinned up, not cut off.

And the welcome home she'd given him…

He chuckled into the silence. Handcuffs.

She hadn't been in a laughing mood tonight, but if she was still the Darcie he'd known, she would laugh about it before long.

Was she the Darcie he'd known?

A lot of years had passed, a lot of things had happened to him, that was for sure. That's probably why he'd had that spur-of-the-moment urge to give her the CD with the pre-release version of Z-Zap. Just to show her what he did these days. But what about her? A lot of things could have happened to her, too. Lots of turning points, perhaps some even more memorable than making love together for the first time.

He closed his eyes. A puff of memory vibrated his nerve endings. Pale, soft skin. Eyes as wide as the moon. A burning pain under his breastbone at the glint of tears trailing off smooth cheeks.

He turned on his side.

God, it really was silent. How could a house be so quiet?

His own bedroom wasn't usually this— And then it hit him. He got out of bed, set his laptop on the old desk and plugged it in.

The faint light and soft hum brought instant familiarity. He climbed back into bed and fell asleep immediately.

Darcie pounded up the stairs to her apartment over the garage, barged in the door—she really should lock it—and grabbed the phone on the fourth ring, barely beating the answering machine.

It was Jennifer.

"Are you okay? After last night?"

"Last night?" Darcie repeated, stalling.

She and Jennifer had talked about a lot these past several years, but not about Zeke Zeekowsky. Even while plotting to get Zeke here, Darcie hadn't ventured into his feelings for Jennifer, or Darcie's feelings for him. Simply because it was all so long ago. Last night had been an automatic reaction, like an amputee feeling a twitch in a leg that was long gone.

"I thought the chief was unnecessarily rough on you."

"Oh, that was nothing." Darcie switched the phone to the other ear, untied one shoelace and levered off the shoe, letting it thud to the floor in her tiny kitchen. "He was being restrained because we had an audience."

"Then I'm glad I decided to come," Jennifer said. "When Corine called me and said Zeke was in town—" Ah, that explained how Jennifer had known Zeke was at the police station, but still left Darcie wondering how the younger set had found out. "I was too curious not to come."

Jennifer was being tactful, not mentioning Darcie putting the Lilac Festival Grand Marshal, Chief Judge and Guest of Honor in handcuffs.

"Sorry, Jen." Darcie set to work on the second shoe. "If this screws up our plans about Zeke, I'll be really unhappy, but I would do it all over again."

"Oh, no—I didn't mean—I absolutely agree, Darcie. With that monster out there with that little girl, you did the only thing you could do. And I could see last night that Zeke understood."

He did take it pretty well. Didn't get all huffy and *I'm An Important Person.*

"I called because Mildred wants to see the Patterson house again. I can't take the schedule to Zeke this morning. You'll have to do it."

Darcie closed her eyes and lied. "It's okay. Sorry about Mildred."

"Yeah, me, too." They both chuckled. With Drago's economy somewhere south of depressed and as low person in the real estate office hierarchy, Jennifer got the worst tasks, including taking Mildred Magnus for viewings of a house everyone knew she had no intention of buying. "I'm disappointed. I hoped this would be a good opportunity to establish some rapport with Zeke."

"Rapport?" If Zeke had had any more rapport with Jennifer last night, the man would have been drooling. "I don't think you need to worry about it, Jen. In fact, you should spearhead this thing. I know we said I would—"

"It has to be you, Darcie. You're his friend."

That was part of the plan. They would first ease him back into Drago life during the festival, with Darcie showing him the need in town and planting the idea that he and his foundation could do so much to help, because they hoped he'd be more receptive to those ideas from a friend. Then, when they felt he was ready—or if he never seemed ready, then just before he left—Jennifer, as the soothing presence and the better salesperson, would set out the specifics of the grant program they'd drafted.

"A long time ago. Haven't talked to the guy since graduation." The early morning hours of the day after graduation, to be precise.

"Judging from last night, you two picked up right where you left off," Jennifer said. "You take the schedule over this morning. We want smooth sailing with the festival to soften him up for the kill."

Darcie had to force herself to join Jennifer's chuckle. Even as she gave in, she was chewing over that sentence: *Judging from last night, you two picked up right where you left off*.

That was the last thing she wanted.

Zeke didn't look as if he'd slept well. Good.

But from the smell of it, he was eating just fine.

After her knock on the front door was answered by a cheery "Come in!" Darcie followed that smell to the tiny, immaculate kitchen. There she found Mrs. Z bustling around and Zeke hunched over a stack of waffles that nearly obscured the postage-stamp-sized table against the wall.

"Good morning, Darcie. How wonderful you come to see us this morning. You want tea?"

"Thank you, Mrs. Z. I'd love tea," Darcie accepted quickly, trying to slide past the insinuations in the older woman's smiling eyes over the word *us*. Remembering her hostess viewed tea as merely a vehicle to soothe her sweet tooth, she added, "But no honey, thank you."

Zeke frowned at her.

"Where are you manners, Anton?" his mother scolded. "Say good morning to Darcie, and give her a chair."

Zeke didn't move fast enough for his mother, because she swooped toward the table. Another chair—obviously hers—faced Zeke with a third chair at right angles to them. This one held a sleek, slightly dangerous looking laptop, which was Mrs. Z's target.

"No, Ma." Zeke dropped his waffle-laden fork, twisted on the wire-backed chair that appeared ready to collapse, spread his hands protectively over the laptop and said, "If you touch it, the security alarm will go off."

"Tsk. Then you move it, Anton. And give Darcie waffles."

Darcie truly intended to turn down the offer—she'd have to run another five miles tonight to work them off—but Zeke heaved such a martyred sigh as he tapped several keys, closed the lid and took the laptop onto his lap that she changed her mind.

She thanked Mrs. Z for a plate and fork, speared two waffles off Zeke's stack and smile sweetly as she asked him to pass the strawberry preserves. He scowled. Possibly because she could have reached the jar of homemade sweetness herself, possibly because he didn't want to share.

Mrs. Z was muttering away about the crash of civilization brought on by people bringing machines to the breakfast table, and how Zeke's father used to bring the newspaper to the table every day, but only to read interesting pieces to her. To bring a humming, whirring monster—no. Machines!

"Ma, you're using a machine to make the waffles," Zeke said.

Mrs. Z dismissed his irrefutable logic with a wave of the spatula she was using to scrape the batter bowl and a spate of her native language.

"Ma?" Zeke interrupted. "Where's the DVD player I sent you?"

"Ah, it must be in the basement. I've no need for such things, Anton."

"And the VCR—the one I had somebody come and set up for you before the DVD player? The guy did come didn't he?"

"Yes, such a nice man. I tried to introduce him to my hair-dresser, but he had a fiancée." She opened the waffle iron and with the tip of a knife flipped perfectly cooked squares onto a plate. "Not such a good girl for him, I fear. Too much she thought of the dancing, the parties."

"Ma. The VCR?"

"I've no need for such a thing, either. There is not so much on that TV that I want to see that I need to store it up like a squirrel with nuts."

"Ma!"

"Anton." She stopped guiding the remaining batter into the waffle iron and raised the spatula in warning. "I cook or I answer question. One—you choose."

Darcie met Mrs. Z's eyes, and her stomach sank. *Oh, no.* His mother hadn't told him. All those times Darcie had asked, and Mrs. Z had assured her that Zeke was fine with it...

"Ma—" he protested again.

"One."

He flicked a look at Darcie and she saw the humor and love for his mother. "All right, Ma. Cook."

Any thought of opening her mouth evaporated. It was an issue between mother and son. It was not her place—or her responsibility—to interfere.

"That's good. I cook." Mrs. Z smiled. A smile Darcie thought turned a little sly as the older woman dropped her gaze once more to the batter. "What do you and Darcie do together today, Anton?"

"Oh, no, Mrs. Z," Darcie said quickly. "Zeke and I don't have plans. I'm here to drop something off on my way to work."

Zeke stopped chewing. "What?"

"Work? My job? Drago's finest? Jennifer wanted to bring it over herself, but another obligation prevented that," Darcie said, smiling brightly. She would not let her ego—over a high school crush, for crying out loud—interfere with Drago's best interests. "She should be done by noon, so this afternoon—"

"What did she want to bring over that you brought instead?" Zeke asked with impatient precision. She used to hate that tone.

"Your schedule for your three weeks in Drago, with all the times and places." She set it on the table.

"Schedule?"

"Schedule, itinerary, whatever you want to call it. A listing of where and when you need to be for festival events. First—"

"Stop," he ordered with the voice she remembered from chem lab. The voice that said she was about to mix two chemicals together that should never reside in the same test tube.

With a frown sharpening the angles, his face looked more the way she remembered. She used to imagine it as the work of a talented artist who'd sketched only stark lines—jaw, cheekbones, chin, brow bone. Time had finally painted in the rest—except for when he frowned like this.

"I don't need a schedule," he said. "I'm going to be here at Ma's getting work done in peace and quiet, and then show up to be Grand Marshal for the parade and Guest of Honor at some dance two weeks from Saturday. I can remember that without a schedule."

Not according to his assistant, Brenda, he couldn't.

Darcie didn't say that out loud because Brenda had strongly suggested she not mention their alliance, forged over several phone conversations set up by Mrs. Z.

"Think again, Zeke. You're forgetting you're head judge for

the Lilac Queen finals. That means finalist introductions, then the judging rounds, official presentation of the court and eventually the coronation. Plus rehearsals, a meeting for parade participants, interviews and—"

"Oh, my God." His voice matched his frown.

"Zeke, you know what a big deal the festival is for Drago, and we gave you all the details in the packet we sent."

"I didn't read that."

His mother's tsk stopped the admission. He flicked a look at her, then returned to Darcie, clearly considering her the easier touch.

"Darcie, I'll go to the dance and the parade, but all this other stuff…"

The CEO of Zeke-Tech, the genius of the New Technology was shaking in his boots. She would have laughed, except she remembered the last time she'd seen him look this lost. The early October day in senior year when they'd buried his father.

Now his eyes asked her to take this burden away. She was racked by the knowledge that not only could she not remove this burden, but she had every intention of doing her best to shove a whole lot more onto his shoulders.

"Sorry, Zeke. You signed on for the whole deal. Starting this afternoon with being interviewed by the *Drago Intelligencer* at the Community Center, and then introductions to the contestants and preliminary run-through."

"This is impossible, this—"

"You give me this schedule, Darcie," Mrs. Z said. "Friends come to say hello soon, then I send him to the Community Center right on time. Don't worry, Darcie, I keep Anton schedule ticking like bomb works."

Zeke groaned.

* * *

"Can you look over here, Mr. Zeekowsky?" the young photographer from the *Intelligencer* asked.

"Why?"

The young man's pimply face emerged from behind the camera. "To get a better angle."

"It would be the same angle if you stood in front of me and I looked straight ahead."

If the photographer had sense, he'd be snapping away, because Zeke's face expressed the first flicker of interest in twenty minutes. Apparently the photographer didn't have much sense.

"Straight ahead puts half your face in shadow. Plus, turning your head angles the light across the eyes."

"Huh," Zeke said, then lapsed into his zombie-in-concrete face.

Darcie sighed from her seat ten feet away. She would give a lot not to be here in the Community Center's main room. But here she sat, on duty, in uniform, assigned to stick by Zeke today, just in case.

Just in case *what,* she had no idea. But that had been Chief Harnett's orders when she'd started her shift at noon.

She'd gotten out one word of protest—*but*—before being hit with the Harnett stare.

She'd arrived at the Community Center at the same time as Zeke, who'd been spurred, no doubt, by Mrs. Z. Darcie had thought she'd seen pleasure in his eyes as she'd explained her assignment today.

Then the young, attractive female reporter from the *Intelligencer* hooked on to Zeke like a native spearing a fish. In fact, Vicki Constable was so attentive to him that Darcie was beginning to doubt her gossip sources that the reporter was having an affair with her editor.

While Darcie faded to the background, Vicki directed Zeke to a chair. She shed her jacket, showing off shapely arms improbably tanned for the last week of April in Illinois, and draped it over an extra chair. That left her photographer to dig gear out of a bag on the floor.

Vicki demanded of her colleague, "Are you done?"

"Not quite," he mumbled. "Mr. Zeekowsky, could you, uh, smile?"

"No."

Zeke's flat refusal was drowned out by noisy arrivals at the far end of the long room.

Cristina Wellton swept through the double doorway first, the acknowledged beauty of Drago. She'd been Miss Everything-and-Anything since she'd been old enough to say *tiara,* and was the hands-down favorite to be Lilac Queen. Sort of the Jennifer of her generation, Darcie thought, but without the brains or personality.

Ashley Stenner's gaze followed Cristina's entrance with attention so rapt that Darcie half expected her to break into applause. Until last month, Jennifer's daughter had barely known Cristina existed. However, ever since Ashley was named Junior Princess—a position once held by Cristina—the younger girl had developed a staggering case of hero worship.

When Jennifer appeared, Darcie saw her gaze travel from her daughter to Cristina. Jennifer was worried, but treading lightly for fear that trying to wrest Ashley from Cristina's shadow would make the girl cling even more tightly.

Then the other four queen candidates, various mothers, festival officials and the two remaining judges filed in, with enough emotional crosscurrents to sink a battleship.

Vicki touched Zeke's knee to reclaim his attention, which had predictably shifted to the other end of the room when Jennifer entered.

"I found yearbooks from your days at Drago High, and I must say, Mr. Zeekowsky, you—" the reporter chuckled "—have certainly improved with age."

Darcie bristled. Maybe Zeke hadn't been a conventional hunk in high school, but anyone who had seen his intelligence, passion, sorrow and determination would have been a fool not to see how appealing he was. Besides, Vicki wasn't helping their chances of winning over Zeke by reminding him of high school.

"Your hair for one thing," the reporter said.

Okay, she had a point there. Zeke's thick mop of medium brown hair had been tamed into an appealing, young-JFK-in-the-wind look.

Zeke eyed Vicki with a distrust usually saved for dogs foaming at the mouth. From a strictly self-preservation angle, what he should have been paying attention to was the approach of Cristina Wellton.

Ashley trailed her. Everyone else remained on the far side of the room. Cristina zeroed in on Zeke with a smile beaming so brightly that the photographer seemed blinded from the peripheral rays.

Zeke glanced at her without a flicker of interest, then looked back to Vicki.

Darcie perked up. Cristina had an ego big enough to swallow all the cornfields in Drago County. This might be an entertaining shift after all.

"My assistant takes care of that," he said replying to Vicki's comment about his hair. "She gets this guy to come in."

"This guy? *This. Guy!*" Cristina surged forward. "Jon le Breque is an *artiste,* a miracle worker, a monumental talent."

"Who are you?"

"I am Cristina Wellton." Her tone and bearing would have worked if she'd declared, "I am the Queen of Sheba."

A flicker crossed Zeke's gray eyes, and Darcie knew something had caught his interest. "How'd you know the name of the guy who cuts my hair?"

The photographer, with a rare show of sense, urgently snapped away, as Zeke's curiosity broke through his stiff mask of discomfort.

"*Everyone* knows Jon le Breque cuts your hair. You are one of the few clients he takes on outside of Hollywood or New York. It's in all the magazines," Cristina said.

Zeke frowned. *Snap, snap, snap.* "I've never read about Jon. What magazines?"

"*Vogue, Elle, People, Cosmo, Hairstyle—*"

"There's a magazine about hair?"

Cristina's mouth dropped open, a distorted mirror of Zeke's astonishment, like two aliens encountering each other for the first time. Darcie couldn't help laughing.

Every face turned to her. Vicki and Cristina glared—Vicki on general principal, Cristina because she expected adulation, not amusement. The photographer peeped over his camera, then dove behind it to click off shots.

Zeke's look was the hardest to untangle. There was something of the young Zeke the first time she'd talked to him— really talked to him—in class, when he'd looked as if he thought he might like a friend but didn't really trust her. Also, yes, deep down, a hint he might like to laugh with her, even if he wasn't entirely sure what she was laughing at.

Darcie's throat squeezed shut, strangling the laugh.

The cause of her throat-squeezing switched in an instant when Ted Warinke, one of the other two Lilac Queen judges, plodded up on Zeke's blind spot, clapped him—hard—on the shoulder and said, "Well, if it isn't my old friend Zeke the Geek!"

Ted wasn't a bad person. Although, if he could have been arrested for terminal lack of sensitivity, he'd be serving a life sentence. Ted had been a Lilac Queen judge for years because his hardware stores sponsored the parade, *not* because he was fit to judge anyone's social graces.

Having recovered from the unexpected blow, Zeke looked from Ted's extended hand to his face and said, slowly, "Do I know you?"

Great, just great.

First, Ted blabbed Zeke's hated high school nickname, which would probably show up in the paper, reminding him why he'd never come back before. Then, Zeke used that I-have-no-interest-in-ever-knowing-you tone, which was sure to make Ted defensive, which would make him take verbal potshots at Zeke, which could make these weeks like leading two elephants through a minefield.

"Zeke, this is Ted Warinke," Darcie desperately filled in. "He was several years ahead of us in school. You probably don't remember him."

"Yeah." Ted guffawed. "We didn't cross paths much."

"No surprise." Zeke's voice told Darcie he was about two seconds from adding, *because I avoid idiots.* Or something even less subtle. Something Ted couldn't miss. Then Ted, of all people, saved the moment.

"Yeah, I was buddies with this one's brother. Isn't that right, Jennifer?"

Jennifer glided up, smiling graciously at everyone, including Ted, even as she sidestepped his attempt to wrap an arm around her waist. "You and Mark were friends."

"Damn straight. And Eric, even before he was the best quarterback Drago ever produced."

"Yes, well, you'll have to excuse us everyone," Jennifer said. "We need Cristina to join the other candidates, and let you continue your interview."

She took Cristina's arm in an apparently casual gesture that Darcie admiringly noted got the girl moving.

"Yes," Vicki said, clearly none too pleased at Young Beauty and Mature Beauty, not to mention Old Jock horning in. "This is a *private* interview."

Ted was impervious to such snubs. Cristina's unshakeable belief that everyone loved her as much as she loved herself deflected any and all barbs. So they departed with equanimity.

As Jennifer led them away, collecting Ashley, too, Darcie heard Ted say something that included "Zeke the Geek" and "brain too big for his body."

But Cristina's voice was clearer. "I thought he was supposed to be so smart? He doesn't know anything!"

Chapter Three

"What are you going to major in?" Ted Warinke asked Cristina.

Big surprise. He'd asked every finalist that question since becoming a judge thirteen years ago, after Darcie's father had died, leaving the opening. Darcie had once speculated to Jennifer that Ted had used "What's your major?" in college, the resulting pickup had become Mrs. Warinke and he'd stuck with the line ever since.

"Oh, I'm not going to college," Cristina said airily. "I can't waste my best years in college. I'm going to model."

Ted blinked. The other judge, Mrs. Rivers, who had taught dance and deportment in Drago at least since covered wagons reached the area in the 1830s, sucked in a breath. Zeke's brows contracted. Even Darcie, sitting as far to the side of the room as she could without leaving, straightened.

"After all, international travel is the best education, and my modeling career will take me all over the world and get me started on my own business. Look at all the old, old models who have businesses. Like Tyra Banks."

Since Banks was about Darcie's age, she did not appreciate *old, old.*

"What kind of business are you interested in, Cristina?" asked Ted, apparently mollified that she wanted to be a business mogul, like him.

"Oh, I don't know that yet. Most of the models seem to go into developing their own clothing line or makeup. But there's a lot of people already doing that stuff. I mean, lately, when you go to the mall, it takes longer and longer to go through everything that's there. I want to do something different, something that says *Cristina,*" she said. "Maybe jewelry. I'm sure something will occur to me. It's bound to when one is in the fashion industry. One would learn so much in that world."

"You can't learn technology," Zeke said flatly.

"Technology? Why on earth would I—" Darcie practically heard the click when Cristina's self-preservation instinct caught up with her mouth. "I, ah, technology, of course, is utterly fascinating. I feel such an affinity with you, such a deep, abiding connection with your work."

To Darcie's knowledge, Cristina's affinity with technology consisted of e-mail and shopping online.

"No one could have success like you, though. Why you've gobbled up all the money and fame there is in technology, so what would be left to a small-town girl like me, Zeke?"

She batted her lashes, looking deeply into Zeke's eyes. She was really quite good, Darcie thought. Did she practice in front of a mirror?

Most of the others—especially the three contestant mothers lurking just out of the judges' sight—sucked in breaths when Cristina called him Zeke, but he stared back expressionless.

"Somebody's got to make the next great discovery," he said, "push the envelope, create a breakthrough."

"You're so right," Cristina said earnestly. "Without that, why, fashion would just *die*."

Zeke's head pounded. His shoulders ached. His throat was dry, despite the water he'd chugged during this break before they did something the schedule ominously called Court Presentation Ceremony: First Run-Through.

He'd felt fresher after a seventy-two-hour straight blitz to streamline code on the Z-Org hot sync program.

"Can you believe this?" He shook his head, sinking down next to Darcie on the steps to the stage at one end of the room.

She gave him a look. For some reason the look reminded him that the woman carried handcuffs and knew how to use them. And not in a fun way.

"What does that mean, Zeke?"

"All this energy and time going into some beauty pageant. Why not do something worthwhile?"

"The Lilac Festival *is* worthwhile. It brings in more visitors to Drago than every other event combined. That helps the businesses and increases donations to everything from the park to the library to the police department, including the Drago Chest to help our neediest families."

"Fine, great. It's all about philanthropy." How had they gotten so far off what he wanted to talk about?

Darcie's dark eyes narrowed. "I thought you were cranky because Ted Warinke had brought up 'Zeke the Geek,' but that sarcastic tone makes it sound as if you've got something personal against the festival."

He opened his mouth to tell her "Zeke the Geek" hadn't bothered him in years. If it had, he'd have killed his college roommate in the first few months of freshman year instead of having Quince become his closest friend.

"It's not personal," he lied. "It's concern for these girls' futures. Without this festival they might have real ambitions—not silly dreams of modeling."

"Don't blame Cristina on the Lilac Festival. It doesn't stunt the girls' ambitions and abilities. In fact, it's supposed to reward them. I was a Lilac princess, and I didn't do so badly."

That memory of watching the Lilac court's float came again, but this time he saw Darcie sitting below Jennifer's elevated seat, her head turned toward him as if their eyes could meet despite the distance.

"Yet you came back here after graduating from Penn State. You could have gone anywhere. I don't get it, Darcie. You have the ability. Why you never gave yourself credit for—"

"I didn't graduate from Penn State." She looked away. He followed her gaze and saw that kid from last night at the police station. Wayne, Walt, W—something. He was fiddling with wires to a video camera they'd used to tape the candidates. Zeke was about to snap his fingers in front of her face when Darcie added, "I left in my sophomore year. When my father died."

He hadn't been prepared for her words. Pain sliced him before he could stop it, pain of remembering his loss, imagining hers. He pushed it away. "Why didn't you finish?"

"Right, I'd go back to college and leave Martha Barrett dealing with life on her own." Her sarcasm eased with her next words. "She's not like your mother, Zeke. I had to take care of things for her. I came back, commuted to Mid-Northern and started working."

"She's—"

"She's fine. Still in the house and her life hasn't changed much. That's all beside the point. You said this festival is a waste of time, but it's not. It promotes Drago, and it's a chance for girls to show what they've accomplished and to consider how they present themselves to adults."

Okay, he wasn't all that attuned to people, but it seemed like she'd dragged the subject away from her family with both hands. But who was he to go digging into something she didn't want to talk about when he'd led her away from an area *he* didn't want dug up?

But damn, he wanted to know what was going on inside that head of hers. Or maybe it was what was going on in her heart.

His gaze dropped to the vicinity of that organ.

Her name was spelled out on a brass bar that rested where her breast curved the shirt. Her breasts had been so smooth, so soft. The first sensation against his fingers had nearly pushed him over the edge.

"Zeke?"

"What?" He jerked his gaze up from her breasts.

"Have you heard a single word I said?"

"Hearing it doesn't mean I agree." Quince had given him that line, and it had rescued Zeke more times than he could count.

"You don't agree that the Lilac Festival scholarships help these girls?"

He shook his head. "There are better ways."

"It's a tradition and it helps the town and the girls—"

"Get wound up and crazy."

Now that she'd reminded him of it, he remembered Darcie's nerves before the court was announced and then again when the queen was named. Even though she'd said over and over that she wasn't nervous, because everybody knew Jennifer would be voted queen.

Darcie hadn't believed in herself much back then. At first, he'd taken her self-evaluation at face value, but after a month of chem lab junior year he'd realized she was a lot smarter than she said she was. Eventually he'd realized she was a lot smarter than she believed she was.

What she'd lacked was confidence. He wondered if she remembered that she'd finally applied to Penn State after he'd heckled her into it.

At least she'd lacked confidence in some areas. When it came to badgering him to talk, she'd had all the confidence in the world.

Now, he shook his head again, partly in futility. "All over some small-town title."

"When you live in a small town, that's all you know."

She'd snapped the words, but he took them at face value. "My point, exactly. They'd be better off getting out of here than worrying about what passes for important in Drago."

"How do you suggest the adolescents of Drago do that? Not everyone is a genius, Zeke. And what would happen to the town if everyone walked away—the way you did? No, don't answer that. I know what you'll say. But take it from me, other people do care what happens to Drago. And some kids are never going to leave because they don't want to leave, so what about them?"

"Do I get to answer this one?"

She made a face at him. "Be my guest."

"They outgrow it."

"I just told you—"

"Not the town, though that, too. But I meant they outgrow worrying about who was Lilac Queen. Five years down the road, who'll remember?"

"Who was Lilac Queen our senior year?"

"Jennifer."

She made that told-you-so face that used to irritate him so much. It still did, but for some reason it also made him want to laugh.

"Okay," he conceded. "Jennifer was everything that year, but that was an unusual circumstance. It won't be like that with these girls. They'll all forget. It's a fleeting thing, like whether you get a parking spot you want."

Darcie stood quickly. "You are so not a girl."

She started past him, up the stairs where he still sat.

"Thank you," he twisted to call after her, then added, "I think."

His words lost energy because his attention was devoted to something else entirely. Darcie's rear end as she climbed the steps.

The uniform pants were far from formfitting. But from his angle, he could see the motion as her rounded hips shifted under the fabric in a rhythm that had him trying to remember how to breathe. Whether she'd meant it as a slam or not, he was so glad he was male right down to his atoms, so he could enjoy a sight like that.

Then his gut dropped about a foot as a voice fluted, "Oh, Zeke."

"I'm busy." He snapped off the end of his sentence when he couldn't remember any more of the contestant's name than Cris-something.

Jennifer's daughter was right behind her, giving him dagger looks for some reason. Cris-something trilled a laugh.

"Of course you are, Zeke. Oh, I hope you don't mind that I call you Zeke. I feel I must—truly I must, since we have so much in common."

Zeke had his mouth open to refute that, when a new arrival crossed his peripheral vision. Jennifer. Frowning and looking tired, she still was beautiful.

"Cristina, you know it's inappropriate for a princess to contact the head judge outside of the formal situations until the queen is selected."

"Oh, if Ashley hadn't wanted to talk to him so desperately,

I never would have approached Zeke," said Cristina, eyes wide and innocent. "She was too shy to come on her own and she begged and she begged."

Jennifer looked at her daughter a long time before saying to both girls, "This is against the rules. Go back with the others now."

Cristina's smile tightened, but she turned away with grace. Ashley glowered and followed.

Jennifer gave Zeke an apologetic look. "I keep hoping there'll be time for us to talk, to really catch up, but…" She tipped her head toward her daughter. "Later?"

"Sure, later."

"Brenda," Zeke said into his cell phone, "I want you to come out here to help me with some things."

There was a pause, then, "What things?"

"Uh, you know, things with projects I'm working on."

"You're not supposed to be working on projects, you're supposed to be relaxing. If you're working on projects, Quince is going to quit, and Vanessa might be right behind him. Besides, I never help you with projects."

"All this stuff with the Lilac Festival, then. If you organize that, it would free me up for other work—you know, like normal assistants."

He knew the gibe was a mistake as soon as the words left his mouth. How come he never knew it before they left his mouth?

"If you had a normal assistant, you'd be curled up in a corner of a closet gibbering. Normal assistant? You can't *take* a normal assistant."

She sounded like Jack Nicholson delivering his "You can't handle the truth" line from *A Few Good Men*. The scary thing was Zeke didn't know if she meant to imitate the actor or if it was all Brenda.

"For one thing, a *normal* assistant would have told you right off that she was on vacation. That's *vacation* as in not working. Hell, a normal assistant wouldn't have arranged her vacation for your convenience. A *normal* assistant wouldn't have left her cell phone on when she was on vacation."

"You're on vacation. I forgot."

She snorted. "Of course you did. As for the festival, your schedule should be all set. Mrs. Barrett made sure everything was well organized."

The Barrett name caught his attention. "You mean Darcie."

"I mean her mother, Martha Barrett. She's handling the festival from the country club's angle, and she has everything organized."

That didn't sound like the mother Darcie had talked about. On the other hand, if Brenda placed her "organized" stamp of approval on someone, there was no chance in hell she was wrong.

"…so," Brenda was saying when he tuned back in. "I can only assume this has nothing to do with work projects or the festival, What's up, Zeke?"

"I told you. It's work. And this festival."

"It's a woman. Got to be. I remember this tone from when that Lane Vawlet was crawling all over you."

Of course, that's who Cristina reminded him of. Right down to the teeth-baring smile.

Brenda blew out a breath. "You can handle any Lane Vawlet clone, Zeke. But now that you're back among people who have always known you don't let your automatic defenses block them out. Listen, I gotta go. Tomorrow we're going to the mountains, so you won't be able to get me." She muttered, "At least I hope not," before hanging up.

For once, Brenda had failed him. He was on his own.

* * *

"Well?"

Darcie finished pouring coffee but skipped a chocolate doughnut because it was such a cop cliché, before facing Jennifer. "Well, what?"

"Softening up Zeke. How's it going?"

"Not well. He hates everything to do with the Lilac Queen, the Lilac Festival and Drago."

"Oh, dear."

"You could say that." Oh, the hell with avoiding clichés, Darcie picked up the biggest chocolate-covered doughnut and bit into it. "On top of that, he's not real fond of me."

"Oh, now there I know you're wrong. Unless… Darcie, you weren't, you know, untactful?"

"I was totally tactful. He was being a jerk about the Lilac Queen and Drago. Like nobody with half a brain would stick around in this town."

Darcie took a quick, hard bite from the doughnut that left crisp teeth marks in the chocolate that would provide a perfect impression if she happened to take a bite out of a certain someone and they had to match the bite marks to pin it on her.

"Darcie." Jennifer closed her eyes for a second. "You have to hide your irritation. I know it's hard. Lord, do I know."

Darcie remembered then that Jennifer had spent the morning showing Mildred Magnus a house she wasn't going to buy, and felt a little guilty for not being more patient. "Sorry."

She shook her head, as if to say the apology wasn't necessary between them. "We've got to win him over."

"I know. That's why you should be leading the way with this. Who could possibly resist you?"

Jennifer's smile twisted, and Darcie wanted to kick herself, because Eric Stenner had resisted, in the form of leaving her after a series of affairs.

Before she could apologize again, Jennifer was shaking her head and saying, "I know you'll get through to him, Darcie. I'll help, of course, but you two were always so close. You were the one he was always talking to."

Darcie pretended great interest in her coffee cup.

Yeah, but you were the one he was dreaming about, even as he made love to me.

Darcie ordered herself not to laugh. Even though she really deserved this laugh as reward for spending the day shepherding the Lilac Festival's Guest of Honor, Head Judge and parade Grand Marshal.

Right now, Zeke looked like Gulliver with the Lilliputians crawling all over him. And Gulliver wasn't happy.

He deserved it.

Dismiss the importance of the Lilac Festival and lo, the Lilac Festival gods inflicted their wrath.

Zeke had barely tolerated listening to logistics for Friday's presentation of the Lilac Festival court—at Lilac Commons Park if the weather was good, here if it wasn't. Darcie had watched, idly wondering how soon his tank of patience would hit empty.

Especially since Warren, who was operating the light board, kept putting the spotlight on Ashley, prompting looks from the senior candidates that ranged from amusement— Mandy—to confusion—Traci—to concern—Nancy Lynn— to interest—Becky—to irritation—Cristina—not to mention making Ashley blush so furiously that Darcie feared the kid would faint from lack of blood anywhere but in her cheeks. The director kept stopping the action on stage to correct Warren, which slowed the process to a pace a snail would disown.

Then Cristina started a campaign of don't-you-think-it-would-be-better-ifs and if-Zeke-stands-here-by-mes, with each suggestion involving her putting her hand on his arm or moving close to look soulfully into his eyes.

Mothers of two other contestants surged onto the stage to protest. Then Ashley defended Cristina, which drew Jennifer in to keep her daughter out of the other mothers' paths. The pageant director had tufts of hair standing straight up from grabbing hair in his fists then explosively spreading his fingers in agonized supplication. "How? How can this be?"

At the center of all the arm-tugging, hand-waving and shrill voices, Zeke grew stiff and more distant.

"Uh-oh," Darcie muttered under her breath when she saw him wrap one hand around Cristina's wrist and detach her hand from his sleeve.

"Excuse me," he said to the pageant director. "I'm done."

"Oh, but, Ze-eeke," Cristina started in a wheedling tone, cocking her head and moving as if to rub her check against his sleeve.

"Don't." He didn't shout it, he wasn't sharp, but he meant it. The shock of anyone talking that way to Cristina silenced everyone.

Zeke walked off stage into the wings.

Cristina was the first to speak. "Poor man. Some people aren't cut out for the tension and pace of pageants."

She was either brilliant or deluded. Darcie was betting on the latter.

For a beat, it seemed that would be the end of it. Then, to everyone's astonishment, Ashley burst into tears and ran off the stage to the left. In a chain reaction, tears erupted across the stage, sometimes mothers, sometimes contestants and even the director.

Jennifer made eye contact with Darcie, who tipped her head toward Zeke's exit. Someone should go after him. If he tried to leave from that side of backstage, he'd set off the fire alarm. Besides, this seemed an ideal time for Jennifer to start softening him up.

Jennifer shook her head and pointed to Darcie.

Darcie shook her head and pointed back. Jennifer made a small gesture toward where Ashley had disappeared and touched her chest, then pointed again at Darcie and tipped her head toward the exit Zeke had taken.

Darcie sighed and stood.

What could she do when Jennifer played the motherhood card?

She made a face at Jennifer, then climbed the stairs and crossed the corner of the stage, walking between two rows of curtains, on the hunt for Zeke. It would have been more challenging if she hadn't heard him swearing.

"Zeke?"

He swore again. She followed the sound around a trio of plywood trees to find the genius of technology rattling his handheld like a martini shaker.

"What's the problem, Zeke?"

"Damn this town. It's like a black hole. My laptop's acting up, my cell isn't working right and now this."

She knew a misdirection vent when she heard one. Oh, sure, he was frustrated with whatever glitch he'd encountered with his gizmo, but it hadn't been technology that drove him here.

"The problem that made you leave the stage?" she specified.

"I felt like a hunk of meat in a tiger's cage."

"I have a feeling you've encountered that before, Mr. Zeekowsky." He didn't respond, so she tried again. "What's the real problem, Zeke?"

He swore again, but this one lacked steam. He eased his

hips against a railing, and sighed. "This whole damned thing. What am I doing here?"

"Being honored by your hometown for your accomplishments."

He said something under his breath.

"What?"

"I said it boils down to them sucking up because I've got money."

Guilt and fear simultaneously cramped Darcie's insides—guilt because she definitely wanted something from him and fear that she wouldn't get it for Drago. "Has anyone asked you for money?"

He shrugged. "Not yet. They will."

"You've become cynical, Zeke," she said. Accusing him was a lot more comfortable than acknowledging her own guilt, which lingered even as the fear ebbed. "That chip on your shoulder about this town is stupid."

"It's not a chip. It's reality. Why in hell my parents settled here, I'll never know. They could have found a community where they'd be accepted. New York, Chicago. San Francisco. Instead of in the middle of cornfields, where we were outsiders. Always will be."

"Your mother is not an outsider. Neither was your father. If you are, it's because you never let anybody inside. Don't you know that your mother is loved, and so was your father? Do you remember your father's funeral?"

Pain flickered in his eyes, and she suspected that what he remembered of the days after Mischar Zeekowsky collapsed in his shop early in their senior year in high school was a haze of pain without detail.

"Everyone was there, Zeke," she said gently. "Everyone pitched in, helped your mom with arrangements, brought food, made sure the insurance came through and your college fund was set. There wasn't a seat left in the church—don't you remember? Because everyone loved your dad."

"The funny shoemaker with the comical accent?"

"No! They weren't making fun of him, and I won't let you think that. People loved your dad because he was always nice, always smiling. He'd ask people how they were, and he cared about the answer."

She was on a roll. "Don't sell your mother short, either. She is well-regarded in Drago. Just because you've made a pot of money and been on magazine covers doesn't mean you can neglect her and people won't notice."

"I do not neglect—"

"It's not all money, you know. It's not buying her VCRs and DVD players and computers and other gadgets. You can't deal with your guilt that way. You're not even looking at her as a person. You're—"

"Wait a minute. How do you know I've given my mother those things?"

For half a second she froze—how was she going to explain her comment about the gadgets?—then *Eureka!* She smiled blindingly. "Getting forgetful, Zeke? You were demanding an accounting from her this morning."

"I was not demanding an accounting." His handheld gizmo interrupted with a rude beep. He banged it with the side of his hand.

"This is the best a tech genius can do? Thump it? Is that something Zeke-Tech makes?"

"Not yet." He slid the thing into his shirt pocket. "It isn't ready to be released. Not like some other Zeke-Tech products."

He looked at her as if he expected something from her. But she had no idea what.

His frown dropped a couple degrees deeper into gloom. "The point is, I quit," he said tersely. "No more festival, no more—"

"You've spent an afternoon being made a big deal of by people from your hometown, some of whom remember you as a kid."

He snorted, and she knew she'd hit a sore spot. Mrs. Rivers had announced to all that she'd once changed toddler Zeke's diaper while visiting the home of her good friend Rosa Zeekowsky.

But she wasn't going to let that verbal pothole stop her. "And some of whom look up to you, and the only explanation you can find is that they want something from you. And because of *that* you're ready to give up?"

He levered his hips up and sat on the slanted railing, his feet hooked on the lower rung, extending his knees into the narrow stairway. Since she stood two steps above him, she no longer had to tip her head back to look at him.

"Okay, it's not because they all want something from me— that's not all that different. But this isn't going to work, Darcie."

Maybe because his position put them eye-to-eye, maybe because she was no longer looking at him through a seventeen-year-old's crush, she saw in his eyes something that squeezed her heart even though she couldn't define it. It was like the Drago River—amid so much smooth-flowing water, there would be a streak of foamy discord. Even though you couldn't see the submerged rock, had no idea of its shape or origin, you knew one was there.

"What's not going to work, Zeke?" She kept her voice even.

"This." He jerked his hand toward the stage. "The judge stuff, the interview, the parade—any of it."

"You're telling me that the man who won over investors with the force of his certainty when everyone else was bailing out of tech stocks, the man who opened the stock market with a world-wide audience, the man who testified before Congress on the technology in classrooms bill…" She sucked in a breath. "You're telling me that man is afraid of a handful of teenage girls?"

"And their mothers," he muttered.

Tact, clearly, was called for. Tact and understanding and a deft touch.

She laughed.

The first burble caught her unaware and after that there was no holding it in. It rocked her ribs, shuddered her shoulders. He glared as she propped herself next to him for the railing's support. Then the glare splintered, and she heard his deep chuckle. But she sensed pain remained. It would take more than some laughter to reach that deep.

"Okay, it's funny," he conceded. "It's also true, Darcie. I'm lousy at this sort of thing."

"You can't be. All the financial articles talk about how the executive team of Zeke-Tech are the darlings of Wall Street *and* the government regulators and how pleasing both is practically impossible to do. So you must be good at charming people."

"The charm comes from Peter Quincy, my public relations VP. But what really matters are profits for Wall Street and scrupulous records for the regulators, and both of those are because of my partner, Vanessa Irish."

Oh, yes, the brilliant partner whom rare photographs showed as attractive despite a style so rigorously severe it made Darcie's uniform look frivolous. But if she'd been looking for any hint of more between the partners than business, she had never found so much as a whisper.

"All the interviews you've done? Magazines and newspapers and TV. That one where they had you for an entire hour—"

She bit off that reference. Partly because she remembered that at the beginning of the interview Zeke had been so stiff that she'd ached for him. Partly because she didn't want the mention of interviews to stir up whatever reasons he had for never mentioning his hometown to the media.

And, finally, because she'd rather not have him know she'd caught every interview of his that she could.

"They're talking my language," he said. "It's about what we're developing, or at least about the business. I have something to say and that overcomes…"

She waited, but he didn't add the remaining element to that sentence—the important element. "Overcomes what, Zeke?"

He glanced at her. "It's not like I'm telling you anything you don't know, but I don't like people. Never have. And they don't like me."

"Seems to me the problem today has been people liking you too much."

He didn't respond.

Okay, she had a better idea of what the submerged rock was made of—though still no clue how it had gotten there and how deeply it had lodged. Not that she had any specific interest in making sure his river flowed smoothly, only a generalized interest in the welfare of a fellow human being. But mostly her interest in submerged rocks stemmed from this important boat carrying a lot of people's unknowing hopes that she needed to steer clear of hazards.

"You've got a problem then, don't you, Zeke?"

That got his attention, though no verbal response.

"What are you going to do? You can't quit. Not only would it be a disaster for Drago, but it would be rotten publicity for Zeke-Tech. And, yes, certain members of the festival committee would see to it that word got out."

"Who?"

"Me."

"You wouldn't!"

"I would. And you'd deserve it." She gave him her best I'm-a-cop-and-you're-not expression. "But the real reason you can't quit is because it would break your mom's heart."

The cop look hadn't budged the resolve in his gray eyes, but her last reason put a good-sized dent in it. Darcie pressed her point.

"Do you know how thrilled she is? First to have you home, and second to have Drago honor you."

"Honor," he scoffed. It seemed to rally him. "You must have had a backup—I didn't agree until last week. So what were you going to do?"

She sidestepped that, going with her best weapons. "Everyone knows it's you now. Your mother spent the three days before you arrived cleaning, cooking and telling everyone about her boy coming home."

His shoulders didn't slump, he didn't sigh, he didn't swear. But she knew she had him.

"You'll do fine, Zeke. You aren't as bad with people as you think you are. You make it sound like your only contacts with people are through business." Another aspect struck her and was out of her mouth with distressing speed. "You can't tell me you haven't been involved with people—romantically involved. What about that woman from the State Department?"

"Ginger," he said. "She called it off because I missed too many events."

Thank God he hadn't asked how she knew about that. She'd resisted the issue of *People* magazine for two full days after hearing about an item with Zeke's picture. She'd driven all the way to De Kalb to pick up a copy. There'd been a single photo, with a glamorous blond in the foreground, and tech mogul Anton Zeekowsky in a tuxedo turning away from the camera. She'd studied the photo a long time. Then she'd thrown the magazine away before driving back to Drago.

"I'm sure you've had other relationships. With money like yours, there must be women clamoring after you."

"That's one of Brenda's jobs—my assistant. To keep the clamor away. Never should have let her go on vacation," he added under his breath.

"All very interesting." Darcie saw no need to listen to how Brenda held all the women after him at bay. "But the solution to your problem is really simple. Follow the schedule and—"

"That's it!"

She jumped. Not in reaction to the suddenness or volume of his words, but because he'd twisted and grabbed her shoulders, drawing her down the two steps and between his bent knees so they faced each other.

"What's it?" she got out.

"You. You're the solution to my problem."

She had never before fully understood the phrase "That does not compute." Now she did. She knew his words meant something, but the meaning eluded her.

What was the big deal? His knees bracketed her hips. So what? "This makes no sense."

"It makes perfect sense," Zeke said, which was when she knew she'd spoken aloud. He breathed in through his nose. "You can be my Brenda."

"What? No." She broke his hold and stepped back, but the opposite railing didn't let her get far. "I have a job, remember?"

"I don't mean on a professional level. I don't need that kind of help while I'm here. I mean on a personal level. Run interference for me, keep people away, that sort of thing."

"Oh, *that* makes it better."

"I know," the dolt said, totally missing her sarcasm. "I could work. Not a lot, but some. If I have six uninterrupted hours a day—"

"No."

He frowned, as if he didn't hear the word often. "No?"

"No, Zeke. First, I have a job."

"You could get the chief to agree if you explain it right."

"I doubt Chief Harnett would commit himself to agreeing with me if I said cars really should stop at stop signs."

"Then I'll talk to him. It's simply extending today's assignment."

"Maybe I don't want to spend that much time with you, Zeke." Didn't want a front-row seat. Only this time it wouldn't be the gawky, brilliant boy longing for the class queen. "You're used to everybody fawning over you, but I don't find that side of you the least bit appealing. Maybe I liked the guy you were before you left town and never looked back."

Something crossed his eyes, and Darcie's sharp anger—at him, at herself, at the unfairness of the heart—melted.

Then he stood.

She might have been able to read whether the move was a prelude to walking away better if she'd stood her ground, but that would have put them practically thigh to thigh in the narrow stairwell. She backed up a step.

He didn't seem to notice. "In that case, you're right, Darcie, my mother *will* be heartbroken. Because I am not going through three weeks of this."

Nothing like planning a guilt trip for someone else and finding yourself shoved on board for the return trip.

Then, the plans she and Jennifer had in store for Zeke rushed into Darcie's mind. She released a gust of a sigh and returned to the railing, gesturing him back to his spot safely two feet away. She waited to speak until he complied.

"Okay, here's the deal. You don't need people kept away from you. It would defeat the purpose of the festival even if it could be done. So that's out. But I will help you."

"How?" He'd never been the most trusting of people, but when had he become so suspicious of *her*?

Bad question. No reason he'd think of her differently from anyone else.

"I'll steer you through the worst of it and help you deal with the people you need to deal with. Who knows, you might learn something."

"Okay."

She snapped her head around so fast her neck twanged a complaint. That came awfully easy. It made her cop instincts prickle.

It didn't matter. She wasn't about to look a gift billionaire in the mouth. Especially when the corners of his eyes crinkled as he grinned at her surprise.

"Deal." She stuck out her hand.

"Deal." He wrapped his hand around hers, but he didn't shake it.

"Oh, there you are," Cristina cooed from the top of the steps. That *you* was definitely singular.

"Don't tell me I have to deal with this one," he growled, loud enough for Cristina to have heard if she'd been paying any attention to anything other than descending the steps with maximum hip swinging.

"I'll get you out of it this time, but you're going to have to come up with a long-term solution." Darcie kept her voice low. Partly so Cristina couldn't hear and partly because she couldn't talk loudly while she was biting the insides of her cheeks to keep from laughing.

"Cristina!" Darcie turned. "Oh, my God, Cristina!"

The dramatic introduction broke the laserlike focus on Zeke. "What?"

"You can't be around any of the judges, especially the

Head Judge, except during official functions. Didn't you read the agreement you signed?"

"I...but as long as you're here—"

Darcie shook her head and started guiding the girl toward the stage. "It doesn't matter—no contact outside official functions. You better go. I'd hate to see you disqualified."

"They wouldn't dare!" But her certainty had been dented.

Before Darcie ducked around the curtain, she looked back at Zeke and mouthed, *You owe me.*

Chapter Four

Zeke stepped out the back entrance and into evening sunshine.

Darcie had gotten that girl who clung like a leech away, but was this a fair trade-off for giving up his soul for three weeks? A deal with the devil.

Well, no not the devil. A deal with Darcie.

He'd forgotten how small her hand felt in his. Small, yet strong and competent.

He'd held her hand just once. That night.

After they'd maneuvered back into the front seat, she'd sat next to the door. He'd felt the absence of her against his side as if he were used to it when, in fact, he'd never experienced Darcie pressed against his side. That intimacy was reserved for couples, and that they'd never been.

When he drove her home, though, he'd gotten out of the car over her mumbled protests, swung wide the car door she'd partially opened, took her hand and walked her to her front door.

That was where his store of how to act had run out.

…you left town and never looked back.

He shook his head, shaking off the past, along with Darcie's words.

Look to the future, that was his motto—like what in hell had he committed himself to with this deal? Three weeks in Drago, with people he didn't like and giggling girls. He'd rather be back working in the unheated garage where he'd started Zeke-Tech, living for months on Ramen noodles and peanut butter.

On the other hand, there was an upside here. He would make his mother happy and spend time with Darcie.

First he had to talk to Chief Harnett about Darcie's assignment.

He got in the car and listened to the well-tuned engine with satisfaction.

Maybe it wasn't such a bad deal after all.

Especially if he could experiment with a few things rattling around in his head that he never seemed to have time for. With Darcie steering him through the festival mess, he'd surface only when he had to.

Oh, yeah, and he'd take Jennifer to dinner. Because God knew they'd never talked in high school. Not like he and Darcie had, and were doing again.

Maybe I don't want to spend that much time with you, Zeke. You're used to everybody fawning over you, but I don't find that side of you the least bit appealing.

On the other hand, maybe he didn't want Jennifer to be quite as comfortable as Darcie, who said anything she wanted to him.

Darcie couldn't believe her ears when the call came over the radio as she made rounds delayed while she'd kept watch on Zeke all afternoon.

Zeke had been stopped for speeding by the Drago Police Department's lone rookie.

Corine's voice broke into her thanks that Darcie wasn't involved this time. "Chief wants to see you, Darcie."

They were in the chief's office. Zeke looked torn between irritation and satisfaction. The chief had settled on irritation. The rookie looked terrified.

Chief Harnett grunted acknowledgement of her arrival, but kept his focus on Zeke, who interrupted himself only long enough to nod at her.

"Then the officer asked where *we* were going in such a hurry. I had no idea where he'd been going, and I told him that. He didn't give me an opportunity to tell him that I was coming here to see you, as I explained before, Chief. He started writing the ticket."

The chief looked at the rookie, Kurt. "Is that what happened?"

He swallowed mightily. "Yes, sir."

Darcie felt an odd connection to the chief in that moment. They both had enough experience to envision the dynamics of this traffic stop. The rookie had likely been torn between a righteous delight at stopping such a flashy car and a preemptive defensiveness that its driver might throw his weight around. So the rookie used that condescending "Where were *we* going in such a hurry?" line, even though Darcie had warned him during training not to indulge in such posturing. When Zeke called him on it, Kurt slapped him with a ticket.

What the rookie clearly didn't understand, what the chief might not guess, but what she knew for sure was that Zeke had responded strictly in the interests of accuracy—he didn't know where the officer had been going, so he couldn't speak to *we*.

"You're dismissed, patrolman," the chief said.

Kurt shot Darcie an agonized look. She tipped her head

toward the door, hoping her expression blended sternness with this-isn't-the-end-of-the-world reassurance.

When the door closed, she spoke. "May I ask Zeke a question?"

The chief nodded.

"Were you speeding, Zeke?"

He met her eyes. "I was going thirty-five."

"Then you were speeding. It's twenty-five on Elm."

The chief dropped his hand onto a pile of papers with the air of a man pointing out he had a lot of work and it was late. "Two times. We've stopped the festival's Guest of Honor two times in less than twenty hours."

"This time was his fault," she pointed out.

Harnett glowered at her. "It doesn't change that our guest appears to be having trouble getting around town. Mr. Zeekowsky has made a suggestion, and I agree. Darcie, you are hereby assigned as Mr. Zeekowsky's detail, including driving him to and from official events." He shifted his eyes to Zeke. "If you get stopped on your own time, you'll get a ticket."

"Full time?" Her pitifulness didn't appear to move Harnett.

"I can't imagine I'll need her full time, Chief. Especially—" Zeke shot her a glance of triumph "—when I'm working."

"Fine. When you're not occupied with Mr. Zeekowsky, call in for assignments. Otherwise, make sure nothing else goes wrong until he leaves Drago."

Zeke looked up from his handheld only when Darcie got back in and closed her car door with a decided "thunk."

Maybe he *was* a tech genius, because apparently thumping it yesterday had fixed the thing. He'd had his nose buried in it ever since she'd picked him up this morning. Day Two of indebted servitude to Anton Zeekowsky.

Only she wasn't indebted, not yet. She just wanted to be. Wanted the whole town to be.

She'd announced she had errands to run before they went to the Community Center for more queen candidates interviews. He'd said fine and whipped out the annoying little gadget and completely disengaged from his surroundings—her and Drago.

He'd turned down her suggestion that he accompany her at each stop with little more than a grunt. In fact, all he'd given her was a symphony of grunts. Satisfied grunts, exasperated grunts, intrigued grunts and impatient grunts, all aroused by his intense interaction with his handheld.

Now, he looked up as if surprised to find her beside him. He leaned forward to peer out the windshield at laden branches of blooms.

"Lilacs," he said as if he'd made a discovery.

"That tends to be what you find at Lilac Commons. The park with all the lilacs that have made Drago famous, that bring visitors in from all over. Remember?"

"You said you were going into the library."

"Zeke, with all the time you spent in this library, you had to have noticed that a park surrounds it. For heaven's sake, you can't get inside the library without walking a gauntlet of lilacs."

"Oh, yeah. You could smell them in the spring. April," he added.

She shook her head. "Peak's in May. In the two-and-a-half minutes we have of real spring." She was talking mostly to keep him from sinking back into the world where she couldn't reach him. "I never understood why people rhapsodized about spring until I went to Charleston, South Carolina. The azaleas and the dogwoods…wow. We have great summers and falls, and winter can be beautiful, along with testing your mettle so you don't become a weather wimp. But spring—it's like three months in a mud pack."

"You mean 'April is the cruelest month'? You recited that poem in Mrs. Edwards's English class at the end of junior year."

"How on earth do you remember that?"

"You kidding? You practiced it every day for a month in chem lab. All that stuff about lilacs and hyacinths and dead people? Something that creepy's hard to forget."

She laughed. "And I only did the first part. There were four more sections to *The Waste Land.*"

"Oh, my God."

She laughed again, no longer irked at him. Maybe because the handheld rested unnoticed in his big hands while he looked around Main Street.

She slowed the car, but not enough to draw attention to the fact that they were passing what used to be his father's shoe repair shop. When Mr. Zeekowsky had been alive, there had been a bench next to the front door where anyone was welcomed to rest awhile, and sometimes, after closing, the shop owner sat and exchanged greetings with passersby.

One of her earliest memories was standing on tiptoe at Mr. Zeekowsky's counter, fingers curled around the wooden edge, trying to pull herself up to see what produced the rich earthy smells she now knew as leather and saddle soap, and the creased, gentle smile of the man behind the counter as he handed her a section of orange from his lunch.

Now, the narrow shop was among several that were boarded up.

"This town doesn't look too good," Zeke said dispassionately.

Irked came back in a flash. She resisted the urge to hit him over the head or to ask him if he'd had his eyes closed since he'd returned.

He didn't seem to notice her struggle. "Didn't the town used to get all spruced up for the Lilac Festival?"

"Yes."

"Skipped this year, huh?"

"No. That's why there are murals on the boarded up windows of businesses here on Main Street." Josh Kincannon, the high school principal, had come up with the idea as an art class project and Ted Warinke had donated the paint and brushes. A win-win situation—the festival had free labor for masking gaping plywood eyesores and the art classes had materials provided, stretching their emaciated budget a little.

He grunted. "The flowers look different."

She stopped to let Mrs. Richards cross the street with her walker and looked at the square concrete planters marching down wide sidewalks. In their heyday they'd held a profusion of blooms from May to October. Over the years some had succumbed to the freeze-thaw cycle of Illinois weather. Last year, they'd consolidated them, so four blocks at the center of town didn't look gap toothed.

What a project that had been. But the town had rallied around. That's what Drago did. Rallied around, despite fewer and fewer resources.

"The flowers don't all match," she said. Now that Mrs. Richards was safely on the sidewalk, Darcie pulled to the curb and lowered the window.

"'Morning, Mrs. Richards. On your way to the library?" The old woman wore a down vest over her sweater.

"Good morning, Darcie. Yes, for some reading." She peered into the car.

"Mrs. Richards, this is Zeke Zeekowsky, Guest of Honor for the Lilac Festival. Zeke, this is Mrs. Richards."

"Hello, Mrs. Richards."

"Hello, young man. It's a pleasure to meet you, after hearing so much about you from your mother. Of course, I knew your father, too. Wonderful man, wonderful."

"Yes, ma'am." Mention of his father always seemed to expose that bruised look in Zeke's eyes.

"We need to get going, Mrs. Richards," Darcie said. "Just wanted to say hello." She drove a block before stopping to jot a note on her unofficial pad.

"What are you writing?" Zeke asked.

"A reminder to myself about Mrs. Richards. She's going to the library to spend the day because her house is cold. I need to check that she hasn't turned her heat so low that it's dangerous, or worse, that it's been turned off for nonpayment. That happened the winter before last."

"Good God. Why don't people help her?"

Again, she wanted to hit him. The metal form-holder would make a nice satisfying sound against his thick skull.

"It isn't that people wouldn't help her. Last time the church council came through, but she refuses to let anyone know when she needs help."

That's how Drago itself was—refusing to acknowledge it needed help. So, after a series of intense talks interspersed with research into available resources, she and Jennifer had formed an ad hoc committee of two to Do Something About Drago. The sole item on their agenda sat beside her.

So maybe she better not hit him.

"Now the church council is hurting for funds. All the groups who help people are about wiped out. Ted Warinke's donated a lot, but business is starting to hurt at his hardware stores, too, so I don't know how much longer he'll be able to help."

She sensed a downgrade in his mood. So, before he could get defensive or—worse—dismissive, she added, "The town used to plant purple and white pansies."

"What?"

"You said the flowers looked different. That's because the town used to plant pansies, then tulips, followed by petunias.

Neither the town nor the Lilac Festival Committee could afford them the past few years. So volunteers grow them from seed indoors. Only this year we had a late frost and they had to fill in with whatever they could get."

"Huh." This grunt indicated either absorption in what she was saying or absolute lack of interest.

Oh, hell, she couldn't sit here guessing, and she couldn't wait forever to start the pitch.

"This town's struggling, Zeke. Small farmers were the reason Drago started, and they've been its backbone for a long time, but small farmers are fighting the tide of agribusiness giants. The economic downturn hit Drago a second blow. It about brought this area to its knees."

She turned right on Hickory.

"Drago hasn't given up. What it needs most are ways to join in the new economy—not letting go of its farming roots, but supplementing them. Something that can coexist with farming."

"Darcie."

"What?"

"According to that schedule you gave Ma and she's been drumming into me, we'll be late unless we get to the Community Center in four minutes."

"Warren," Darcie said under her breath, as if in answer to something she'd been mulling.

"Who?" The idea for the handheld that had come to him had potential but needed to perk, so he'd resurfaced to find they were at the Community Center. And Darcie wasn't talking about Drago's economy anymore.

"Warren Wellton," she said.

Zeke followed her gaze as she cruised for a parking spot. It was that kid helping with the festival. "What about him?"

"I was wondering how Ashley and Warren knew you were at the police station that first night. Cristina was the instigator to get them to go there, but how did she know? That's the interesting question."

Not especially interesting to him, but he'd play along. "So you think he found out somehow as a favor to his sister?"

"Nope. He did it to impress Ashley," she said immediately.

Zeke watched the kid go inside. This was getting complicated. He tried another tack. "What makes you think he'd be able to find out I was at the police station?"

"Because he reminds me of you."

"Me? He's a fireplug and I'm a beanpole."

"Not anymore—but I'm not talking about appearance. I'm talking about what goes on in your heads. He's shown a lot of aptitude. He rigged Benny's radio and played havoc with the middle school's computers last year. I also suspect he's behind Mildred Magnus's conviction that she's seen ghosts. Warren is too smart and too bored for his own good, just like you were. It's why he gets in trouble."

"I never got into trouble."

"You never got caught."

He nearly smiled. Darcie knew things nobody else did.

"Maybe you were too smart for Drago's police *then*." She clearly didn't consider him too smart for at least one current member of the department. "You left in the nick of time before that restlessness in you exploded."

His eyes cut to her. He hadn't left before another kind of explosion. The kind when two sets of adolescent hormones combine and ignite a reaction he would never forget.

"But you're back," she added with an odd brightness. "And you have the chance to change what didn't happen back then."

"Like what?" he asked cautiously.

She laughed. Not her usual laugh. "Oh, c'mon, Zeke. This is your old pal, Darcie. I knew all your ambitions in high school. *All* your ambitions."

He'd been thinking she knew things about him no one else did, now it seemed she might know things about him *he* didn't know.

He'd wanted to get out of Drago and that had been no secret. Neither had his ambitions. So what was she talking about?

The swell of voices and commotion at the doorway announced the arrival of the horde. He looked over his shoulder. From the midst of the group Jennifer gave him a rueful smile.

He turned back to Darcie. She was watching him.

"What?"

She opened her mouth then closed it. "Nothing more than what I said. I knew all your ambitions."

"I have to make a couple stops before I take you home."

"To my mother's," he muttered reflexively.

He wasn't particularly surprised by Darcie's announcement. Detours had become her MO. The first two days she'd picked him up early at Ma's, then discovered errands she just had to run before they arrived at the Community Center. He'd tolerated stopping at the library, driving past empty buildings, visiting with clergy expressing concern over the community emergency fund's diminishing balance and detouring to a grade school that needed painting. Yesterday she'd managed to "need" to stop at Yolanda Wellton's beauty salon, which was a converted garage on the back of her house that sat practically atop the highway out of town.

For once, Darcie hadn't invited him to come in with her. That didn't mean he'd been spared.

About a minute after she'd gone inside, she and Yolanda

emerged. From the look Darcie shot at the car, he'd guessed she'd decided that having this talk in front of him was preferable to having it in front of whoever was inside.

Yolanda had dark circles under her eyes and slashes of red across her cheeks and nose that created a startling contrast to the rest of her pallor.

Darcie handed the older woman a purse, talking sternly. Yolanda tucked it under her arm, wrapping her loose sweater around herself. Without looking at Darcie, she nodded, but even Zeke could see she didn't mean it.

He'd looked away, and caught the twitch of the curtain at a window in the flimsy connector between the house and salon—the kid, Warren. There'd been something said that first night at the police station, something about his mother driving Warren and Ashley there and that she'd been okay— what had that meant? And where was the kid's father?

It was that moment—the moment of finding himself wondering about family situations that he usually had no trouble shutting out—that Zeke had made his decision.

This morning, when Darcie would have hustled him out of Ma's kitchen for a round of her Social Services Tour of Drago, Zeke had declared he needed to make a business call, then kept it going—despite Vanessa's efforts to wrap it up—until five minutes before they were due at the Community Center.

Now, Darcie *just had to* do something before dropping him back at Ma's. Tomorrow he'd schedule phone calls before and after his festival duties.

Except this time she'd brought him to a residential part of Drago that didn't look as if it were suffering.

The area seemed familiar, though he hadn't had cause to be in this part of Drago when he'd been growing up.

Darcie braked behind an unwieldy truck trying to back into

a narrow drive between a wall and garden. She drummed her fingers on the wheel.

"If you're in a hurry, go around the delivery truck," he proposed.

"I'm afraid it's picking up, not delivering." That sounded strained, but her next words sounded more like her usual tart self. "It's your time I was concerned about. No doubt you want to get to your mother's to work."

"No problem. Relax."

She put the car in neutral and stopped the finger drumming.

He looked out his window. A soft yellow house sat well back from the street. A planting of tall maple trees with landscaped bushes and what he suspected would be blooming flowers during the summer divided the front yard from the street. The drive was a backward *h,* with the straight line connecting to a garage set well behind the house, and the hump of the *h* curving up to the front porch before returning to the street.

The porch's broad steps led to a glossy door set in an arch of glass. Fanlight and sidelights—he remembered from the months when he'd looked for a house and Brenda had insisted he know things like that.

"This is nice," he said.

"Thanks. So what's your house like?"

Her response clicked on the light for him. This was her house—that's why the area was familiar. He hadn't been here often, and that last time, that night after they'd made love, God knows he hadn't been taking in landscaping and architecture.

"Zeke?" she prompted. "Your house?"

House. Right… Only at this moment all he could recall was his office.

He should have tried harder to get Brenda to select the house for him. He suddenly thought he would have liked a front door like this one.

"It has a three-car garage," he said with something akin to triumph. Then he saw her expression and the triumph faded.

"There's a porch." Which he seldom used, because he was seldom home when it was daylight, and what was the point if you couldn't see what was around you? "A lot of trees, especially down by the creek at the back of the property. Uh, bushes that bloom in the spring. Pink. And white."

"Azaleas, maybe?" He'd never understood how she did that. She was laughing at him, no doubt about it, yet it didn't remind him why he generally preferred machines, software and theory to human beings.

"Yeah, that sounds right," he said with a half grin. "The best thing is I can turn the TV screens in the den or my bedroom into giant computer monitors. So I can work from bed if I get an idea during the night."

"I bet your overnight guests love that feature."

He almost said that his rare overnight guests had their own rooms, then he realized she meant women. As in women who shared his bed. The urge to tell her how few of those there had been bubbled in his chest.

"Like It Or Lump It—that's my motto," he said instead.

She grimaced. "Mister Chivalry, aren't you."

"How about you?" he heard coming out of his mouth. "Any overnight guests? I mean guys. Anybody serious?"

"Now? No."

"Ever?"

"I was engaged at the end of college."

A sensation gripped him like that time he'd lived on chili for five weeks because all his money was going into starting up the company.

"At last," she added as the truck cleared the street.

"What happened?"

"He didn't approve of my wanting to be in law enforcement. If I insisted on dealing with the criminal element, I really should be a lawyer." From the prissy tone, he disliked the unknown guy even more.

She negotiated the turn into the drive with easy familiarity. "And," she added with the air of a knockout blow, "he refused to settle in Drago."

Now *that* Zeke didn't hold against the unknown fiancé.

"You couldn't have found a compromise?"

At the end of the drive, two bay windows peeked out over double garage doors. A path ran from the drive to a narrow green alleyway between the side of the garage and an evergreen wall marking the lot line.

"No. I told him from the start I was going to stay here. *Had* to stay, for my mom. So she could keep the house."

"Ma said your mother's working. At the country club."

"Oh, right, like that would be enough to cover the house costs. Besides— Never mind. Stay here. I'll be right back." She jumped out of the car and was gone. No invitation to join her this time.

She'd put the brakes on her words so hard he had practically heard them squeal. Because they were talking about her staying in Drago.

Okay, he could understand how family finances after her father's death pulled her back. Temporarily. And he certainly understood about mothers who wouldn't budge. He'd been grateful his father had paid off the little house on Ash Street, and left Ma some income. But he'd worked two jobs to keep himself at Stanford.

Darcie could have managed, somehow, to get out of Drago, join the FBI and be on her way. You didn't let anything stand in your way.

He frowned, remembering.

Darcie's plans had formed only after he'd dragged her

dreams out of her. It had taken weeks of her sidestepping and evasion before she'd blurted out that she wanted to be an FBI agent. Then she'd tensed like she expected him to make fun of her. Just like with applying to colleges—when he'd asked where she wanted to go, and she'd said it was more a matter of who would let her in—she'd been reluctant to name big career goals.

Was this all part of what he'd first noticed in chem lab? That Darcie hadn't had a lot of faith in herself?

Maybe what she'd needed to get out of Drago was him, pushing her, the way he'd pushed her through chem and into applying to Penn State.

He got out of the car, turned the corner of the garage she'd disappeared around and headed for the stairway attached to its side, with some half-formed notion of beginning the pushing process immediately, when he heard Darcie clattering down the stairs.

She spotted him and raised one eyebrow. Then her gaze shifted to over his shoulder, and she gave a little stutter step and slowed.

He looked around and saw Martha Barrett closing in fast.

"Mom. We were just, uh…" Darcie seemed to come to a decision, not one she particularly liked. "Mom, this is Anton Zeekowsky, the Lilac Festival Guest of Honor. Zeke, this is my mother, Martha Barrett."

"Of course I know Zeke." She took his hand into both of hers and smiled up at him with charm and warmth. "How are you? It's been too long."

Zeke felt nearly as surprised as Darcie looked. He had met Mrs. Barrett a few times, mostly when he'd helped out his father on a Saturday at his shop and she'd come in as a customer. He'd tried to avoid those Saturdays. When he couldn't, he'd tried to avoid interacting with customers, but he hadn't been entirely successful.

"Hello, Mrs. Barrett."

Zeke wouldn't have picked Martha out of a crowd as Darcie's mother. They didn't look alike. Or sound alike. Or move alike. Martha was pretty enough, he supposed, if you liked thin, languid women, but Darcie had vitality.

"We're all so pleased you've come home for this well-deserved honor, Zeke. We're all so proud of you. I hope you're looking forward to the ball."

"Ball?"

"The dinner-dance at the country club," Darcie said. "Mom helps arrange events at the country club, so she's involved with that."

"It's the Lilac Ball," her mother said so sweetly it could be possible to miss the firmness. "And you, of course, are the Guest of Honor, Zeke."

"You're going to freak him out, Mom. We're only telling Zeke one day at a time what activities are coming up. Don't want to scare him into running away from Drago and never looking back. Again."

Zeke knew he wasn't the most attuned to people's nuances and subtext, but he heard something lurking under Darcie's words.

"Nonsense," Martha said with conviction. "You should enjoy every minute. It's not every day your hometown celebrates your accomplishments. Your mother is so proud."

He barely stopped from asking how Martha would know his mother.

A loud voice from across the street made them all look down the driveway to the house with the big truck parked beside it. Two men were maneuvering a large, dark piece of furniture out the front door with difficulty.

"Tip it, Bob. Tip, not drop," one of the men said sharply.

As Zeke turned back to Darcie, he caught a look between her and her mother. Darcie seemed to be asking a question, and Martha Barrett gave a slight nod. "I gave Marabelle the information," she said in a low tone.

Darcie looked away, but not before Zeke saw pain cross her eyes.

"We have to go." Darcie backed toward the car. "We've got another stop before I get Zeke home. See you later, Mom."

Darcie's cell phone rang as they got in the car. It did that a lot.

Police calls came over the radio. These calls were part of the Darcie Barrett Outreach Program. Usually she used a small headset so she could talk while she drove. But she'd taken off the headset when they pulled in, so she answered the phone directly.

She backed down the drive one-handed holding the phone to her ear, but she didn't pull into the street. She flicked a look at him.

"Okay. Yes. I'll tell him. See you tomorrow."

She turned off the phone, reconnected the headset, backed into the street and started off. Martha stood in the driveway, watching.

"Jennifer says hello," Darcie said, not acknowledging her mother, maybe not seeing her, "and she's looking forward to seeing you tomorrow for the run-through at the country club."

He grunted. *Run-through at the country club* sounded ominous. Mrs. Barrett had said something about the country club, too. Maybe he'd better look at that festival schedule his mother had been doling out a day at a time.

"You'll get to spend more time with her tomorrow," Darcie added.

He turned his head to look at her. There'd been significance to those words, but damned if he knew what.

"Jennifer seems distracted," he said.

"What makes you think so?"

"Ah." He didn't know. He'd been puzzling over Darcie's behavior and simultaneously fighting a rising dread of the public functions awaiting him. Somewhere in that, the thought had come that Jennifer seemed distracted.

"She hasn't had the easiest time of it, starting with marrying an asshole." She waved that away. "Okay, okay, I know, that was definitely a minority opinion here in Drago for the longest time."

"One I shared," he said grimly.

"Yes, you did. But because of who he was or who he was dating?" She continued so quickly that her words ran together. "Never mind. You were asking about the past few years."

She was saying he'd considered Eric Stenner an asshole because he'd been dating Jennifer. She was saying he'd been jealous.

"Darcie—"

She ignored his protest. "She's a woman alone trying to raise a kid. That's never easy, especially one about to be a teenager. Her family hasn't been the most supportive, while Eric's parents have been downright hostile, so it's a good thing they'd moved away when Mr. Stenner retired. Anyway, she doesn't have much help. She's starting a new career—real estate. That's more stress."

"The Stenners were always so rich. With the dealership and everything. I'd think the settlement from Stenner would leave her set."

"That's what a lot of people thought."

"They were wrong, these *a lot of people?*" he pursued.

"Eric's brilliant management drove the dealership into near bankruptcy."

He whistled. Stenner Autos had been the flagship of the family's prominence in town, a prominence Eric Stenner had flaunted as a birthright. Now it was gone. And so was he.

Odd. Zeke would have expected having the small world of Drago turned upside down to feel more satisfying. It simply left him empty.

She pulled the car into a parking spot with a view of athletic fields. A baseball diamond, several soccer fields and a trio of tennis courts in the far corner. All teemed with kids.

"I might be here awhile," Darcie said without looking at him, "why don't you come along and stretch your legs."

He could have said no thanks.

He could have kept letting her drag him from place to place where he was supposed to look into the faces of the people of Drago and take them to his bosom, while opening his wallet wide.

He faced her, waiting for her to turn to him. It didn't take long.

"I'm not interested, Darcie. I wasn't interested in the kids of Drago when I lived here. Why would I be now?"

Quit thinking everything revolves around you and your old hurts, Zeke. Even if you were right about those hurts— and you're not—what did these kids ever do to you?

Good thing she'd gotten out of the car after blurting that out, Darcie decided as she searched for Josh Kincannon, the high school principal at his daughter's soccer game. Or she might have said more. A lot more.

Josh had called two days ago, worried because Fay O'Hearn had come to school with another black eye. Darcie wanted to update him—she and Sarge had arranged it so Fay would stay with an aunt for the rest of the school year.

Good news never took long to deliver, and she could have returned to the car right away, but she decided to wind along the paths between the fields, saying hello, watching interactions, observing the people of her town and thinking.

She'd been going about this all wrong. Darcie was irritating Zeke. That had always been her role—irritating him until he poked his head out of his shell, agitating until he responded.

Tomorrow, Jennifer would have a different effect on him entirely. The guy would do about anything the fantasy girl asked.

She didn't mean that as cynically as it might sound, Darcie told herself.

Because if Zeke looked beyond his fantasy, he would see in Jennifer a good and kind and interesting woman.

Darcie looked up and realized her wandering had brought her back to the car where Zeke sat, his dark head bent in concentration over the handheld. He probably hadn't looked up once.

Thank God, she'd long ago come to her senses about Zeke and had become friends with Jennifer. Because at this point, it seemed Jennifer was their only hope to get Zeke to help out his hometown.

Drago Country Club was a lot smaller than Zeke had expected.

The lobby and dining room were ordinary. The outdoor pool was empty and the diving boards had been removed for the off-season.

Somehow, in his imagination, the country club pool was always open. Always uncrowded. Always glittering. Unlike the community pool, where he'd learned to swim and dive as a kid.

He sidled away from the discussion of how the queen and her court would be introduced the night of the dinner-dance— Lilac Ball, Mrs. Barrett corrected. He was grateful the dispute gave him the chance to get away.

From here they were going to Lilac Commons for the official presentation of the court, though he couldn't imagine who would come out on a cool night for this. Thank God tomorrow's schedule was entirely clear. He'd have the whole day to himself and finally get some work done.

He saw Darcie sitting, making notes. As he approached, she glanced up, but returned to her work immediately.

Zeke straddled a chair so he could lean his crossed arms on the top of the back. Darcie had that look of determination she used to get in chem lab. *Do not tell me the answer, Zeekowsky. I'll get it. Just give me a darned minute.*

He used to like to watch her face when she got that way. To see her mix impatience, doggedness and intelligence to come up with the solution. When she did, it was as if lightning sparkled from inside her.

She had changed remarkably little for all the years that had passed. There was a little less softness in her face. A more serious line to her mouth. An added steadiness to her eyes.

But still that skin… Not until he'd touched her cheek the night they graduated had he realized he'd spent years wondering if it could possibly be as soft and sweet as it looked. It had been even softer and sweeter.

Then he'd found skin so soft and sweet it had exploded his senses.

"Why are you looking at me like that?" Darcie demanded.

Unfazed by being caught staring at her, because she couldn't possibly know what he'd been remembering, he continued to regard her.

"I was wrong. I thought yesterday that you didn't look like your mother, but you do." When they stood side by side, he'd seen the differences, now he saw similarities.

"You're crazy."

He'd said the wrong thing. "Maybe look isn't right. Not like you're a replica, but I can see the—" he'd almost said *same source code* "—resemblance."

She shook her head.

He persisted. "Gestures, expressions—people in the same family can share those things."

She grimaced. "You mean I've copied her mannerisms?"

"I didn't—"

"Hell, you're probably right." She hadn't heard or didn't care about his protest. "When I was a kid, I would have groveled at your feet if you'd said I reminded you of my mother. I tried everything to be more like her."

"Why?"

"Real funny, Zeekowsky."

She seemed to think his *why* had been sarcastic. "So, you wanted to look like your mother?"

"Only in my dreams. Even as a kid, I could see I wasn't made from the same material. Sometimes, it didn't seem like she was human. Oh, yeah, it was great fun growing up being Martha Barrett's daughter. Beautiful, ethereal Martha Barrett. Jennifer should have been her daughter instead of me. Ethereal is not something people say about me."

What was so damned good about ethereal? "She's thin."

"You know what they say, you can never be too rich or too thin. At least she's got one of those covered." Darcie's shoulders lifted and she sat straighter. "When I grew up, I recognized that being a carbon copy of Martha Barrett was not a good idea. After my father died…well, this family couldn't afford two people without their feet on the ground."

Darcie always had had her feet on the ground. "You're sturdy," he said.

"Sturdy. Thanks." But she chuckled.

"You don't look like you'd break if someone touched you."

"I wouldn't."

He caught something in her words. "You think your mother

would? That's really why you came back." He shook his head. "I think you're wrong."

"After meeting her, what—twice?" she scoffed. "Look, she's not like your mother. Mrs. Z left everything she knew behind and came to a new country and made a life here. That takes tremendous courage and strength."

And sacrifice. But he didn't want to talk about that. Instead, he tried to sort out what Darcie was saying and what she *wasn't* saying. God! Give him a dozen hard drives to reformat any day.

"This all has to do with the Lilac Queen stuff, doesn't it." His words gained confidence as he went on. "It's still about a beauty queen contest when you were seventeen."

"It's *not* a beauty queen contest," she mumbled. "The princesses are supposed to be chosen as the best representatives of Drago—grades, poise, charm. I was a fool to enter."

"Not a fool," he said. "You had advantages over Jennifer— leadership, academics and talking to people. It must have been a tight vote."

Darcie noticed he didn't say anything about her looks making it a close race. No surprise there.

"Tight? No. Unanimous for Jennifer." Odd, after all these years, to still feel that blow.

"Ah. And, what? You're still letting that determine how you feel about yourself? A beauty queen contest when you were seventeen?"

She bolted upright with indignation. "And you're not?"

"I've never entered a beauty contest in my life."

She swatted his arm. "No, you're just lusting after the beauty queen."

His expression shifted into something unreadable.

She wished she'd kept her mouth shut. Or should she say more? Present her theory that he was operating on some unconscious notion that by winning over the beauty queen he could make his whole high school experience—maybe his whole life in Drago—change retroactively?

No. Because what if he got past the adolescent crush and found something real with Jennifer? There were no two people she more hoped would find happiness. She just wished they would do it out of her sight.

"You can't mean that Cris girl?" Zeke sounded so horrified she laughed.

"Not Cristina." But before Darcie could add *Jennifer,* Jennifer herself called Zeke to the front of the room.

He was in Jennifer's hands now. Darcie would fade from view and Jennifer would take over, starting with giving him a ride home from this session. Jennifer would succeed in persuading him to help their hometown.

It was best all around this way.

"Brenda?"

"Who's calling please?"

"You know who's calling—Zeke." He kept his voice low. Not that the clot of women debating whether the princesses' tables and the queen's table should have the same centerpieces were likely to listen, even if they noticed him on his cell in the far corner of the dining room. Darcie was nowhere in sight. "What are you doing in the office? It's Saturday. And you're on vacation."

"Apparently not."

"Why?"

"The wild lure of working without you interrupting pulled me back. And yet," she continued, "here you are interrupting me, again."

"I was going to leave a message, but this is better. I want you to ship me a D prototype handheld by overnight. Maybe you better send me a couple."

"A couple? R&D will not be happy."

"Make it four. Just in case. Send them to me at Ma's. The address—"

"I know your mother's address. What do you want them for?"

"I have an idea."

Brenda made a choking sound. When she spoke again, he knew she wasn't talking to him. "He says he's got an idea."

Zeke recognized the answering groan.

"Quince wants to talk to you," Brenda said.

"No. I don't have time."

"Zeke." Quince's voice came on the line. Zeke gave a fleeting thought to what it would be like to have an assistant who did what he told her. "This trip is strictly to keep you out of temptation's way until the announcement. You are *not* there to have ideas. I can't take any more of your ideas."

"I'm not going to stop having ideas because you feel overworked, Quince. I want to see if—"

"I want to talk to you about these rumors."

That stopped Zeke. "What rumors?"

"Rumblings someone might leak our news before the announcement."

"They say that every time."

"I know. But there's something about these… My bad-news-is-coming knee is throbbing like hell. Just don't say anything to anybody."

"Who would I tell?"

"You're in your hometown, you get relaxed, your guard comes down around people you trust."

"Outside of Zeke-Tech, I don't trust any—" It would have been untrue to say he didn't trust anybody here. Two anybodies. Ma and Darcie.

"Who'd you tell?'" Quince demanded.

"Nobody."

"Zeke, I know that tone."

"I didn't say anything except *nobody.*"

"That's enough." Quince sounded grim. "You've got to keep this quiet a few more weeks, Zeke. Don't get tempted, just don't get tempted. And don't lose that laptop. Never should have let you take it in the first place."

"I've gotta work," Zeke protested.

"No, you don't. That's the whole idea of this trip."

He hadn't lied. He hadn't *told* anyone. But he had given Darcie that disk with the trial program on it.

Thousands of techies would give a limb for a look at the new Zeke-Tech product before its official introduction. Darcie hadn't said a single word.

"Warren?" Darcie peered at the boy in the gloom of the back hallway.

He jumped and spun around, putting a black gizmo resembling her cell phone headset behind him.

She'd come to peek into the dining room to see if everyone had left. She'd excused herself earlier, leaving the path clear for Jennifer and Zeke to pair up. But something wouldn't let her risk stranding Zeke. *Just in case.* Possibly the something was the wrath of Chief Dutch Harnett.

"What are you doing, Warren?"

"Fixing the sound system."

Sound system? Out here? "I didn't know it had a problem."

"I'd already fixed it," he said. "I was checking it was okay."

"Is it?"

A satisfied smile lit his pudgy face. "Yeah."

"Good. Then you better get going before everyone leaves."

"Yeah, okay." He grabbed his bag and headed off.

She pushed the curtain open.

Neither Zeke nor Jennifer was in sight. The centerpiece controversy raged on. Her mother was trying to soothe the crowd.

Darcie edged around the room, heading for the exit. She did not want to get caught in this dispute.

She would make sure Zeke had left with Jennifer. So what if she might see Zeke with his hand on Jennifer's back or looking down into her face with his characteristic concentrated attention.

She'd be glad they were together. She would. Because it would be good for Drago. Although it would be easier to be glad if she hadn't had the dreams about the night they made love. Actually, twice.

He'd levered himself up, and the thought had torn through her like a sob that he would get up and act as if nothing had happened. Instead, he'd maneuvered around doing something in the dark that only later had she realized was disposing of the condom. Then he'd come back and put his arms stiffly around her. She'd curled into him, her face into his shoulder so he couldn't see her expression, so she didn't have to see his.

She had no idea how long they'd stayed like that. And no idea which of them started moving. It seemed, though, that with the first friction of skin against skin, the fire roared again.

Afterward she lay with his weight on top of her, and she knew then that she could live a good life, love other people, be happy. But she would never completely get over Anton Zeekowsky.

Chapter Five

"You ready?"

Darcie swallowed a gasp but couldn't control her body's jolt, an automatic reaction to Zeke's voice from behind her shoulder. She spun around to him.

"We're not going to stay here all day, are we?" His eyes were half-closed as he breathed in deeply through his nose.

"I thought you'd go with Jennifer."

"Why? You and I, we have a deal. You brought me, I go back with you."

All pretty simple to him, by that tone. The unfairness of it burned through Darcie. Because their *deal* didn't include being dragged around like a third wheel.

She drove out under a twilight sky dotted with puffs of navy clouds trying not to grind her teeth.

"Darcie? Are you okay? I mean is there something…"

The length of his silence drew her gaze despite herself. "Something what?"

"You know, something wrong."

"No, I don't know. What could be wrong?"

He looked at her the way he'd looked at her back in chem lab when she'd recited poetry. Like there was something in front of him he didn't understand, but, unlike unknowns in math or science, he wasn't sure he wanted to try to understand. "You seem edgy."

"I am not edgy."

He fell into another silence. A silence during which he studied her in a way that *made* her edgy. She hadn't been when he'd first said it. Not really. So she wasn't going to amend her statement.

"Sometimes it's just like when we were kids," he said abruptly. "And sometimes it's not."

"Things were bound to be different after all these years." But things would have been different even without all the years. Because some things changed a relationship forever. "You can't expect the awkwardness to just go away."

"You said that before. Well, not that exactly, but you said putting me in handcuffs got us past the first awkward part. What awkward part?"

Faced with such a direct question, she felt obliged to answer equally forthrightly. "Seeing each other again."

He looked astonished. "Why did you think it would be awkward?"

"Gee, I don't know," she snapped. "Maybe because you never contacted me after…after—oh, hell, after we had sex."

His forehead creased. "You knew I was leaving. The next day, for that summer program at Stanford. You knew I didn't plan to ever come back. You knew—" His eyes widened slightly, as if he'd been hit by a recognition for the first time. "You knew better than anyone how much I wanted to get out of here."

Wasn't that just like him. He not only didn't respond to her bringing up their making love, but he also ignored it completely.

"Sometimes, Anton Zeekowsky, you are one of the densest human beings on the face of this earth. Of course I knew you were leaving. I wasn't expecting you to stay, for heaven's sake. But a phone call? A letter? It is possible to have communication with those in Drago without being sucked back into its deadly vortex, you know."

He squinted, as if he could see the past. "I guess I was so focused on what I was heading toward that I didn't think much about what I left behind. Besides," he added, "you were going to leave, too."

Even if she'd stayed at Penn State, he could have reached her at home over holidays and the summer. And if he'd ever tried, he would have known that she'd come back. All she said was, "Right."

"Why didn't you leave Drago for good, Darcie?"

"I told you."

He shook his head. "If you'd really wanted to leave, if you'd wanted to leave as much as I did—"

"I didn't." They'd come to a stop sign and she looked at him, level and reasonable. "You wanted to get out no matter what. I wasn't willing to get out at any cost."

"What do you mean at any cost?"

She looked both ways on the highway, which meant she couldn't look at him anymore. "You left and you never looked back." She eased the car into the turn. "I'm not criticizing you, Zeke. You did what you felt you had to do. I'm pointing out our paths were different. *We're* different."

She refused to let this silence or the knowledge that he was studying her face—again—get to her. She paid attention to the road. Being distracted was the number one cause of accidents. So what if hers was the only vehicle around. Focus was good.

"Sorry, Darcie," he said after too damn long. "Especially, I'm sorry you haven't had a chance to pursue your dreams away from Drago."

She shrugged. "Things work out for the best. Probably saved me from finding out I wouldn't have made it. This way I can still dream about it."

Wouldn't have made it, his ass. Of course she would have made it. She had to know that. And she *would* know it if he had anything to say about it.

Zeke would have told her that right then if Darcie's cell phone hadn't started again. Mildred Magnus and some nonsense about ghosts. Somebody had a hang nail and they all expected Darcie to take care of it.

By the time she'd finished the call, they were at Lilac Commons and a swirl of people never let him alone the rest of the night. Who knew all those people would put on their winter coats to watch five goose pimpled teenage girls introduced as "royalty"? He'd been prepared to slip away when Mr. Carter, his old chemistry teacher, had stopped to say hello. Ma insisted Mr. Carter come back to the house, along with a "few friends." He'd had a great talk with Mr. Carter and enjoyed seeing old neighbors, though he'd kept hoping Darcie would show up. She never did.

Lying in his old narrow bed later, his mind had gone back to Darcie's comment. He'd decided showing her was far better than telling her. Words were messy, action wasn't.

But even he had known action should wait until this morning. He slept, but woke early and crept out of the house silently.

Now, he hit speed dial for Brenda. His assistant could be pushy and maddeningly independent, but she'd find out everything he needed to know.

She didn't answer. But then the sun hadn't risen yet here

in Illinois and it was Sunday. He left a detailed message and replaced the cell phone, shifting more comfortably on his perch on the top fence rail.

He'd been so focused on Darcie and his plans he'd barely taken in his surroundings, the whole reason he'd driven here at dawn.

"'Morning."

The male voice jerked Zeke's head around, but his muscles instinctively rebalanced him, so he didn't tumble.

Under a blue baseball cap with a Chicago Cubs insignia, the man was white-haired and seam-faced. His right shoulder dipped lower than his left.

"Sorry. I'm trespassing. I'll leave,"

"Didn't say that. Just said *'Morning.*"

Zeke relaxed some. "'Morning."

The man nodded, then rested down-jacketed forearms on the top rail beside Zeke. "Nice spot."

"I used to ride out here from town on my bike as a kid," Zeke confessed.

"I remember."

Zeke looked down at the man, who continued to stare toward the horizon. "You knew I was here?"

"Yup."

Yet he'd never shooed away a trespassing boy he didn't know.

"You weren't hurtin' anything," the man said, as if he'd heard Zeke's thoughts.

"Thank you. I used to come here to think."

"Good place to do it. Been doing it all my life."

Zeke looked at green plants rising from black loam. As a kid, he'd taken for granted that the earth could give so much. Seeing the hard red clay, thin sandy dust, rocky iron-dotted ground of other areas of the country had made him remember the rich black earth around Drago.

"Yes, it is a good place. You must love this farm to spend your life here."

"Wouldn't be worth much anywhere else." The old man snorted. "Not worth much here anymore. Can't run the place myself. My nephew was running it, but he's gone, and his widow, she's stubborn as the day is long, but she's a woman."

Zeke thought of Darcie, then his mother and Vanessa and Brenda.

"Don't sell her short because she's a woman."

The farmer shook his head. "It's tough going now. Not like when I started out. Most farms need somebody working another job. That's what Anne would have to do, too—no matter what that stubborn woman says—*if* there were jobs for the getting 'round here."

"Then she'd give up this farm?"

The man's mouth twisted. "Nah. Even if she wasn't born to it, she feels it. We do what we gotta do to keep it breathin', even on a respirator."

Zeke wondered about feeling that passionately about a place, as passionately as Darcie felt about Drago. Passion about ideas—that he knew.

"There she is," the farmer said.

Zeke looked around, before realizing the farmer meant the sun. It crested the horizon, light streaming down rows of newly planted corn toward them like extended rays of a child's drawing.

"That's somethin'," the farmer said. "That's really somethin'."

A man who must have seen this sight a thousand times, still felt its thrill.

"Yeah, that's really something."

* * *

"Mom? Mother!" Darcie called as she came in the back door.

No answer. She checked the kitchen, then went to the bottom of the stairs and called again. No Martha Barrett.

On her return trip to the kitchen to leave a note about the sudden need for two vegetarian plates at the ball after Ashley's instant conversion when Cristina announced she no longer ate meat, light slanting across the glass fronts of her father's cases in the library caught Darcie's eye.

She hesitated at the doorway before stepping inside.

She huffed out a small breath. It actually looked like a library. Her mother had put in a pair of reupholstered easy chairs from the basement rec room with a floor lamp for each and a desk with another good reading light. Books filled the empty spaces in the cases that must have struck a blow at her mother each time she'd looked at them.

When Gordon Barrett had been alive, the cases had teemed with art he'd collected. A few small paintings, but mostly Japanese and eighteenth century French porcelains. He'd spent hours each night in this room with his collections, the door closed.

Everyone had thought his collections were a sign of how well the Barretts were doing. Darcie had known, at some level, they were a sign that he preferred inanimate objects to her.

After his death, they'd discovered how wrong they'd all been about the first premise. What her father had collected most successfully was debt.

She'd had no idea. Clearly, neither had her mother.

After Gordon Barrett's death, Darcie had been torn. Wanting to return to school, unable to leave wraithlike Martha to make the decisions.

"I'm sorry, Darcie. So sorry. We'll have to sell it all," she'd said of the collections. "I'll call Riesners."

"No," Darcie had said. Even with her limited experience, she had recognized that shock was behind Martha's stunning declaration. "I'll do it."

True, they had to sell to relieve the debt. But Darcie couldn't let her mother's grief and lack of business sense send her father's lifetime of collecting to be unloaded through the local antique emporium for a pittance.

So Darcie had gone over his possessions item by item, contacting three galleries in Chicago and two in New York. Then another reality had hit. The paintings Gordon Barrett had bought were knockoffs, few of the porcelains were Japanese or French and none were eighteenth century. She adjusted her thinking and set about getting the best prices she could.

Her mother had artfully arranged the items of Gordon's collection no one had been willing to buy in splendid isolation in the library cases.

"They look better this way," Martha had said, a tear on her cheek.

That was the moment Darcie knew she couldn't leave her fragile mother. She certainly couldn't let the house be sold out from under her.

So Darcie withdrew from Penn State, enrolled at Mid-Northern Illinois as a commuter and used the bulk of her college fund to pay off the mortgage.

"Why did you do that? Why, Darcie?" her mother had asked, tears streaming down her face.

Darcie had shaken her head mutely, not having the words to explain without walking on her mother's fragility like someone in army boots tromping on a sore toe. They had not talked about it again.

Even with being careful about household expenses, the remnants of Darcie's college fund, which was all they had left, had dwindled shockingly by the time she graduated. If she'd left then, what would her mother have had to live on, much less pay taxes?

So she'd applied to the Drago Police Department.

After a couple months, she noticed her mother was spending less time at home, and the household account had barely budged. That's when Martha told her the manager of the country club had asked her to help organize and arrange social events there, and he insisted on paying her.

"I know your father wouldn't have liked it," she'd said apologetically.

Darcie could almost hear Gordon Barrett's cool tones. "My wife being paid to, in essence, serve our peers? Absolutely not."

Tough. He'd landed them in this mess, so he'd forfeited any right to dictate, especially from the grave.

"Do you like the work, Mom?"

"Yes. Yes, I do."

"Great. And the money doesn't hurt."

Martha had stared a moment as if she'd said something shocking, then chuckled.

They'd gotten on better after that. Maybe they'd both been too busy to fret much about mother-daughter conflicts. As they both earned more money, things had eased enough for Darcie to fix up the apartment over the garage, and move into her own space.

She'd ventured past the main house's kitchen infrequently enough to be caught by surprise by the changes in the library.

It looked like a different room. She liked it.

Cars lined both sides of the street all along Mrs. Z's block. Darcie got lucky, the vice-chair of the church council was leaving and waved to indicate her spot was opening up.

So much for Zeke's quiet Sunday afternoon to work. Apparently Mrs. Z and the rest of Drago had other ideas. Darcie grinned. Mrs. Z was missing no opportunity to fill her house with guests.

Darcie spotted a clot of people around the back door, making that entrance an obstacle course, so she went in the front. Another dozen people milled around the living room, including most of the town council and their spouses. Her progress was slowed by hellos, questions and comments, but she gained a spot outside the doorway to the kitchen, which was populated even more thickly.

She saw Zeke's head above everyone else's in the kitchen. Jennifer was beside him. Surrounding them were mothers of Lilac Queen contestants, as well as two members of the church council, the head of the library board and Vicki from the *Intelligencer.* Amid the voices, Darcie heard Mrs. Z's, excited and happy, with a crowd in her house to feed and fuss over—especially the tall one in the middle.

Darcie couldn't see Zeke's expression, because he had lowered his head to listen to Jennifer. There wasn't a chance he was actually happy, but at least his body language didn't convey rage. That was good.

Josh Kincannon gave a pained grin as he slid between people to emerge from the kitchen and join her in a sliver of space.

"Couldn't take the crowd, huh, Josh?"

"It is crammed. And I didn't have any reason to stay." His grin twisted. "I took a shot with our giant of technology. No go. He's tough, isn't he?"

Uh-oh. "Sorry, Josh." She winced in sympathy as they both stepped back from the doorway in search of more breathing room. "Zeke can be, uh, blunt. He doesn't realize—"

"Don't worry, Darcie. He didn't leave any scars." This

time his grin had less twist to it. "He did it really well. Never turned nasty, but didn't budge an inch. In fact, I wouldn't mind the kids being exposed to Mr. Zeekowsky and seeing how a truly powerful man can handle himself."

She hadn't really thought of Zeke that way before. A genius, sure—she'd known that since high school. And obviously he was rich. But somehow she hadn't quite melded all that together into the idea of Zeke being powerful. Wielding that kind of power had to affect a man, had to change him.

"He'd be a great role model for them," Josh was saying. "He's got to be tough to have gotten to where he is, but he's not mean."

"You don't think so?"

He wrapped his hand around her arm above the elbow and smiled at her. "Just because he doesn't do what you want doesn't mean he's mean."

"I suppose not." Maybe not mean, but a real pain in the patoot when he wouldn't do what she wanted—what the town needed.

Josh chuckled at her morose tone.

"So tell me about this plan he turned down," she ordered.

He launched into a description of his proposal for a multi-leveled program to provide computer access and training. It sounded great.

Josh was a far cry from Mr. Grandhier, the principal when she and Zeke had been in school. Mr. Grandhier had been about a hundred years old. Josh was about her age, and had more on his plate than any one person deserved. In addition to being principal, he had three kids and his wife had left them.

"Looks like you're in Mr. Zeekowsky's sights," Josh said.

She looked around and saw Zeke making his way through the kitchen crowd, trailing mothers still extolling their contestant daughters. Jennifer remained by the counter, talking with Mrs. Z.

The clog of people at the doorway stopped Zeke's progress. Over their heads, Zeke's eyes locked with hers, and she read his request clearly.

She excused herself from Josh and reached the living room side of the doorway. Zeke sidestepped to the near edge and bent to speak into her ear.

"Did you have something to do with this? All these people showing up."

"Me? I just arrived. Could barely get in."

He glowered down at her, apparently not buying her innocence, though, really, she was innocent this time. Mostly.

After Mrs. Z had made the suggestion, she'd only said a few words to a few people...true, a few carefully chosen people. That was one benefit of living in a small town. You knew who to talk to.

"You shouldn't have answered the door if you didn't want to socialize."

"I didn't open it. Ma did. And she insisted I join everyone."

She chuckled. Then he leaned closer. His breath stirred her hair, whispering across her ear. The chuckle stuck in her throat.

"I've got to get out of here, Darcie. It's been like this all afternoon. Besides, I need a steak. I'm about to explode from all Ma's sauces."

Was it a memory that made her imagine the sensation of his lips on her ear, kissing around it, under it, tugging on the lobe... Or a wish?

"We wouldn't want that," she said, amazed at how normal her voice sounded. "Steak sounds like a good idea."

"Yeah. So I'm taking Jennifer out to dinner."

The cold water of his words went down Darcie's back, freezing it rigid. "Makes sense. Have a good time. See you later."

She turned away. She thought she heard him say her name, but she kept moving. She had to be out of here before he and Jennifer left together.

Besides, she had somewhere important to get to. Her bathroom. So she could look in the mirror to memorize exactly what she looked like when she was being a first-class idiot.

At Loris's Café, crowded with people who'd spent Sunday afternoon visiting Lilac Commons Park or on historical tours, Zeke looked across the table at Jennifer. She was even more beautiful than in high school.

The first time a beautiful woman had chased him had been a rush. That was also the last time it had been a rush. And Jennifer was far from chasing him. Besides, she was as bad as Darcie. All she wanted to talk about was Drago. Odd, when Jennifer did it, it didn't get under his skin nearly as much. But it didn't entertain him as much, either.

"Who was that guy Darcie was talking to?" he asked in the first lull.

"What guy?"

"At my house—my mother's house. Medium height, dark sport jacket." He'd wrapped a hand familiarly around Darcie's arm. She'd looked up into his face as she'd smiled a warm welcome.

Jennifer laughed. "Only you would say Josh Kincannon was medium height, Zeke—he's got to be six-one. And you know who he is. You talked to him for ten minutes. He was telling you about his students who'd really benefit by having more computer access. He's the principal at Drago High."

"Oh, yeah."

The guy had seemed nice enough. Sure, he'd wanted Zeke to fund the computers, but Zeke had requests like that all the time, and the guy had done it well. He'd even taken Zeke's refusal with a no-hard-feelings acceptance.

If it had been a school anywhere else, Zeke probably would have directed him to the foundation. But he'd said no to Josh Kincannon. Because he was the principal of Drago High School.

Quit thinking everything revolves around you and your old hurts, Zeke. Even if you were right about those hurts—and you're not—what did these kids ever do to you?

"Zeke?"

He became aware Jennifer had spoken his name only after she touched his hand.

"I was—" *Listening.* No, he wasn't. "Oh, hell, Jennifer. I'm sorry. My mind was on other things."

"I know."

He found himself staring. Not because her beauty or her smile stirred him, but because of the comfort he felt with that smile. There weren't many people he felt comfortable with. The chances of Jennifer joining their number had never occurred to him. He'd worshipped her, been tongue-tied around her and mooned after her. It was a jolt to realize now that she was nice. Beautiful and very nice. And didn't stir anything in him except liking.

"You and Darcie have always had a connection," she said.

"What?" When had she changed the subject to Darcie? Or had he?

"A connection," she repeated. "I remember how different you always were when Darcie was around, like you plugged in." She chuckled. "Or more like she dragged you out into the light."

His mouth twitch. "Dragged, pushed and zapped me with a cattle prod sometimes." Sort of the way he'd pulled the shade off her academic ability.

"She is determined."

"About some things," he said.

Probably saved me from finding out I wouldn't have made it.

Darcie still needed prodding, and he was just the man to do it. As soon as Brenda lined things up.

He found Jennifer giving him a look that reminded him of his assistant.

"But that doesn't mean— We're not…you know," he said.

"That's okay." She patted his hand. He didn't like this smile nearly as much as her previous one. "You'll figure it out, Zeke. I have faith in you."

Yeah, it was the Brenda smile that meant he was missing something.

The best way he'd discovered to avoid being told what he was missing was to change the subject. "I can't believe Stenner left you."

She chuckled ruefully. "You don't beat around the bush, do you, Zeke?"

"No. But if you don't want to talk about it, I'll shut up. Otherwise I'll tell you that even for Eric Stenner, it was a stupid move."

She studied her hands, folded on top of the table. "Oh, I'm certain some people believe the only reason a hometown hero like Eric would leave his wife and child would be because he discovered something horrible."

"Bullshit. Darcie said you haven't had the easiest time."

She withdrew her hands across the tablecloth toward her lap, her gaze following the motion. "Oh, at the start, sure. But Ashley and I are doing fine."

He put a hand over both of hers before they could disappear. "Child support?"

She looked up, clearly surprised at the directness. "I have a job, Zeke. Once I get established in real estate, it'll be fine. I'll make it fine for Ashley."

He heard fierceness. He recognized it as the fierceness

he'd felt in his determination to make something of himself, to escape Drago.

"I know you'll do great, Jennifer. I'd sure as hell buy real estate from you if I were in the market here. But sometimes, when you're starting out, you need something to carry you through. If you need help—"

"No." She tried to smile and didn't achieve it. But the next words were softer. "Thank you, but no."

"Do you mind if I… I mean… What the hell happened? Darcie said Stenner Autos is nearly bankrupt, and he left. Was he crazy?"

"Thank you, Zeke. You're sweet."

"I'm not trying to be sweet—I mean it. What happened?"

"Let's say Eric became more of himself."

"That's a shame."

She started to laugh.

"So, how was dinner with Zeke?"

Darcie's words came out before she could pull them back. Almost as if she'd followed Jennifer to the refreshment table looking for an opportunity with no audience to ask that very question.

She wouldn't have asked, except Zeke had seemed odd about it on the drive here for the second round of queen candidate interviews.

She'd picked up a vibe while he'd asked question after question about Josh Kincannon. At first she'd answered, thinking he was interested in Josh's proposal for a computer lab in town. But when he'd zeroed in on Josh's dating habits, she'd stopped answering the Zeekowsky inquisition.

If he was worried that Jennifer and Josh had something going, he'd have to ask Jennifer. On the other hand, if there was tension between him and Jennifer, she had a duty to find out. For Drago.

"Dinner was interesting and pleasant, but not particularly productive, and the aftermath was a near disaster."

Darcie felt a squeeze of nausea. "Aftermath? You and Zeke—?"

"Not Zeke. The aftermath was with Ashley." Jennifer sighed. "She was furious with me for going out with Zeke."

"Why? She hasn't had trouble with your other dates."

"Please, don't let her hear you call it a date. I assured her it was two old friends catching up. It was either that or be accused of heinous crimes against the sisterhood." Jennifer must have seen Darcie's puzzlement. "Ashley sees Zeke as belonging to Cristina."

"Oh, my God."

Jennifer nodded. "Stop laughing. You don't have to live with her. I don't think Zeke will think it's funny to know he's been cast in this grand romance. You'll never guess where Ashley got the idea."

"Cristina, of course."

Another nod. "Whatever Cristina says is gospel with Ashley. She's already outraged at the horrible behavior of the other contestants."

"Huh?"

"Because they fawn all over him."

Darcie gaped. How could anyone fawn over Zeke more than Cristina?

Jennifer giggled first. Darcie was sure of that. But then the contagion hit, and they both stumbled down the hall with their hands over their mouths until they reached the open back door, where they gave in to the amusement.

Finally, wiping her eyes, Jennifer said, "In a way Ashley's got a point. Some of the other contestants have started following Cristina's lead."

"And the mothers," Darcie added. Another giggle erupted. "Poor Zeke."

Instead of laughing, Jennifer sighed. "I'll tell you, Darcie, I wish to heaven I'd refused to let Ashley be the junior princess. I know it's an honor, but it's like she's gone straight from little girl to the deep end of the teen drama pool, and she's not ready. If she can't even see what Cristina is, how will she ever cope?"

Darcie patted her shoulder. "She's got a good head on her shoulders. She'll come around about Zeke. Don't worry about that."

Jennifer waved that off as an issue. "Sorry. I've been giving in to maternal panic when I should be answering your question about dinner. This could be harder than we thought, Darcie. I kept trying to bring the conversation around to helping out Drago but he was less than receptive. He wanted to know all about Josh Kincannon."

Voices from inside reached them. Darcie thought she heard Ashley calling.

"Yeah, he was asking me about him, too," Darcie said. "So he might not be as closed off to the proposal as Josh thought. The computer lab would be a great start to—"

Jennifer shook her head. "What Zeke wanted to know about was if there's something going on between you and Josh."

Darcie replayed Zeke's questions. "Why? Where on earth would he get the idea something was going on between me and Josh?"

"Where he got the idea, I don't know, but as for the why— come on, Darcie. That's so obvious."

Darcie would have requested more explanation, but then Ashley came through the doorway, demanding her mother return because *everyone was being just horrid to Cristina.*

Chapter Six

Zeke had developed moves since he'd returned to Drago that would have made an NFL ballcarrier proud.

Darcie watched as he eluded Ted Warinke, sidestepped earnest Nancy Lynn, then deked a pair of mothers, safely reaching Jennifer on the far side of the gathering on the stage. The second round of judging interviews was over and they awaited the director's return from sorting out technical problems to give them two sets of instructions for the remaining ceremonies, one if the weather was good and one it if wasn't.

Jennifer gave him a distracted smile and continued watching the interaction between Cristina and Ashley.

It was a one-sided interaction. The older girl's drama eclipsed everyone around her, but it left Ashley practically invisible. Not even the director gave her instructions anymore. Only Warren's single-mindedness kept Ashley within the realm of the spotlight, although no longer singled out.

At that moment, Cristina, with Ashley in tow, headed for Zeke.

Darcie's muscles tensed in preparation to run interference. She consciously relaxed them. Not only had he improved at fending off Cristina, but she'd be an idiot to go charging in when Jennifer was right there to provide aid.

Cristina grasped Zeke's arm and ran her hand down it, as if checking for damage to the goods.

Without looking at the young woman or interrupting whatever he was saying to Jennifer, Zeke shrugged, dislodging Cristina's hold, then sidestepped her attempt to reattach.

Cristina pouted, and immediately moved between Zeke and Jennifer—she clearly wasn't going to waste a perfectly good pout on his back.

However, Zeke's back remained the target of Ashley's glare of outraged dislike. Boy, Jennifer hadn't been kidding about how Ashley felt about him. Would Jennifer even consider a relationship with Zeke if her daughter felt that way?

Lost in these thoughts, Darcie was only half aware when Zeke strode away from the little group and headed into the huddle at center stage.

"Darcie."

She jumped at his voice. Or maybe at the warmth of his hand wrapped around her elbow.

"I want to talk to you about that guy," he continued, at the same time pivoting her and propelling her toward backstage.

Darcie double-checked, first over her shoulder at a stage full of females, then ahead of them.

"What guy?"

"That guy you told me about."

"A guy I told you about? Warren?" Or did he mean Josh?

"That kid? No, the guy you were going to marry."

"Oh." That guy. To say she hadn't expected this was like

saying she hadn't expected the sky to be brown this morning.
"What about him?"

Dredging up memories, she geared up for an unemotional
APB rundown of height, weight, coloring, age and distin-
guishing marks. Then Zeke caught her off guard for the
second time in half a minute.

"Do you ever hear from him?" he asked.

She cut him a look and found him staring. "Not since we
broke it off."

His lips barely moved, but she thought she heard a curse.

"It was mutual. We were after different things. When it
came down to it, we were too young to get married. It's a good
thing we realized it in time."

"Do you think about him?"

No. "Why are you asking me this stuff?"

"To gather data. It's a crude method, but convenient."

Data. Great. "I have something more important to talk to
you about than some detached scientific interest in my past
relationships."

"*Relationships*—plural?"

She ignored that. "This is about something right now and
important. Zeke, you need to talk to Cristina."

That stopped him. In fact, it seemed to freeze him in place.
"Talk to her? I thought you were going to run interference for
me with all these people."

"Oh, no, you don't. I said I'd help you so you could
handle stuff yourself, and that's what I'm doing by telling
you that you have to make it clear to her that you don't return
her feelings."

"Feelings?"

You'd think she'd said a dirty word. Darcie waved a hand
in front of his face, checking if he was in a trance. "Hello?
Zeke? Are you in there? Have you noticed how she treats you?"

"She's a kid."

"She's sixteen. That's not much younger than..." No, maybe better to skip the topic of how he'd lusted after Jennifer since that age. Before Darcie arrived at an alternative, he spoke.

"Not much younger than when we first made love."

One sentence. That's all, and it provided about a thousand things to react to. That he'd referred to it at all. That he'd said it with such ease. That he'd called it making love. That he'd said first as if there might ever be another time.

"But that's the point," he continued. "That means I'm old enough to be her father."

"For God's sake, don't say that to her! That's just what we need. Major Cristina drama all over the place. As if most of this year's court aren't already basket cases. For the sake of the festival, will you please tell her the score. Diplomatically."

"Are you—?" His gray eyes seemed to deconstruct her component parts so he could reassemble them in a way that made sense to him. She knew that look. He hadn't heard half of what she'd said "—are you jealous?"

"Jealous?" Not even Zeke could think she was jealous of Cristina Wellton, but if he was thinking along the lines of her being jealous, had she given something away? "Why would I be jealous?"

"Because those girls..." He clearly was thinking through this possibility he'd raised. "Because they have a chance at what you wanted—to be Lilac Queen."

That was his opinion of her? She stood straight, confident that no sign betrayed her. Training from the police academy had taught her to shake off physical blows and training at her father's hands had schooled her to show no reaction to emotional blows.

"For a genius, you are one idiot male, Anton Zeekowsky. I am not jealous of these girls. I am concerned that the festival goes on without a hitch, and that includes one of our princesses having a hissy fit like you've never seen. Listen to me, Zeke."

He was focused on something over her shoulder in the direction of the stage. She put her fingertips to his jaw and turned his face toward her. The touch was a mistake. His skin was too warm, the flesh too firm, the bone beneath it too hard. She jerked her hand away, tucking it behind her back until the tingling subsided. "Are you listening to me, Zeke?"

Now she had his complete attention. She wasn't sure this was an improvement.

"Cristina has set her sights on you. You might not take that seriously, but she does. She definitely does. And she is not accustomed to failing. It's going to be a jolt for her. You've *got* to think of a way to tell her, and soon. You've— What?"

He was shaking his head. "I'm not good with words. I wouldn't know how to talk to her about feelings. I told you, I like..." He locked gazes with her and a blaze of something crossed his face. "...doing."

Focus, Barrett. Focus. The object of this conversation was to avoid a major Cristina meltdown. Possibly to leave enough of a bridge between Ashley and Zeke that if he and Jennifer... Better not to think too much about that.

"I know you're not all that comfortable with words, Zeke. But in this instance, I don't think action is the solution."

"Darcie?"

She looked up. "What?"

Zeke was leaning into her. He was going to kiss her.

A kiss on the cheek. That's all. She'd had them before. Thousands probably in her lifetime. From relatives, friends' parents, longtime neighbors and from guy friends. The kiss would land on her cheek and he would continue on toward her ear, then glance off, like two cars brushing bumpers.

But he didn't. He pulled back after touching her cheek.

Straightened. Leaned in again. His lips met hers, warm and hungry.

That was their sole connection at first. It was enough, too much.

Then his hands lightly cupped her shoulders, and she had the sides of his jacket fisted in her hands, holding on so she didn't grab him, his body, his skin.

His hold tightened, his arms wrapping across her shoulders in a circle he made smaller and smaller. She had to release his jacket or have it bunched around his throat.

She felt the heat of him, the intensity, through his mouth, into hers, Her now-empty hands curled with exquisite sensation.

A piercing alarm broke through her fog. Was it not just her on fire, but the whole building?

No…no, the sound was human. Almost human. Familiar. Like…

Ashley.

Darcie pushed weakly against Zeke, not putting any distance between their bodies, but at least disengaging their mouths.

"How could you? How could you?" Ashley screeched. "You horrible, horrible man! How can you betray Cristina?"

"Who I kiss has nothing to do with her," Zeke said.

Ashley gasped, tracks of tears marking her cheeks. Tears of rage, Darcie realized.

Jennifer came around the corner, abruptly stopping as she took in the situation.

"Ashley," Darcie stated in her everybody-stay-calm tone.

It failed miserably.

"And you!" Ashley wailed. "Stealing another woman's man! That's the lowest of low."

Somewhere under the ongoing assault on her nerves and the recognition that it would not help the situation, Darcie felt an urge to laugh.

"Ashley." Jennifer's tone warned her daughter not to go too far.

"No!" the girl cried. "They've betrayed her! Cristina *loves* him."

"If she loves anybody, it's herself," Zeke said. "Not me."

Ashley's mouth gaped with shock.

Zeke appeared unaffected. "Darcie was my first love. She's the reason I came back to Drago."

The shock she'd seen on Ashley's face descended on Darcie like a contagious disease. She felt numbed, unable to process what she'd heard.

At a distance she was aware of Ashley's tears renewing, then giving way to gulping sobs. The look Jennifer gave them—Zeke still with his arms wrapped around Darcie—could almost be interpreted as fighting a grin, before she guided Ashley toward the privacy of the back exit.

Then shock fell away, and Darcie shoved at Zeke's chest with the heel of her hand. More than pushing him away, she pushed herself away. Far enough away so she wouldn't grab him and hold on.

"Darcie?"

"I told you to talk to Cristina. I said—"

"She was heading this way, too. I didn't think it would only be Jennifer's kid who saw me kiss you. I thought if Cristina saw us—"

"I said talk, not lie. Lies never make things better. Never."

"Darcie."

She kept going.

He'd thought it was a great opening.

In fact, made to order. A way to show her what he'd been feeling these past days without having to dredge up words.

When Darcie had said he had to talk to that girl Cristina it fit with what Jennifer had been saying.

It had started with Jennifer hinting about Zeke-Tech donating stuff to the town. He'd been doing pretty good ignoring those hints, when she'd said she supposed the request came as a surprise, since Darcie wouldn't have let on how desperate the town was.

"Darcie doesn't hide much," he'd said dryly, thinking how she'd been driving him around town, showing him Drago's problems. What she wanted was crystal clear.

Jennifer had tipped her head and squinted. "Darcie? Darcie Barrett?" she'd said, as if unsure they were talking of the same person. "You find she doesn't hide much?"

"I can tell what she's feeling more than with most people. So she must not be hiding stuff."

Jennifer laughed. He didn't think she was laughing at him, precisely. She sounded too delighted to be mocking him. But he had no clue what she was laughing about.

"I'm sorry. I didn't mean to— It's just so…sweet."

"What is?"

"You and Darcie. Darcie could be one of those guards in front of Buckingham Palace, with nobody getting any reaction she doesn't want to give. Including me. And have you ever seen her with her mother?"

Oh, yeah, he had seen that. "Maybe with her mother—"

"Most people, Zeke. So, either she lets you see more of what she's feeling than she does with other people, or the two of you are connected, like I said last night."

He shook his head. "All Darcie does is give me grief. I think she's still hung up on that guy she was engaged to."

"Oh, Zeke," she'd said with a soft smile. "You two need to talk, you really need to talk. Let her know how you feel."

That's when Cristina and Ashley had come up, making it impossible to get more information from Jennifer.

So, he'd gone to talk to Darcie. But she'd gotten onto that stuff about that silly girl.

But when he'd said, *I wouldn't know how to talk to her about feelings. I like doing* he'd meant *Darcie.* As he'd looked down into her face—in those seconds before his mouth had touched hers, deleting all coherent thought—he'd thought she'd understood.

Apparently not.

Oh, hell, maybe he hadn't been thinking. He'd looked into her face…and he'd wanted to kiss her. He'd needed to kiss her.

All this flashed through his brain in the moment after she walked away, he said her name and she kept going, one arm extended, palm out in a clear order not to follow her.

But that didn't stop him from watching.

Some insight hovered at the edge of his consciousness. But it took a back seat to the visuals of the current moment blending with memories of a certain backseat.

The woman had one fine rear view. Her strong, straight back going down to the smooth roundedness of her buttocks, then the flow of slender curves in her thighs and calves.

He'd felt the warmth of her back just now. But once, he'd touched her in all those places, and more. It hardly seemed real except for the stirring of his body reminding him how real it had been. Urgent and fumbling and terrifying and spectacular.

Each reaction rolled together with the others. Each of them and all of them connected in his memory to the sensation of Darcie's skin under his hands, against his body.

And another memory, more elusive. Something of Darcie that had never left him. What was that?

Pushing out the exterior door, Darcie shot a look over her shoulder, as if she'd felt his regard. He smiled at her.

Maybe in the hope that she might hold those memories as good ones, too. Mostly because he couldn't help it. It had become a conditioned response in only these few days. He saw Darcie's face, and he smiled.

She quickly moved out of sight.

The thought that had been hovering at the edges of his mind finally found an opening: He would never understand women. Never had, never would. Great hardware, but their software was plain screwy.

He wouldn't try to build a bridge because he didn't have those engineering skills. He wouldn't try to play the cello because he didn't have musical talent. When it came to women, he had neither the skills nor the talent. So he would stop trying to solve that particular mystery.

As soon as he figured out the cause of that…what? Hurt? Sorrow? deep in Darcie's eyes.

He needed to think. There were three places in Drago he used to go to think. But it wasn't anywhere near sunrise. And he hadn't set foot in his father's shop since the day he'd died.

That left one.

Darcie passed under the wrought iron arch that arose from stone pillars at either side of the entrance to Old Cemetery.

Before she headed home on the second half of her usual morning run, she liked to do a never-the-same-twice zigzag among the grassy paths and lilacs. It kept her lateral motion sharp, and gave her a chance to say hello to her grandparents, a few former teachers, a favorite neighbor and the mail carrier from her childhood, as well as acknowledge early residents of Drago. Today, though, it was her nearly-sunset run, squeezed between Zeke duty and putting in a few hours tonight so Benny could go to his daughter's grade school spring concert.

She'd handed it to Zeke right on a plate. "Why would I be jealous?" The perfect opportunity for him to say, *You have no reason to be jealous because you're the one I truly want.*

And what did he say? That she was jealous of those kids over the Lilac Queen competition. As if she wanted to live through that again! So much for Jennifer's hints about Zeke having feelings for her.

No, she wouldn't think about that. She would concentrate on the here and now, even in this place devoted to the hereafter.

Monuments to family names—Stenner, Truesdale, Fletcherton and others—rose tall. But smaller markers could tell as much of a story.

Here a young mother died, followed two days later by her baby. There her husband's second wife lived well into the next century. In the northwest corner, a husband and wife born in Vermont in the early 1800s who died here late in the century. Under a maple, six children in one family all dying within three months in 1918. Throughout, tales of sacrifice and loss.

She slowed, then stopped in front of another grave. A simple headstone, a name, dates and three words, one to each line:

Husband
Father
Friend

Darcie couldn't say if she had consciously noticed this headstone before. Definitely she remembered when Mischar Zeekowsky was buried here.

It had been a bright fall day. Colors so crisp they seemed to crackle. The nearly silent crowd of black-dressed townspeople had spread among gravestones like a dour cloud below the scarlet and gold of the leaves and blue of the sky.

Darcie had come alone. The first funeral she'd attended where she wasn't surrounded by family, shifted from home to funeral to burial amid a knot of relatives.

Attending the funeral of Zeke's father had meant a decision to take time off school. Her mother had listened to her defiant declaration that she was going, and quietly said she would go with her.

Odd, Darcie had forgotten that.

So she was wrong—she hadn't come to Mr. Zeekowsky's funeral alone. Martha Barrett had said so little that in Darcie's memory she had faded into a colorless drop amid the ocean of townspeople who had turned out. Friend.

She remembered Mrs. Z, standing at the doorway of her little house, taking the hands of each visitor between her own and thanking them. Husband.

But the stark, clear vision for Darcie of that day had been Zeke's face. Gone to granite and shut off from the world. Father.

He'd been harder to reach after that. And far, far more determined to leave Drago. To become someone important, successful, admired.

He'd practically hummed with impatience to get on with it. While she'd tried time after time to pull him back into the here and now of their lives.

She sighed.

Did Mischar Zeekowsky approve of what his son had achieved? Did he admire what Zeke had created away from Drago? Did he, like Zeke, believe this was a place to escape? Or was he glad to have his boy home?

She wished she knew. More important, she wished Zeke knew.

She touched the top of the headstone, then resumed her run.

"Darcie?"

Her mother was coming out of the side door of the garage as Darcie finished her cooling-off jog down the driveway. Darcie grunted a greeting.

"The vegetarian dinners for the ball are taken care of," Martha said, pulling off gardening gloves. Not lightweight Lady of the Manor cutting flowers for arranging gloves, but battered leather that looked as if they could stop a pickaxe.

"Good. I, ah…what were you doing?"

"Adding compost for the roses. I apologize if I carry the smell, but manure really is best for roses. The lilacs have done particularly well—"

"Mom, you should have told me."

Her mother cocked her head in the patented Martha Barrett Look. "Why would I tell you, dear?"

"Because you shouldn't have to do that. I'll do it."

Her mother looked amused. "It's done. Besides, I intend to keep doing that and other yard work as long as I'm in this house and able."

Yard work? Darcie never really thought about the yard except for paying a neighbor kid to mow the lawn. "But with Dad gone—you shouldn't do the heavy stuff. If I'm not here—"

Martha laughed. "Darcie, your father's been dead fourteen years, and he never dug in manure in his life. I've always done most of the yard work, when he was alive and after. He wasn't interested."

Of course Gordon Barrett wouldn't have done yard work. Darcie couldn't imagine him lifting a shovel. But then, she couldn't imagine her mother doing it, either. How had she missed that all these years?

She blinked, looked at her mother again, not as her mother, but as a woman. Say, a woman she'd encountered in her police duties. What would her impression be then?

Attractive. Of course.

Fit. Sure.

Intelligent. Yeah, she supposed so, though she'd never really thought about it before.

Capable.

Capable. The woman standing before her had a definite air of being able to handle things. And... Oh, my God. A restrained sensuality.

Who was this woman?

Martha Barrett.

Her mother.

"Darcie? Is something wrong?"

Darcie opened her mouth to demand answers, to find solutions to puzzles, to holler, *Who are you?* All that came out was "Thanks for taking care of the vegetarian plates."

The dispatcher's call interrupted an entirely uneventful half shift filling in for Benny. Darcie practically sobbed out her thanks to Corine for the distraction. Between thoughts about her mother and thoughts about Zeke, Darcie had been about to go nuts.

"Mildred Magnus saw lights on in the high school again. She says they're not moving this time," Corine reported. "That's got her real rattled."

Ever since the paper had printed some legend about the hill the high school was built on having once been a campground for Native Americans, Mildred had decided spirits of the dead came back to light their campfires.

Very adaptable spirits, apparently, since they used electric lights.

Darcie acknowledged the call and drove across town.

The orange sports car was parked by the side entrance to the 1970s addition to the venerable original building of Drago High School. Great.

It was almost certain Zeke was the source of Mildred's lights. But almost wasn't certain enough to make Darcie forget caution.

It wouldn't be the first time Zeke had slipped into the building after hours. She could think of at least three times when Mr. Grandhier had refused to let Zeke do some experiment in eleventh grade that Zeke had his heart set on. Back then, Darcie had volunteered—like a sap—to be his lookout.

This time she would roust him out. She would have preferred wrestling with a rabid dog. It would have posed less threat to her emotional well-being.

The lab door was ajar. Light arrowed across the floor. She drew a breath, and eased the door wider.

Zeke sat at his old seat at the lab table, a battery-powered lantern beside him. He seemed to be staring at the huge poster of the Periodic Table of the Elements.

"Hi, Darcie," he said without turning.

She stifled surprise. "I didn't think you heard me."

"I didn't. I smelled you."

She was not going to ask what on earth he meant by that, or why he sounded so almighty pleased with himself. She was here to do her job.

"You've frightened some of the neighbors. Light bobbing around the hallways has fired up overactive imaginations. You need to leave, Zeke."

He didn't move. He seemed weary. She wanted to close the distance between them and stroke his hair.

It made her next words staccato. "It's late. Your mother'll be worried."

"Bingo night." His mouth twisted. "I remembered this time. But I'm not used to anybody keeping track of me, except my assistant, and she's used to me working all night."

"Is that what you were doing, Zeke? Working?"

"No. Trying to remember that once upon a time I did get some work done." He spun around on the stool to face her. "I feel like I've forgotten how to work. When I'm not smothered in lilacs, Ma's letting a cast of thousands troop through the house. Letting? What am I saying? She's practically dragging them in off the street."

"You need to take a break." So they weren't going to talk about what had happened this afternoon. That was good. Better than good. She was on duty. Even if she'd wanted to talk about it, which she didn't, she couldn't. But he could have. He'd been the instigator after all. "To connect with people."

He twisted a grin at her. "People are vastly overrated."

She didn't grin back. "You use work to avoid people, Zeke."

He opened his mouth. Closed it, then said, "No, I don't," as he switched off the lantern.

"You always have. You used to try to do it to me in chem lab."

For the moment they were both blind, stuck in place, waiting for the memory of the lantern to stop strobing and for their eyes to adjust to the dim light coming through the blinds.

"I like to work. That doesn't mean anything other than I like my work."

He was crossing the area between them, cautiously, slowly. She backed into the hall, a deeper shade of dark than the classroom.

"When I used to try to talk to you in class, at the beginning, you'd dive into work like some men dive into the newspaper to avoid conversation at breakfast."

"I was interested in it." He closed the door behind him, cutting off even that patch of dimness. Both of them held still again, reacclimating.

"And didn't want to talk to me."

"I didn't know you. Then." His voice was low. They were almost whispering, as if the darkness demanded that.

She backed up another step. "Yes, you were interested in your work, but you lost yourself behind it. You withdrew behind it. I see you doing it now, too."

"Darcie..." He stepped closer, then stopped, more than an arm's length away.

"The only one you don't do it to is your mother."

Or maybe he had. Something clearly weighed on him, but rather than talking to his mother or someone else, he'd closed himself up here. An odd pain welled in her—a double-edged pain, both for him and caused by him.

"Darcie."

He did whisper that. And he took another step toward her.

The silence around them abruptly shattered with heavy footfalls rapidly advancing down the hallway that intersected with the one they occupied.

Darcie had her flashlight out, holding it well to the side of her body, in case a desperado had dropped into the hallways of Drago High School.

The intruder turned the corner and headed right for them. She switched on the light and had two shocks, one minor, one not so.

The first was that the frozen-in-midstride intruder was Warren Wellton. That was the minor shock. If she'd listed people who might be in the high school building when they weren't supposed to be, he'd make her top five.

The not-so-minor shock came from Zeke turning on his

lantern only seconds after her flashlight came on, and then trying to put himself between her and Warren, as if to shield her.

"Stop that." She sidestepped Zeke, keeping a clear view to Warren.

"Darcie?" The boy sounded as if his lips had gone numb.

"Yeah. What are you doing here, Warren?" He'd shown a moment of relief when he recognized her voice, but now guilt suffused his face. "What are you up to?"

"Nothing. I…I only—"

He spun around and ran as fast as Darcie had ever seen him move, back around the corner and out of the range of their lights. Apparently he felt being out of sight gave him safety because his footfalls stopped.

She spun around into the beam of Zeke's lantern. "Don't ever do that again, Zeekowsky. Ever. And don't turn on your lamp in a situation like this unless you're instructed to by the police officer."

"I acted on instinct." He clicked off his lantern.

"Well, don't," she said crossly. Could that be what he'd done this afternoon, too? No, that had been a calculated effort to shake off Cristina. "Now, let's get out of here."

She headed in the direction Warren had taken, intending to sweep him out of the building ahead of them. Zeke hadn't moved.

"Darcie, I have something I want you to see." He spoke in his full voice. The whisper, along with the moment, gone. "It's back at the house—at Ma's. Can you come by tonight when you're off duty?"

"Zeke—"

"Please."

"Fine. But you have to do something for me."

"What?"

"Prove you're not a ghost to a very spookable woman."

* * *

After a night at bingo that Ma had characterized only with, "Bah!" she dozed off on the sofa watching TV, so when Zeke heard a car stop in front, he switched on the front porch light and went outside to meet Darcie.

"Hope you don't mind staying out here," he said after telling her his mother was asleep.

"Not at all. It's a nice night. Warmed up a lot since Saturday."

He hadn't noticed. Had other things on his mind. He drew in a breath that held a spicy sweetness.

He held out a device balanced on his palm. "Here."

"What am I supposed to do with your handheld?"

"Go on, take it." He reached out, poking her with the fingertips of the hand holding the device. Finally, she took it. "It's not my handheld. It's a mock-up for a new device for police. It's so you don't have to write notes like you did about Mrs. Richards. Or dates and times of ghost sightings the way you did with Mildred tonight."

She looked at him for what felt like several minutes before her gaze dropped to the small screen. She poked around on the keys.

Looking over her shoulder this way, he only had to turn his head to see the porch lamp's glow glinting on the varied coloring of her shining hair. She'd taken it down now that she was off-duty, and the breeze stirred it, along with that subtle, spicy scent of hers that had fluttered at the edge of his consciousness. Finally, tonight, sitting in the chem lab, it had clicked into place.

At first he'd thought he was remembering. Then he realized she was there, and his pulse had rocketed.

"Multiple choice?"

"Yeah. It'll save time to check which applies. Then you can

file it, forward it or copy it to other people. You can select a reminder date to pop up."

"All that's great, Zeke. The reminders and being able to file and copy it, but there are too many variables."

He nodded. "That's why I added drop-down menus under these—see? It's like a decision tree."

"Those are your decisions. You're forcing me into a mold. You can't make my decisions. It needs to be simpler, Zeke."

"But—"

"Did you hear about the big hospital out in California that instituted a computerized system? After a few months, the doctors rebelled. The machine couldn't make the nuanced choices and decisions the doctors did. The machine constrained the doctors instead of helping them. The system was set up to be convenient for the system, not for the users."

He looked at her a long time. Long enough to make her edgy, he saw. "You have a really good mind, Darcie Barrett."

She blushed a little. "Thanks."

"I mean it. You should meet Quince. He's our VP of PR, but he's also the one who keeps Vanessa and me aware of what customers really need. He and Brenda." He considered that. "And a department of customer advocates Quince and Brenda instigated."

Darcie chuckled. "Sounds like Quince's somebody I'd like."

He frowned. "You're interested in Quince?"

"Interested? I haven't even met him, remember?"

"Yeah, I know. I only thought…" He wasn't sure what he'd thought. Except he hadn't liked the idea of Darcie being interested in Quince. The logic that they'd never met hadn't stood in the way of his not liking it.

Darcie picked up the handheld again. "What you should be doing, Zeke, is asking this consumer what *she'd* want from a gadget like this."

"What would you want from a gadget like this?" he duti-
fully asked.

"Give me a place to write a note, *then* the options of what
to do with it."

He kept asking questions, digging and assessing, figuring
out what she did and how he might make it easier for her.

"Stop! That's enough, Zeke. You'll go on with questions
all night."

"You always think you can figure out what I'll do."

"I've always been pretty good at reading people and I've
honed the ability as a cop." She spoke easily, but didn't look
at him. "You have to be able to anticipate what people are
going to do."

"Really?" He didn't like her lumping him with *people* any
more than he'd liked the idea of her being interested in Quince.
And he didn't like that she was good at reading everyone,
while the best he could do was be partially literate with her
alone. "Can you anticipate what I'm going to do now?"

He saw the knowledge in her eyes a second before he
closed his own eyes and took her mouth.

She would have stepped back, but his hand had curved to
cup her head, and his mouth came down on hers again. Now,
instead of drawing away, she stepped into him, so the only
thing between them was desire.

He'd thought that kissing her this afternoon was an
impulse. Now the need went much deeper than any impulse.

Maybe back to a June night in his parents' car. No, before
that, because when he'd kissed her then, he'd found the need
waiting for him, driving him.

But that was looking back, and he was a man who looked
to the future. This was a future he'd been looking forward to
for…it couldn't be measured in time. Only longing.

Overhead, the porch light abruptly went out, wrapping

them in intimate darkness at the same time it proclaimed his mother's presence just inside the door, and her approval.

Zeke smiled, even as he kept kissing Darcie. She made a small protesting sound and might have thought to back away from him, but he remedied that by putting a hand to each side of her face and opening his mouth over hers.

He lined her lips with his tongue. Found an opening and stroked inside to the warmth and spice and heat that was Darcie.

She made a sound deep in her throat and leaned into him more, so he needed a half step back to balance them. With equilibrium regained, he consolidated the new closeness, backing her with one leg advanced between hers. He eased her up to the porch pole and pressed against her, no longer restricted by balance.

He felt the cushioning curves of her breasts against his chest, the welcoming hollow between her legs. He slid one hand down the back of her thigh, drawing it up, wanting to be closer, deeper.

She gasped. He stroked his tongue deeper, felt her hips rock once against his in answer.

Then she stilled. Only half a second, before she was twisting to the side, pushing against his chest enough so she could slide away.

"Wait. Wait. "

He reached for her. "Darcie—"

"No. Wait." She half stumbled to the far side of the porch. "A minute."

He followed. She was breathing hard. He liked knowing he'd caused that in her. He was breathing hard, too. He more than liked how she'd caused that reaction in him. He didn't like how she held him off with an outstretched arm.

"I know it's been sort of intense, coming back," she finally said. "This afternoon, when you kissed me, and even, well, you know. Graduation. When we… There were a lot of emotions. Things get confusing in the middle of, uh, things. But there's Jennifer, too."

He hadn't considered it particularly confusing until she stopped kissing him and started talking.

"Jennifer?"

"Look, I know—I knew then—how you felt about her. How you've always felt about her."

"You mean in high school? Jennifer was an ideal. I never viewed you that way."

"Thank you very much."

When they were kissing, the dark had wrapped them together. Now, with her out of his arms it became a barrier between them, masking expressions, making words harder. He drove his hand through his hair.

"I didn't mean it that way. I meant…she wasn't real. She didn't exist for me, not as who she really was. She was only this image I had in my head. I never knew who she was as a person. I don't think I cared. Not until I came back. Now I see she's a nice woman with many fine qualities."

"Yes, she is."

"But she's not you. You were never an image in my head, Darcie. You were always real."

In the darkness he still thought he saw shock on her face. Then she spun away, the line of her shoulders straight and tense.

"Darcie, there's something between us. There always has been. I can talk to you—you make me talk. And when we kiss—" He stepped close. "I don't want to stop."

She jerked around to face him. "This—we can't. Unless—"

With his heart suspended—first by *we can't,* then, no less suspended, but not quite so hopeless, by *unless*—he looked into her intense face.

"Unless what?"

Her words came out in such a rush he could barely

separate them. "Zeke, this town needs your help. I've shown you every way I know how and now I'm asking—please, will you help Drago?"

His heart kicked back in, a stuttering, uneven pace.

He knew this moment. In developing any new product there were stops and starts, points with multiple possibilities, of going left, turning right, zigzagging or zooming straight up. There was also a decisive point to commit to one path in order to move forward. His gut told him when it was that moment, and which path to take.

This was that moment in an entirely different enterprise. But this time, his gut hadn't declared the time. Darcie's ultimatum had. *We can't. Unless.* Unless he committed to bailing out the town he'd never wanted to see again.

He had to make a decision. And his gut was echoingly silent.

Chapter Seven

"I don't owe this town anything."

"I know that."

Darcie kept her voice steady even though her insides felt like late night on the Fourth of July. Every once in a while an errant kaboom went off, reminding you both of the glory you'd seen, and that it had ended.

Not that this was a big deal. It wasn't like they'd made love. Just a few kisses. And it wasn't like she didn't have experience getting over Zeke.

But Drago wouldn't get over not having his help.

"It's not a matter of owing," she said, looking into his still face. "It's giving a hand so people can get started on a new path. People you've known most of your life."

A sharp grunt expressed his opinion of that connection.

She sat back. She could try to go around his attitude, but that had rarely worked with Zeke as a teenager. Coming at him straight on had always been most effective. Possibly because he wasn't used it. His glower kept most people from trying.

Now the glower was backed by maturity, power and prestige. An intimidating combination.

"Zeke, I know you felt you and your family didn't fit in, but your mother doesn't feel that way. I tried to tell you in high school that they would be friendlier to you if you'd be friendlier to them. Okay, not all of them. Idiots like Eric Stenner always would have been jerks. That's because he's only smart enough to be jealous of how incredibly smart you are and stupid enough to resent it. Not everyone's like that. A lot of people respected you then and respect you now. Even more respect and like your mom and your dad when he was alive, because your parents reached out to people."

Silence. Not even a grunt.

It seemed to be getting darker and darker. As if a light she needed to read him and his reactions had gone out.

"You could do a lot of good, Zeke. It wouldn't take a lot to reach out to these people and this town. You could— Or Zeke-Tech could."

"No it couldn't."

The coldness in his voice stopped her.

"Nothing personal," he said, and they both knew it was a lie. "It's business."

"We're not asking for a lot, Zeke. Seed money to help us pull more business in. Enough to get us started in the right direction. Jennifer and I have researched how we could set it up as a trust, and it would give you a great tax break, plus the town could pay it back—"

"Darcie." She looked into his eyes, and saw the answer before he said the final word. "No."

* * *

Zeke closed the front door after watching Darcie drive away, and encountered Ma's basilisk stare.

Darcie had said almost nothing at the end, only, "Benny will pick you up tomorrow, Zeke." He'd started to say her name but she'd talked over him. "It'll be better that way. Good night."

He supposed he should be grateful she hadn't said more. He wasn't going to be as lucky with his mother.

"What do you think, Anton? What do you think? I do not know this man who comes home as my son. What your papa would think—"

No. That he wouldn't listen to. He cut across her words as he strode to the hall. "Good night, Ma."

Two more strides took him to the small bedroom. With the door closed, he stood at the desk, one hand on the back of the chair, the other already poised over the familiar keys of the laptop.

What do you think?

The hell if he knew. Kissing Darcie? Definitely not problem solving at a higher level. More like at the most basic level. A chance to hold and kiss Darcie. Yahoo, boys let's go for it.

That certainly hadn't changed since that last night before he left Drago.

…you left and never looked back.

Darcie had said that to him that first day at the Community Center, when she'd agreed to help him out.

…you left and never looked back.

He'd accepted the words without argument then. They were the truth as far as words went. But they weren't the truth of what had been inside him.

He hadn't looked back. He wouldn't let himself look back. For fear…

A dark welling void of fear that he could just catch sight

of from the corner of his eye if he ever let his gaze stray from straight ahead. If he'd actually looked back, it would have swallowed him.

He hadn't thought that then—he hadn't thought of any of it then, he'd just felt it. And kept moving straight ahead.

Moving ahead of the fear. A fear he'd never recognized as existing until now.

Fear of what?

He still didn't know. Maybe he'd be wise not to dig too much. Or maybe he didn't have the courage to find out. But there was one thing he knew.

…you left and never looked back.

That wasn't true, not the way she'd meant it.

Because even looking forward, always forward, the fear had never blotted out his memories of Darcie.

Darcie was not looking forward to calling Jennifer, but she owed her an update.

"You sound awful, Darce," Jennifer said immediately. "Are you sick?"

"No. Didn't get much sleep. Spent most of the night surfing the Web for a charity specializing in bailing out hard-up towns in the Corn Belt."

Let Jennifer think the surfing had caused the sleeplessness, instead of the other way around.

After an aerobic workout in the form of tossing and turning, she'd wandered the apartment. When she'd found her fingers trailing over the case of the CD Zeke gave her that first night, like the memento of a lovesick teenager, she'd yanked back and occupied herself with fruitless surfing.

"I have two questions," Jennifer said. "Any luck? And why?"

"No. And because I blew it."

"I doubt that." Jennifer's warm laugh seemed to hint at secrets only she knew.

Darcie restrained herself from cursing, barely.

"Believe me. I blew it. I tried a gambit and it didn't work." Had she? Or had she tossed out that ultimatum because he'd scared her. She'd scared herself. She'd wanted him. Right there. On his mother's porch. Oh, God. "We had a, uh, parting of the ways last night. Benny's taking over Zeke duty as of this morning. I cleared it with the chief."

"Darcie?"

"It's up to you now." She forced enough enthusiasm into her voice to override Jennifer. "But that's great, with the way Zeke has always felt about you. All you have to do is look at him, and he melts."

Jennifer laughed. "Give it up, Darcie. You've had this fixation that something was going to happen between us ever since we started this Zeke campaign."

"I know Ashley isn't wild about him, but that'll change."

"It's moot, Darcie. Zeke and I have no chemistry."

Chemistry. Sitting across from Zeke in Chem lab. Feeling the miracle of his rare smile all the way to her toes.

Stronger, more volatile, his mouth on hers.

Combustible, his touch on her skin.

Explosive, his body against hers, inside hers.

"Are you listening to me?" Jennifer asked.

"What? Sorry?"

"I said, Zeke and I are becoming friends, and I'm enjoying it. It's fun to have a guy friend."

"Great," Darcie said, wondering what on earth she and Zeke had become. "Then you can persuade your friend, the stubborn mule, to bail out Drago."

* * *

"Zeke, the office is transferring a call from your mother."
The head gardener of Lilac Commons held out a cell phone
to him, and Zeke gladly accepted this reprieve, too.

It hadn't seemed this bad when Darcie was around. At
least he could look at her and know someone else knew what
was going on in his head. But with Benny driving him for the
fourth day, he felt isolated.

He'd jumped at the excuse to get away from the official
picture taking when the gardener, Jerry, had offered a tour of
the grounds, pointing out with pride his beds of tulips, hyacinths and daffodils. There were blooming cherry trees and
huge oaks and pine trees. And of course lilacs. Age, shape,
color, scent, each one different. Most interestingly, Jerry had
identified a particular lilac bush that stopped Zeke dead when
they'd walked past it.

Tinkerbelle. Darcie smelled like Tinkerbelle. God, he'd
wanted to tell her—the one person he was in no position to
tell anything.

He took the cell now from Jerry with thanks. He'd given
Ma his cell phone number more times than he could
remember. She refused to use it. She insisted anything without
a cord and plug was not to be relied on. So she'd obviously
called the parks department, which transferred her to the gardener's cell. If she only knew.

"Ma?

"Anton, that machine of yours, it screeches on your desk."

"I told you, you can't lift it up to dust under—"

"I don't dust!" she interrupted, indignant, as if she hadn't
originated the notion of preemptive dusting. "I am in kitchen,
and it squeals. I do nothing. Box squeals. I go in your room.
Window open. I shake it only a little and—"

"Get out of the house, Ma. Now. Go next door. I'm calling the police."

"Why?"

"Mother. Do it. Please. For me."

There was only the slightest pause before she said, "I do it."

He waited for the click, hung up, handed the cell to the nearest hands, then was on the move. He shouted, "I have to go," to anyone who cared to listen. He had his cell out and was dialing 9-1-1 as he got in his car.

Corine would have kept him on the line after he'd reported the facts, but he hung up and dialed Darcie's cell. He got a message prompt.

"Someone's tried to break in to Ma's house, Darcie. I'm almost there."

His mother and the neighbors were standing on their front porch as he pulled up. "Go inside!" he shouted as he loped toward the house. They ignored him.

He made a circuit of the house, noticing the open window, then came in the back door as a knock sounded at the front.

With the alarm still sounding, he opened the door to Darcie—no, to Officer Barrett. She was definitely in cop mode.

Only deep beneath her professional demeanor did he recognize that she would rather not be here. More precisely that she would rather be anywhere in the world but here. Because he was here.

"Someone broke in. The alarm—"

She nodded and moved past him, gun drawn. She gestured for him to stay where he was. She gave the living room a quick but thorough survey, opening the coat closet, saw that no human could possibly squeeze in among its packed contents, then scanned the kitchen. Her gaze lingered on the basement door, then she turned and started down the hall.

She ducked in and out of the bathroom before he could react. She was already in his room when he followed. Starting with behind the door, she made another room survey, checked the closet then looked under the bed. There was nowhere else to hide in the small room.

She glared at him as she backtracked to the hallway, then repeated the exercise in his mother's neat bedroom.

Nothing. The tension in his shoulders eased but she hadn't relaxed. She came close to him, stretched up and said into his ear, "Can you turn it off?"

Her closeness, the brush of her breath across his ear, put an end to what easing of muscles he'd gained, particularly below his belt. There he tightened and swelled.

Turn it off? Not with her turning him on. He wanted to kiss her. Even knowing how Monday night had ended, he wanted to take her in his arms and—

She stepped back, frowned and moved her mouth as if she'd tsked. She moved into his space to speak into his ear again. "The alarm—can you turn if off? Please!"

He jerked out a nod and went to the keyboard. The silence was abrupt and smothering.

He opened his mouth, but she commanded him to hold it with one hand. She was listening, hard. Apparently satisfied, she strode off, and he again followed. In the kitchen, she locked the door to the basement, then the door to the garage.

He followed her outside, where she took up a position where she could watch the front door, back door and garage.

"How does that alarm work?" she asked.

"If anyone tries to move the computer without entering a code first, it sets off the sound alarm, sends a message to my office and activates powerful, uh, call them magnets, though they're not exactly magnets, they're—"

"The window wasn't open when you left?" she interrupted. "Your mother didn't open it or move the computer."

"That's right."

"Is it valuable?"

"Yes. The computer itself is special, but what's in it is even more valuable."

She still hadn't looked at him. But he sure couldn't complain how she was doing her job.

"Do you have enemies? Professional rivals who might stoop to this?"

"Yes. But none have any reason to know I'm here."

She cut him a look, quick and cool. "Did you cover your tracks? Travel under an assumed name?"

"No, but—"

He didn't bother to finish because she wasn't listening. Another cop car pulled up, and after a quick consultation with Benny, she said, "Never go inside a house in a situation like this, Zeke. Never. Do you know what could have happened if the neighbors hadn't shouted to me that you were inside? Stay here, and if you don't, I *will* shoot you this time."

He wasn't entirely sure she didn't mean it, but more important, he could tell by the way she and Benny moved as she went inside again and Benny took up a position covering the basement door, that this was serious. As much as he wanted to charge after her, stand between her and any bullets, his reason said that getting in her way was more likely to increase her danger.

Darcie emerged from the basement, and Zeke released the breath burning his lungs. After another quick consultation, Benny headed toward the neighbors. Darcie retrieved a camera and clipboard from her patrol car and started around the house, looking down.

His cell phone rang. With no intention of answering, he glanced at the number from habit. Then he did answer, briefly.

"Brenda. It's okay. The computer's okay. I'm okay. I'll get back to you."

At the corner, where the flower bed extended deeper into the yard, Darcie paused, stared at something, then turned around to him.

"Are these your size fourteens, Zeekowsky?"

"Yeah." He moved toward her, and when she didn't object, he fell in behind her as she continued around the house. "I made a quick check before I went in the back."

She grunted. Her path was a good three feet farther away from the house than his had been.

She took several photos, with notations for each. Over her shoulder he saw she had both a drawing of the house where she was noting where she'd taken photos, and a running list describing them.

When they neared the open window to his bedroom, her pace slowed to almost nothing. She snapped photo after photo of the plantings and window. She got low, then onto her hands and knees, looking away from the house.

She shot off another couple of photos. "Those probably won't take," she sighed. "Get down and see if you see anything."

"What am I looking for?"

She shook her head. "You either see something or you don't."

He got down on all fours. Nothing. But she'd been lower…He dipped his head, so he was looking along the surface of the grass. There. A faint track of compressed grass leading directly to the upside-down crate Ma had used as a gardening stool for years. It made a perfect mounting block to hop the fence.

That left a quick sprint between two backyards, then up a grassed-in alley between windowless garages and across the street to the forest preserve where a bike could be stashed for a quick getaway. He knew because that had been his boyhood escape route.

He stood. She looked away, toward the fence and beyond.

"Someone jumped the fence. Headed for the forest preserve you think?"

She nodded. "Someone who had first climbed out of that window."

She crouched again, looking at his footprint that straddled the neat edge between lawn and flower bed. Then, keeping her feet on an area of untouched grass, she propped her hands on her bent knees and leaned way over to peer at the base of a bush.

The position stuck her derriere out and up, drawing the fabric tight over the rounded curves. His mouth went dry, his gut clenched.

"Zeke! Are you with me?"

"What?"

"Did you hear me? I asked who knew you'd be gone this morning?"

Finally, he saw what she was getting at. "Anyone who knew the pageant schedule, which includes anyone who reads the paper. You're thinking one of my enemies, or industrial espionage…"

She was shaking her head.

"I doubt this is the work of a pro. With your mother in the house? Not anticipating your alarm? Daylight? No. Besides…" She shook her head again. "No."

"You're really good at your job, aren't you."

"Just go over with your mother and let me finish my job."

What had he said to make her even madder? The chances he'd figure that out anytime soon were so infinitesimal that the man known for tackling the toughest technological challenges headed to the neighbor's porch without another word.

"Zeke."

He turned back, hoping…One look at her face ended that hope.

"You and your mom will need to check if anything is missing, and you might want to prepare Mrs. Z. I'm going to have to use fingerprint powder and it makes a mess. And give me a list of anyone whose fingerprints you would expect to find in your bedroom."

Darcie heard the storm brewing in the distance, but she was almost done…almost.

For routine crimes—the only kind Drago had had in her years on the force—she or Sarge took all the fingerprints, since they were certified as evidence technicians. Mrs. Z would have a fit when she saw the marks on her furniture, but she should count herself lucky it wasn't Sarge at work in Zeke's bedroom.

Zeke's bedroom.

How many times had she had to yank her mind away from that thought?

You're really good at your job, aren't you.

Right, like the New Technology's Genius was impressed with her.

What she was, was intimately familiar with Drago, Illinois—the last thing on earth that would impress Zeke.

So she had a good idea who might be tempted by a trophy like Anton Zeekowsky's laptop. Someone who knew when Zeke would be occupied. Someone too blinded by hormones to think straight. Someone with enough heft to bend the grass down as he ran, but young enough to jump that fence.

But before you could act on what you thought you knew, you had to know what you thought—and that started with finger-printing Zeke's bedroom, and eliminating the prints she found.

And give me a list of anyone whose fingerprints you would expect to find in your bedroom.

She could explain that she needed to know who'd been in the room to eliminate their prints. Would that make her sound less like a jealous woman?

One good thing from this break-in was it would override any awkwardness with Mrs. Z. That porch light hadn't gone off by itself Monday night. Mrs. Z had ideas about her son and Darcie, and Darcie hadn't been looking forward to confronting that. But now she could safely ignore it in light of more important issues.

She couldn't ignore the storm of rising voices now, it was coming her way.

Benny had taken the duty of getting Mrs. Z's and Zeke's preliminary statements and having them check the rest of the house. She heard him telling someone *you can't go in there,* and she heard Mrs. Z, fast and excited in her native language.

"Darcie."

That was Zeke's voice. Just outside his bedroom.

"A minute," she said without looking up. Last one… Had it.

"That's damned rudimentary, isn't it?" Zeke asked. He was standing in the doorway, blocking most of it, though she caught glimpses of Mrs. Z beyond him, her gestures coming as fast as the words Darcie couldn't understand. "I'd have thought you'd have more sophisticated equipment."

"This isn't *CSI: Drago.* Cutting edge, we're not. What's the problem?"

"There's a lot of stuff missing. They made a haul."

Her eyebrows shot up, her mind shifting to adapt to this new information. "What's missing?"

"Anton, you leave Darcie alone. Don't listen to him, Darcie. You work. We leave." Mrs. Z tugged Zeke's arm. He didn't budge. "Anton—"

"Mostly electronic gear. A plasma TV, DVD player, VCR, massage chair, digital camera, digital camcorder, PDA—I sent those things, and they're gone from the basement. I'll get my assistant to give you a complete inventory."

Mrs. Z, suddenly quiet, peered around Zeke's arm and met Darcie's eyes. The older woman's gaze held fatalism and a faint hope. She saw no way out of this, but her look said, if Darcie did, she'd be ever so grateful.

Darcie didn't.

"You never told him?" she asked, though the answer was obvious.

"Told me what?" Zeke looked over his shoulder at his mother, then back at Darcie.

Mrs. Z tipped her head, eloquently saying that she hadn't been able to bring herself to tell him. The gesture also placed responsibility for informing Zeke in Darcie's hands now.

"Told me what?" Zeke repeated, looking only at Darcie.

"Don't bother your assistant. I can give you a complete list from our records. Your mother's been donating to the police auction to raise money for kids' sports leagues. She's been our biggest donor. All those things you mentioned have been auctioned."

"That's how you know my mother," he said.

It figured that solving a puzzle would be his first reaction.

Before she could relax though, he added, his voice flat and tight, "Everything I sent."

Mrs. Z teared up. "Anton," she whispered, adding something in her native language.

He kept staring at Darcie, his eyes giving her nothing to read.

"Your mother promised me that you were okay with this." She said that she'd told Zeke. That's what Darcie intended to say. Before the words came out, though, she realized what Mrs. Z had actually said every time was *My Anton just wants his mother to be happy.* Not the same thing. "She'd indicated you'd be okay with it. She believed you'd be generous enough to be okay with it."

He turned, sidestepped his mother and started down the hall, forcing Benny to flatten himself—to the best of his ability—against the wall.

"Anton? Anton, where do you go?"

Darcie thought he was going to ignore his mother, then he shot back one word before he stalked around the corner and out of sight. "Walk."

Oh, yeah, closed-off high school Zeke was back. Big time.

"Darcie?" Mrs. Z's tear-filled eyes begged her.

"He doesn't want company. Let him think it through."

"Please. I have so few days with him home. I do not want to waste even one with his thinking."

Darcie could have laughed at that, except the older woman was clearly heartbroken.

She sighed, exchanged a look with Benny, who nodded and stepped back against the wall to let her pass, too.

She went looking for Zeke.

She'd had to run to catch up with him, so at first saying nothing was expedient. She needed her oxygen for breathing.

Even once she was beside him, she was getting plenty of aerobic benefits. Matching Zeke's long-legged stride was a push at the best of times, when he was walking at ticked-off speed, it qualified as a fitness test that would have knocked Sarge off the force.

But there was one more reason for saying nothing.

She could feel Zeke's emotions simmering down, approaching the point where he would admit he had any emotions. Up to that point, it wouldn't have done any good to talk to him.

"I hope to hell you got a good price for those things," he muttered eventually.

"We did," she said calmly. "As I said, Mrs. Z's been our biggest donor."

"Every damn thing I sent."

"Without her, without your gifts, there wouldn't have been athletic leagues for the kids the past few years. The economy's been so bad, all the usual sponsors dried up."

He didn't seem to hear the latter part of that.

"Gifts." He snorted. "What gifts? She won't let me do anything for her. She won't take anything from me."

Darcie wanted to punch him in the arm. Was he listening to himself? Of course, Mrs. Z wouldn't take anything from him. His mother loved him, she wanted only to give to him, not to take.

She kept her mouth shut, and her hands pumping.

"All I've ever wanted to do was to give her a good life, to take her away from here to someplace nice."

Now she *really* wanted to punch him.

"She *has* a good life, Zeke. And she doesn't want to go away."

"You think I don't know that? I've been trying for years to get her to Virginia. Or at least let me build her a decent house here. All I get is *No, Anton. Drago is my home. No, Anton. This house is my home.* It drives me nuts."

"It's natural to want to show your mother that you've made it, Zeke—"

He stopped, squared off to her and glowered. "Is that what you think it's about? Me showing off?"

Maybe at some level she had thought that. The presents he'd sent Mrs. Z had been so outrageously inappropriate for her lifestyle, that she'd wondered how he could be so obtuse. "I think more useful things would have had a better chance of being accepted."

"Useful? Like maybe a can opener? *Oh, no, Anton. I don't need a can opener that plugs in.* Just because the one she has is so old and rusted that it's like opening a can with a finger-nail. She used it last night and I swear dogs from five states showed up. Or like a new washing machine because the old one has been fixed so many times and they don't make parts for it anymore, so it's practically held together with rubber bands. When I tried to bribe the repairman to give her low bills and let me pick up the difference, she figured it out and got the full bill. She won't even take that from me."

He turned away and resumed his quick time march. She hurried to catch the wrap-up of his complaint. "She has got to be the most hard-headed human being on earth."

"And here I always thought you took after your father," she murmured.

He glared down at her, but didn't respond directly.

"Why the hell do you think I give her all that stuff?" She recognized that as rhetorical. "I keep hoping something—anything—will strike her fancy, and she'll start using it and maybe then she'll let me really make her life easier. Even if she does want to stay in this godforsaken town, I could make life easier if she'd let me."

That burst of words might have broken some dam, because when he looked at her this time, his expression had lightened, though his pace didn't slow.

"Sorry, about *godforsaken,* Darcie. We'll have to agree to disagree about Drago."

She fluttered a hand, waving that off. Not because she had any intention of letting him continue to disagree with her about his hometown—Drago couldn't afford that attitude from him. But because she had only so much breath, and first things first.

"I've got to tell you, Zeke—you need to change your thinking about your mother. First, accept and *respect* her choice to stay in Drago because she loves it. No more wisecracks."

He grunted. That would do.

"Second, and as much as I hate to lose the best items for

our kids' leagues auctions—this is vital—you need to stop giving her expensive gadgets."

"She—"

"Nope. No negotiating on this one. Even after she started donating to the auction, she was uncomfortable about getting those things. She's loved helping the kids, but getting those packages from you always makes her unsettled, uncomfortable."

"I—"

"This isn't about what you need to give. It's what she needs to get."

"What she needs." His lips barely moved repeating the words, stripping them of inflection. He drew in a breath through his nose, looked down at his hands then away.

She knew that look. The mile long stare hardening his gray eyes, the shutting off from everything outside himself. Some people confused it for that other look Zeke got—the absorption in tackling a problem. To Darcie the expressions were the difference between pulling down the shades on your windows and closing them off with steel shutters.

They walked in silence for two blocks. At least the pace had slowed and they were headed toward the house and her squad car.

There wouldn't be any more meaningful conversation, so she might as well get Zeke back to his mother while she tackled the paperwork on the intrusion and decided whether she could resolve this situation without putting through the lab work. If might work if she could bluff about finding certain fingerprints. She *was* a pretty good bluffer.

"Did you know my father was a professor?"

"What?" She was buying time to adjust to the shock of Zeke talking after he'd brought down the shutters. And something personal, no less. *Shock* might be too mild a word.

"My father was a professor, before he came to the United States. A professor of engineering. He was respected. One of the top figures at his university. Had a good life. He gave that all up when they came here."

"But, then, why...?"

"Why did he repair shoes? Because he couldn't get a job teaching in this country. His English was never good enough. If he'd been working on cutting-edge technologies, it probably wouldn't have mattered what his English was like, but he wasn't.

"And he knew how it would be before he came over. He knew what he was teaching and working on was behind the times in the West. He knew he had no gift for languages. He knew he was giving up the respect, the prestige, the privilege he'd had there. Knew it and came anyway." He turned haunted eyes to her. "For me."

"He loved you a lot."

"Yeah. And what did I do with his love? His sacrifice?"

"Uh, become a huge success? Become one of the new technology's top minds? Create a company and give people jobs solely with the ideas you thought up?"

"It's not enough. Not to repay him, not to repay my mother. She didn't have the position he did, but she'd been a promising graduate student. If she'd continued working in her own language—I *had* to achieve. I *had* to be a success. All they gave up for me..."

She understood better the drive that had set him apart from his peers and the weight that it had placed on his shoulders.

But he'd had something to help make that weight bearable, too.

"Your parents believed in you, Zeke," she said without thinking.

"Always."

The solitary word struck through her like a cold knife. "You're lucky. You have no idea how lucky." She felt the intensity of his focus on her, and she tried to shift it away. "The important thing about this situation with your mother is to remember—"

"What makes you think your parents didn't believe in you, Darcie?" He wasn't stupid. No, Zeke was definitely not stupid.

"This isn't about me. Your mother's intentions—"

"Were good. They always are." He'd stopped, holding her arm so she had to stop, too. "You've never thought your parents believed in you. Why?"

"I'm on duty, Zeke. This is not the time to dissect my family history."

"But it *was* the time to dissect *my* family history, Darcie?"

He tried to take her by the shoulders, but she eluded the hold.

"Consider it part of the investigation. I need you to look over your laptop, Zeke."

She didn't wait for an answer, but went inside. Mrs. Z peeked anxiously from the kitchen. Darcie gave her a reassuring smile, but had no time to say anything. Zeke was on her heels, intent on continuing the fruitless discussion. She didn't want him bringing that up in front of Mrs. Z and Benny, settled at the kitchen table with coffee and cake, and her best hope of avoiding that was to get Zeke into his bedroom.

She reached the room ahead of him, went to the desk, pointed to the dusted laptop and before he could say anything, repeated, "I want you to look over your laptop. For signs someone fooled around with it."

That caught his interest.

"Nobody but an expert could get through our security, and even an expert wouldn't be able to do it in the time before the alarm went off."

She opened the lid, pulled out the chair and gestured him to sit. "Someone was on your laptop, unless you wiped it clean after the last time you used it, because there are no finger-prints. Besides, we don't know that the person left when the alarm went off. All we know is the person was out of sight when your mom checked it."

"Oh, come on. Who would stick around after that thing started wailing?"

"Zeke, check the computer." She gave him the I-am-a-cop-and-you're-not look. It worked again.

"Okay, okay." His fingers flew over the keyboard. "See I could tell right here if... Well, damn."

"What?"

"Just..."

Darcie sighed. She supposed she should be grateful for that *just.* Even the one word was considerably more than she used to get in high school, when he'd disappear into concentration, leaving her on the surface wondering when he might return and trying not to stare too intently at those fingers, long and strong with interesting boniness.

"Huh!"

Zeke's expelled breath made her jump guiltily, but he still hadn't looked up from the screen, and his fingers hadn't stopped moving.

"What?"

"Someone did try..."

Before he submerged again, she demanded, "Tried what?" followed by "Zeke!" and a cuff to his shoulder.

"Oh. Tried to hack in. Actually, more like planting a kind of spyware."

"Spyware? That can track keystrokes remotely, right?"

"That's a basic explanation. It can be elaborate. They use particularly sophisticated kinds in commercial espionage." He looked up for a second. "Noncommercial espionage, too, for that matter."

"So someone put sophisticated spyware on your computer?"

"Tried. We stopped them."

In those simple words, Darcie heard the man Anton Zeek-owsky had become. No trumpets blaring, no bragging, a simple statement of fact. Yet said with confidence, pride and zest at meeting this challenge.

A pulse of heat infused Darcie's chest, then shimmied through her.

Oh, God, she remembered what had turned her on so much in the taciturn, skinny, hurting boy in high school. That absolute confidence in his abilities, and the resolve to stretch them ever further.

God help her, it turned her on now, too.

The fact that he was no longer a boy or skinny or quite so taciturn made it all the more powerful.

But the hurt…that was still there. It made her want to wrap her arms around him and push his hair back from his forehead.

Not a good combination with being turned on.

She swallowed, moved to put the desk between them. "Okay, you stopped them, but the point is, if this was a so-phisticated attack—"

"Intelligent, but not that sophisticated." His eyes scanned the screen. "It's—oh, yeah, that's good—clever," he concluded. "Not polished."

Her thoughts reordered themselves. "A talented amateur could do it?"

"An extremely talented amateur. Smart enough to use several layers, hoping that if the first or second was uncovered one of the remaining ones would get—"

"Wait. Stop. Be quiet."

He stared, but he obeyed.

Bits and pieces clicked together, forming a picture, a possibility.

She picked up the phone from the desk, looked at the bottom, then followed the cord toward the jack in the wall. There, where the cord dipped out of sight behind the bottom of the window curtain, she found what she'd been looking for.

"What?"

She stopped Zeke with a look. She took the camera out of the kit still on Zeke's bed, shot pictures of it in place, drew the telephone cord up, took more photos and, finally, unclipped the device from the cord.

"Okay?" he asked. After her nod, he added, "A tap?"

"I think it's a more general bug, using the phone for power. What you said about backups made me wonder if our guy had yet another backup."

He whistled. "Maybe this isn't an amateur."

She didn't answer. She needed to think this through. Not only how to deal with Zeke, but the chief.

"As long as you're certain your data's secure?" He nodded. "I need to get this evidence to the police department, Zeke. I'll let you know if we come up with anything definitive."

"Okay, sure. I'll help you with it."

She let him take the case after she'd closed it, and let him follow her out. When she stopped to reassure Mrs. Z that she seriously doubted a dangerous criminal had targeted Drago, she saw that the real reassurance the older woman needed wasn't anything Darcie could give.

Zeke said nothing to his mother, simply waited for Darcie to say goodbye, then followed her to the patrol car.

"Thank you, Zeke," Darcie said gravely as she placed the evidence kit he'd handed her into the trunk. "But you're going to have to go back inside and talk to your mother sometime. Better to do it now."

He growled.

She figured that was the best she could expect.

* * *

"'Morning."

Zeke wasn't surprised this time. "'Morning. And sorry."

"For what?"

"Trespassing again."

"No trespassing on the sky, son, and seems to me that's mostly what you're treading on. Heard you had some trouble yesterday at your mother's place. Somebody broke in."

"How'd you hear about that?"

"Folks look out for Rosa Zeekowsky. Neighbors were upset they hadn't spotted whoever got in."

Before Zeke digested that, the farmer added, "So, what'dya make of yourself, boy? Always figured you for becoming a rocket scientist, sending those telescopes and such into space."

"I've had a little to do with rockets going into space, but I'm not a rocket scientist. I went into technology."

"Oh. Them computers."

"Not exactly computers. Not the hardware anyway." Curiosity nudged him. "You don't like computers?"

The old man hitched his lowered shoulder, a gesture more dismissive than a full shrug. "They got their uses, I suppose. Just not in farming."

"Big operations use computers."

"Sure. Those that are looking for today's profit and not thinking what the soil'll be like for their children, much less their great-grandchildren. There's those that work the soil, and there's those that work machines. I'm not saying machines aren't necessary these days. It's an attitude. Which one you put first, which one you feel here." He thumped his chest.

"Those big operations, they're working the machines. They use computers to take all there is the soil can give. That's not farming. Farming is a partnership, like a marriage or a family. Giving back to the soil so it can keep giving. And knowing if there's a time it can't give, then you gotta give a little more until things turn around."

But surely there were ways technology could help a small farm like this. Not just spreadsheets for finances, but maybe a way to find which market would pay best. Or—

No, this wasn't his concern. Farming? He didn't know anything about farming, he didn't care anything about farming. Certainly not about farming around Drago.

The farmer had started off, but turned back. "I know who you are. You're that genius they're all excited about in town. Think you're going to click some button and save 'em all." His bark of laughter carried no humor. "I suppose I shoulda been hoping you'd turn that genius to makin' farmin' easier. But I guess if you were going to do it, you'd've done it back when you had farms all around you."

"I wasn't…"

Interested. Wasn't interested in making life easier, not for the residents of Drago he'd lived among, not for the kids here now, not for the farmers nearby, not even for this farm, where he'd been drawn so often to watch the sun rise.

Quit thinking everything revolves around you and your old hurts, Zeke. Maybe Darcie was right. Maybe he had become a self-centered bastard. Maybe he always had been one.

"…thinking along those lines."

The farmer grunted. "'Spose not." He shuffled away, raising one hand in farewell without looking back.

Zeke stayed where he was.

I wasn't thinking along those lines. Not as a boy, and not when he'd arrived at this fence line this morning.

But now? Maybe the farmer was wrong. And Darcie, too.

A patrol car with Darcie behind the wheel eased to a stop beside the side entrance to Lilac Commons, where Zeke was taking an unofficial recess from smiling and saying hello at the fund-raising lilac sale. He now knew lilac bushes could live for a couple hundred years, needed sunshine, liked alkaline soil and most bloomed best in climates that had a strong winter freeze.

Zeke watched her get out of the car and saw her focus on something to his right that was masked by a grove of lilacs. Keeping close to the bushes, he edged forward.

Warren Wellton sat on a bench tucked among the lilacs.

"Hey, Warren," Darcie said, talking over the top of the car.

"'Lo," the boy mumbled, darting a wary glance, then returning his attention to an electronic game in his hands.

"Phew." She stirred her hair with the expelled breath. "It's always busy during the Lilac Festival, but this year it's nuts. Everybody's so excited about Anton Zeekowsky coming back to Drago. Guess it's understandable with a certified genius. You must have seen what a zoo it is whenever he's around."

"He's not such a genius. I— Somebody could take him."

"Take him?" she repeated, her expression puzzled.

"You know. Do better than him." The boy kept playing his game.

"Like develop a better software program?"

"Maybe."

"Or find a flaw in a Zeke-Tech product?"

"Maybe."

"Or get into their system, like a spy and see what's going on?"

"Maybe."

"Nobody has, so I guess that does make him a genius."

His head came up and he opened his mouth. "I—" He shut it.

"You what, Warren?"

"Nothin'. I gotta go." He was already moving.

"Sure, see you later," Darcie called after the boy. After a pause punctuated by the fading crunch of Warren's steps on another path into the park, she said, without turning her head, "You can come out, Zeke."

After watching her work, he wasn't entirely surprised she'd spotted him.

"I thought you had him." He leaned against the car's passenger door.

She shook her head. "He's not stupid. A blend of computer smarts and crime ignorance, but not stupid."

"You think he's the one?"

"Thinking's not proof."

"Could you prove it with fingerprints, other evidence you collected?"

"Might have to go that route. He's not a bad kid. He needs guidance. He's fallen for the wrong girl." She broke eye contact, then added, "I might want to try another way and hope the chief goes along."

Even without other things on his mind Zeke doubted he'd be interested in Warren's adolescent love life. And he had a lot of other things on his mind.

Especially what he was about to do. And the knowledge of why.

Not for Drago. Not even entirely for his mother. It was for Darcie. Because those leagues were important to her. God knew why, but they were.

She reached for the door handle.

"Darcie."

She straightened and looked over the car at him. He jammed his fingers in the back pockets of his jeans, palms out.

"About the auctions…you can quit holding them. I'll send you whatever you need for the kids' sports leagues."

A blaze of something crossed her face. So strong, he thought his knees would buckle with it. Before he dropped to the sidewalk, she'd covered it over.

"Thank you, Zeke," she said quickly. "Thank you."

With those simple words heating his blood, she ducked into the car and drove away, as if afraid he'd take back the first gesture of civic-mindedness he'd ever shown toward Drago.

Chapter Eight

At the sound of a car squealing to a stop, Darcie stopped pacing beneath the stairs to her apartment and looked down the driveway crowded with nearly the entire department fleet, even though it was Sunday morning.

The Drago PD didn't like it when someone targeted one of their own.

She caught a flash of orange, but still wasn't quite prepared when Zeke charged toward her.

"Are you okay?" He grabbed her by the shoulders. "Jennifer said someone broke in to your place. I got here as soon as— Are you okay?"

"No. I—"

"Where? Where are you hurt? Have they called the ambulance?"

"Zeke! I'm not hurt," she managed to say. It took some doing because he'd been running his hands over her as he asked those questions, and suddenly she was short on oxygen.

"Not hurt," he repeated, as if testing the concept.

Without warning, his hands returned to her shoulders, tightened and drew her in. His arms went around her, enclosing her in a space that was all Zeke. Her face pressed against his neck. A whiff of soap and some sort of shaving cream braided with the warmth of his skin. Against her cheek she felt the steady pulse of his blood. She went to wet her lips, truly, that was all she meant to do—relieve the sudden dryness. Somehow her tongue flicked against his throat. Just the tip. It was enough. He tasted of salt and man and more of that warmth—lots more of that warmth.

His arms seemed to convulse around her, and she both heard and felt a strangled sound she couldn't categorize. If her tongue touched his skin again, would it produce the same reaction?

She didn't have the opportunity to conduct that experiment—purely in the interests of science—because he shifted his hold. One hand went to the back of her head, guiding her so her cheek rested against his shirt, and she could hear the echo of his heart beating. Hard and…shouldn't someone in as good physical shape as he was have a slower heartbeat than that?

She forgot about his cardio condition because his other hand, very low on her back, had pulled her flush against him. Or they would have been flush if there had not been something growing hard between them.

Was he—?

As quickly as he'd folded her into his arms, he had his hands on her shoulders and his arms extended, putting her at arm's length. Since they were Zeke's arms, she might as well have been in the next county.

She glanced down. She wasn't proud of it, but sometimes temptation was too strong.

His khakis were too loose. Why couldn't he have worn jeans?

"You're sure you're not hurt."

What about you? Feeling any, uh, discomfort in a certain region?

"I'm sure."

"Why the hell did you say you weren't okay?"

"Because I'm not. I'm not hurt, but I'm not okay." He released her, and she stepped back, remembering where they were and why. "I'm pissed."

"Because someone broke into your place."

"Yes. And because they won't let me in there."

He looked up at the open doorway of her apartment, which let everybody else and his brother inside her space while they kept her out.

"Probably to protect the investigation," he said wisely. "So there's no question in court of someone with a conflict of interest being involved."

"Conflict of interest, my ass. My interest is finding out who was in my apartment, and that's in the interests of the investigation, too."

"What did they take? Is there damage?"

"That's the weird thing. They didn't take my TV or CD player or jewelry. And the only place they messed up was around the computer, which they also didn't take."

They'd both been looking up, watching figures move across the opening of the door. Zeke brought his gaze down to her.

"The CD I gave you, did they take that?"

"The CD, you—? Oh." She'd almost forgotten about that. "No, I don't think they took it."

"You have to find out, Darcie."

His urgency captured her complete attention. "Why?"

"That CD has new software on it. New software we're supposed to release at the first of the month."

The bottom of her stomach sank to her toes. "How important is that CD, Zeke?"

"Very. A major investment of time and resources. If our competitors get it ahead of time…it wouldn't be good."

"Oh, my God. If someone took it— Why did you give it to me?"

"I wanted—" He paused. "I thought you'd be interested. Maybe I wanted to impress you."

"Oh, Zeke." How could she say that she'd be much more impressed with what she'd felt—thought she'd felt—a few moments ago? She cleared her throat. "As soon as I can, I'll go up and check. It shouldn't be much longer."

She hadn't thought anything was missing, but she hadn't been focused on whether someone could have broken into her apartment in pursuit of the latest multi-million dollar tech breakthrough.

Why did you give it to me?

A damned good question, Zeke admitted to himself an anxious half hour later as the chief, Sarge and a couple patrolmen he didn't recognize finally left the apartment and said Darcie could go in.

I wanted you to have something that would show you how far I've come. That I've made something of myself.

I wanted you to have something from me. Something that was part of me.

What kept poking him between the shoulder blades was that he'd given it to her that first night in Drago. He'd swear he hadn't had those kinds of thoughts about Darcie then.

Had he?

The door at the top of the stairway he'd seen her coming down last week when they'd talked with her mother opened into her apartment. A short hallway had sliding closet doors on the right, a half-wall revealing a compact kitchen was on the left. Another two strides and he was in the living room.

Straight ahead a bank of windows looked out on the gardens. To the left were the two dormer windows that over-looked the driveway. Matching bookcases rose on either side of them and a fireplace between them.

"Fake," she said when she saw him looking at it. "The fire marshal couldn't be budged on a real fireplace."

She had a desk angled in the far corner with computer equipment. CDs were pulled out of the rack beside the monitor and coated with the same dust she'd used at his mother's house. A couch faced the fireplace. A chair sat beside the bookcases.

The back wall of the living room area consisted of an ingenious arrangement of sliding wood doors that apparently could shut off the room behind them, but they were pushed to one side now, revealing a bed with a cushy comforter and a colony of pillows. He supposed there were the other necessities of a bedroom, but he didn't get past that bed.

"What color?"

Yellow.

Just before he said the word, he realized she was talking about the CD, not her bed.

She was crouched in front of a storage unit of CDs beside an audio unit.

"You thought it was a musical CD?" So much for impressing her.

"I didn't know." Her voice was muffled as she ran her finger along the spine of CD cases.

His gaze returned to her bed. It was a lot wider than the slab in his boyhood room. Not as big as his bed back in Virginia, though. Not that this one wouldn't do. Hell, a backseat would do.

Had done.

"The color, Zeke? Wait, never mind. Here it is." She held up the orange jewel case in triumph. "It doesn't look as if anyone touched any of these CDs."

"Good. Good." He should feel a lot more excitement than he did at the recovery of the valuable CD. But his excitement was not about that.

"Now that we know it's safe, I've, uh, got to go somewhere," she said. "Sorry to rush you out, but you probably want to go check it out on your laptop…."

He looked away from her bed.

"You think you know who broke in, don't you? You think it's the same person who broke in to my place."

He watched her consider sidestepping. Then she said, "Yes."

He felt as if he'd won the Nobel Prize. "And you didn't tell the chief." He didn't need confirmation to know he had that right. "I don't care if he is a kid, I'm going with you."

"There is no need to—"

"I'll take back the support for the athletic leagues."

"You wouldn't. That's blackmail."

"Damn right, I would." What was a little blackmail to keep her from going off on her own?

Abruptly, she turned smug. "I already told your mother. You can't take it back. Besides, you can't come. This is official police business."

"Then call the chief."

That shut her up. Literally. Her mouth closed with a snap.

"Okay then," he said. "I'm going with you."

"Zeke—"

He stopped her by touching her. A brief touch of his fingers to her cheek. He wasn't sure he liked the fact that his skin touching hers brought her to such a complete stop. It bothered him on general principle, but he wasn't going to argue with the result in this specific instance.

"Do I look like I'm gong to change my mind? So let's quit wasting time and get going."

* * *

Zeke had watched Darcie escort Warren into the police department, tell him to have a seat by the dispatch center and she'd be right back. She'd walked off and left the boy to Corine's tender mercies, in which comments about "Always knew you'd come to no good, ordering all those things off the Internet," figured prominently.

After several minutes, Benny directed Zeke into an observation area then escorted the boy to a windowless room with a table and three chairs, leaving him alone. When Darcie walked in, the boy stopped fidgeting, and from this side of the one-way glass Zeke imagined he heard his sigh of relief.

She didn't look at him while she put a tape recorder, pad of paper and two pencils on the table. Then she took the seat opposite him.

Slowly, she brought her gaze to his face, still without a word.

The boy swallowed, two quick bobs of his Adam's apple. He looked even younger than his years. That might have been nervousness. Or the fact that Benny had taken his shoes and replaced them with blue paper booties before leaving him alone in the room to ripen, as Darcie called it.

"She's good," the chief murmured. Harnett had arrived just after Zeke entered the room. He wondered if Darcie knew the chief was here.

"I'm not going to let this go on too long," warned the advocate she'd brought in to protect the boy's interests. It had taken Darcie a long time to persuade the young lawyer not to be in the room with her and Warren. He'd finally agreed on the stipulation that the tape recorder have no tape in it.

"Warren, you know why you're here," Darcie said in the other room.

"No. I don't."

"You know why you're here," she repeated. "We have the evidence."

"What evidence?" Warren sounded smug.

"That was a mistake," the chief murmured.

He should have asked "Evidence of what?" if he really didn't know why he was here, Zeke realized. That and the smugness told a tale.

"There are a lot of ways to trace someone besides fingerprints, Warren. Take purchases online of certain items—those purchases can be traced. Or take damp grass. Did you know that the sole of every shoe is individual, Warren? The way a person walks wears the tread differently."

The boy did his best to keep his face expressionless, but from behind the mirror, Zeke saw him curl his bootied feet under the chair. It spoke volumes about a vulnerability recognized.

"So?" His defiance lost impact when his voice squeaked.

"So, we'll find out soon, won't we, what the soles of your shoes have to tell us. Now, here's another interesting thing, Warren. I know you like computers, so maybe you'd be interested to hear about the tiny video cameras they have nowadays. Some folks use them to check on the babysitter they've left their kids with, or even on the kids. They're so small that unless you know where to look, you'd never spot them. They start when someone comes near. What do you call that?"

"Motion activated." Warren didn't sound happy to have the answer.

"That's right, motion activated. You know Chief Harnett tries to keep the department up to date, to know whether or not to recommend them to citizens. We need to be familiar with running them, so he has us try them out at home. It's not like we expect to catch anything on a camera like that.

"But things we don't expect happen all the time. Like not

being able to find what we came looking for. Unexpected things like that happen, don't they, Warren?" She pointed the pencil's eraser end at Warren. "Don't they?"

"S'pose."

"Now, here's another thing that might not be expected. A system in a computer that tracks and identifies an intruder without even letting the intruder know he's been spotted. Not only that, but this program redirects the intruder so he thinks he's seen the real files, when he's not really any closer than a rank amateur."

For the first time he sat up straight. "No way! Those weren't shadow files. He had no idea I'd—"

He collapsed back into his chair like a balloon pricked by a pin.

"Why?" Darcie asked so softly Zeke almost missed it.

"Everybody's acting like he's God or a TV star or something," Warren grumbled, chin tucked against his chest. "I got sick of it. Sick of hearing 'em talk about Zeke this and Zeke that."

"You mean your sister?"

"Not Cristina," he said with disdain. "She talks herself blue in the face and I don't care."

"Ah."

The boy looked away, misery in every inch of his pudgy body.

"We're going to have to figure out what to do about this, Warren. You're in a lot of trouble. You know that don't you?"

He nodded and looked as if he wanted to cry.

Darcie turned the pad around and slid it toward him, then the pencils. "I want you to write down everything you did, everything that happened."

He looked at the paper then up at her.

"Can't I use a computer?"

* * *

"Are you satisfied you know what's behind all this, Darcie?" the chief asked.

She'd hardly taken in the fact that the chief had been watching her talk with Warren when he'd insisted they confer in his office, leaving Benny to watch Warren toil over his handwritten description of events, then take him home to await their decision. The chief was behind his desk. Zeke's long limbs took up most of the rest of the space in the small room, leaving her and Warren's advocate to cram together.

"Yes. The root of it is Ashley Stenner."

"She's not interested in computers," Zeke said.

"No, but Warren's interested in her. Interested, smitten, gonzo, nuts for, head over heels and totally clueless how to deal with the feelings."

He should understand that, since he'd had the same feelings for Ashley's mother.

"Is he?" Zeke asked.

"Yes. He broke into your mother's house, then into my place to find out what you were doing. He was looking for the handheld prototype—he didn't know about the CD. He'd listened to some of your phone conversations. And he'd heard you say you had something you wanted me to see that night at the high school. He followed you there. He thought it would impress Ashley. So he waited outside your mother's house and listened." He'd said when he left the porch light was on and they were talking, so thank heavens he hadn't seen anything.

"If he'd gotten into the laptop or stumbled onto that CD, he'd have impressed a lot more people than Ashley," Zeke said. "Breaking news about Zeke-Tech's next release would have been a hacker's coup."

What Warren hadn't considered was what would happen after the glare of attention. As in a court case and possible punishment.

"We would have tracked him down," Zeke said, apparently following her line of thought. "He took a dumb risk. And that's odd, because he's quite intelligent. He picked up the crossbar security quickly. The insulated—"

"Zeke, look at me." She backed up the words by taking hold of his upper arms. His eyes were sparkling and intent, yet with a focal point far beyond the chief's office. As she watched, his focus shifted. The sparkling interest mellowed, then deepened.

She swallowed, and dropped her hands from his arms.

"Warren's not operating on logic." She turned to the chief. Odd to think she found him a safer conversationalist than Zeke. But having that look in Zeke's eyes focused on her... "That's why I want to propose something a little unorthodox."

The chief instantly became wary. The advocate said, "Unorthodox? You know that nothing he said—"

"Don't worry. My idea's for Warren's good. It's a matter of redirecting his energies, at the same time taking advantage of his abilities."

The chief got it first. Eyebrows lifted, he looked at Zeke. The advocate saw that and also looked at Zeke.

Finally, Zeke felt the imprint of those stares. He looked from face to face, stopping at hers. "Darcie, I won't—"

"You'll be great, Zeke. Don't worry about that." She knew he wasn't, but the word *worry* caught him by surprise long enough for her to grab the conversational reins. "I can't think of anyone better."

"Whatever you're angling for, the answer is no."

"I'm talking about mentoring Warren. An intensive program during the last week you're here. Then some ongoing contact. He could do work—real work—under your guidance as community service."

"If the kid's so smart, maybe he could tackle fixing our

system so it doesn't crash in a crunch," the chief said. Darcie could hardly believe it. Chief Harnett was backing her up.

"Exactly. Under your supervision, Zeke, it would be perfect."

"I don't—"

"Zeke, there's a chance here with this kid. You said it yourself—he's talented. Do you want that talent turned to mischief? Because that's what'll happen if he's left on his own. There aren't the resources here for a kid like him. Maybe if Josh had his computer program…"

She figured that was about as thick as she could lay on the guilt before Zeke rebelled. She had one more card to play.

"Besides, if he's in trouble, he won't be able to mow your mother's lawn and shovel her walk come winter."

"So, she'll get someone else. I'll pay—"

"It's not the money. The reason she has him do it is to encourage him to exercise. If it's not Warren, she'll do it herself. You know she will."

At that moment, Darcie knew she had Anton Zeekowsky, genius of the technology world, right where she wanted him.

When Zeke opened his mouth, he was aware of Darcie's hands on the steering wheel tensing slightly, as if she expected him to try to wriggle free of this plan she'd embroiled him in.

Instead, he demanded, "Tell me again why you never left Drago. You're good, Darcie. Really good."

She made a face. "I'm a small-town cop."

"You don't have to be."

"Yeah, I do. It's…" She shook her head. "It's too late."

She parked in front of the small house with the beauty salon in the converted garage.

They'd both opened their car doors when Zeke felt her look across the width of the car. He twisted to face her.

"You might have to talk him into doing this," she said.

"No way." But she was getting out of the car, and he leaned across the seat to keep making his point. "I'm not going to beg this kid who broke into your apartment, scared my mother and tried to hack into my system—"

"What do you think about that, Warren?"

Zeke whipped his head around. The kid stood behind him, sour faced.

"Who cares?" The kid curled his lip at her, and Zeke liked him even less.

"The chief told you what the deal is and that it starts in the morning."

Zeke had protested, but it had done him no more good than anything else he'd protested about to Darcie.

"I don't need him to teach me anything."

"You know the first sign of stupidity?" Darcie asked. "Thinking you don't need to learn anything."

"Yeah, well *he* didn't think I was so stupid Friday."

Darcie snorted. "A talented amateur, that's all."

"He said *extremely* talented amateur. And smart."

With her arms crossed under her breasts, Darcie let the silence stretch, long enough for the kid to realize he'd quoted words he could only know if he'd been listening in on the conversation between Zeke and Darcie in Zeke's bedroom after the break-in. And the only way he could have listened in was through the planted device.

The kid squirmed, and Zeke felt a flash of empathy, though the kid's motive and his own for squirming were different. The kid was uncomfortable because Darcie had caught him. Zeke's was more elemental.

Her position snugged the material of her uniform shirt across her breasts. Not tight, just tighter than before. Instead of a vague impression of her breasts, it provided a definitive curve, especially the underside of the curve, where her skin had felt so warm and soft, he'd had to kiss it—

"So, you heard that much before I disconnected the transmitter."

"I didn't say that. I didn't admit anything."

"Save it, Warren." Darcie didn't raise her voice. "We had plenty of evidence, even before this self-incriminating comment. You either take this offer—work with Zeke to his satisfaction and mine and the chief's—or we stop giving you a break. You make up your mind, and you stick with it. You say yes, we tell your mother, and you commit to working your behind off under Zeke's instruction and my supervision. What's it going to be?"

The kid flicked a look at Zeke.

"All right," he mumbled, studying the toes of his battered running shoes.

"No, it's not going to work that way," Darcie said. "You look at me and tell me you appreciate this break and you're going to take it, then you look at Mr. Zeekowsky, and you tell him thank you for this opportunity."

Warren looked up, his face molded into rebellious resentment. Then he encountered Darcie's expression.

The kid swallowed, and his soft cheeks seemed to melt into babyhood.

"I appreciate this break, Darcie, and I'm going to take it." He swallowed again before looking in Zeke's vicinity. "Thank you for this opportunity."

"Sir," Darcie demanded.

Zeke thought she'd gone too far. But once more she proved she did know people.

"Sir," the kid said.

Zeke found himself letting out a sigh of relief, when, not

half an hour ago he was absolutely going to refuse to mentor this kid.

"Okay, where's your mom?"

Oh, yeah, Darcie Barrett was good. And she was wasted on Drago.

From the top of the stairs leading to Corine's domain at the police station, Darcie took in the situation Monday evening.

Zeke and Warren sat side by side in front of the computer screen, Zeke's fingers speeding across the keyboard, while he rattled off language that only occasionally included words recognizable as English. Warren punctuated Zeke's monologue with nods. Neither noticed her descending the stairs, but Corine, displaced to the side of the room, did.

"They've been at it for hours," she grumbled.

"At what?"

"Who knows. I only know they rigged it so 9-1-1 calls come in here." She gestured disparagingly at an ordinary phone at her elbow. "I have to write calls by hand." Clearly the equivalent of chiseling into stone with a toothpick.

"Ah," Zeke breathed, capturing the attention of both women. He leaned back and stretched his arms, like a well-muscled bird in flight. "Now I see how you did it. Not bad, Warren, not bad."

"They didn't even know," the boy said, preening.

"They knew they were crashing when they had a heavy load. If the people who'd looked at it had half a brain they would have spotted it. I saw it right off. Though, it took longer to see how."

"Not that long," Warren said, and Darcie could tell he was impressed.

Darcie walked up behind Zeke and put a hand on his shoulder, to get his attention. That's all.

He turned quickly, his eyes intense and alive.

He regarded her blankly for half a beat. Then he blinked and smiled. She felt the kick of that smile right down to her toes, with some side trips to body parts that reacted a lot more strongly than her toes.

He covered her hand with his, and that sensation also detoured to several sensitive spots. She withdrew her hand.

"Hi, Darcie."

"Hi, yourself. What are you guys doing?"

"We've discovered the drain on the department system." There was a devilment in Zeke's eyes she didn't quite trust. "Warren?" Zeke invited.

"I, uh, tapped into the system to, uh, sort of borrow power."

"I *knew* it!" Corine exulted darkly from the background.

"Ingenious, really," Zeke picked up. "Because his system didn't have the capacity to receive data he was trying to harvest from my laptop. That was one thing that puzzled me. The program had multi-pronged output and—"

"Okay, okay, Zeke."

"With that piece of junk I've got, I hadda do something," Warren said in a man-to-man tone.

Zeke nodded. "Not a bad work-around. And far more efficient for keeping track of police business than a scanner would be."

"Stop." Despite satisfaction at having the answer to how Cristina, Warren and Ashley had known Zeke was at the station that first night, Darcie crossed her arms, and gave them both a quelling stare. Warren appeared subdued, but Zeke's expression was peculiar. As if he was trying for that gone-to-granite expression, but couldn't get it quite right.

"Okay," she continued in no-nonsense mode, "it's a fascinating puzzle, Zeke. But sucking the power from the police computer system is dangerous. People's safety depends on this system. Our safety." She gestured widely to encompass

Drago PD, and noticed Zeke's gaze follow the motion as she returned her arm to cross with the other. "And the safety of everyone in Drago. The night Zeke arrived, while we were chasing a man who'd kidnapped a girl not much younger than you, Warren, our computer crashed."

"I told him that," Zeke said. "He understands the seriousness of what he did. Don't you, Warren?"

"Yes, sir. I'm sorry, Darcie. Zeke says I didn't think it out far enough, about the effects. And that's essential." Zeke nodded approvingly. With that backing, Warren added in a more natural tone, "I never meant to cause trouble."

Corine huffed, but Darcie said, "I know, but it can be really hard to predict what the consequences are going to be of something." Like luring Zeke back to Drago. "Especially if you start messing with other people's lives—or computer systems," she added quickly.

Zeke nodded sternly. "You could have put that little girl in even worse danger. And you *did* put Darcie in danger when she stopped me."

"Put you in danger, too," Darcie said. "An APB stop can go bad in a second. Change lives forever."

Their eyes held, and there was something there. Something about the instant in the near dark of the D-Shop's lot when they'd recognized each other, and felt a connection that stretched back to another dark night.

Darcie broke the look and mentally shook her head. Maybe—maybe—that other night had changed her life in ways she was only starting to acknowledge. But their lives had diverged, separated.

"Did you really put Zeke in handcuffs?" Warren's adolescent voice skidded up with interest.

"That is *not* the point," Corine glared. "A kidnapper on the loose, a child in danger, officers responding to an APB and a civilian—all in danger because of you."

Warren shrank in his chair. "I know."

"We'll finish restoring the police system," Zeke said after a moment. "With a few improvements for Corine as an apology." Corine preened. "Then we'll see about fixing your system so you can do some real work."

From Warren's expression, Zeke had single-handedly made the sun rise.

Chapter Nine

Darcie didn't see Zeke or Warren for the next two days. She heard rumors, though.

From Corine, whose grumbling eased into faint praise as they completed fixing and upgrading the department computer system.

From Benny, who despaired of being able to fit into any of his clothes since he spent so much time in Mrs. Z's kitchen while Zeke and Warren lost themselves in techno nirvana.

From Yolanda Wellton, who insisted on giving Darcie a free trim in preparation for the Lilac Festival's big weekend, with the coronation, parade and ball, but also gave her a headache with unrelenting praise of Saint Zeke.

Then, Thursday, Benny had a family emergency when his daughter was hit in the mouth with a foul ball during phys ed and needed stitches, so Darcie was back on Zeke duty.

She arrived at Mrs. Z's shortly before time to leave for

Lilac Commons for the final run-through of tomorrow night's coronation. Zeke and Warren were in his bedroom, their rapid exchange of techno mumbo jumbo an undercurrent to Mrs. Z's exclamations of concern over Benny's daughter.

Mrs. Z called to Zeke that it was time to leave. He paused in the hallway when he saw Darcie, and for no reason other than his look, she felt heat spreading from the pit of her stomach up through her body, hampering her breathing when it hit her lungs, then stinging her cheeks as it continued up.

His mother's flow of explanations about Benny's daughter and exhortations not to be late covered the fact that neither Zeke nor Darcie said a word until they were in the car, alone, and the silence had stretched long enough to be wearing thin.

As she was about to say something—anything—Zeke surprised her by saying, "It's nice to be your passenger again."

"Thanks. Benny's so used to a carload of kids, he keeps the radio loud."

He nodded ruefully. "Nobody needs a scanner, just wait for Benny's patrol car to go by."

She chuckled. "Sounds like you and Warren have been having a good time—now and the other day at the station."

"I haven't let him forget that what he did was wrong," he said defensively, and Darcie suspected he'd gotten so involved in what he was teaching Warren that he'd forgotten exactly that.

"I didn't say that," she said mildly. "I simply was commenting that it must be fun to teach an enthusiastic pupil."

"I suppose it is." He gazed straight ahead with the unfocused stare of someone seeing something from a new angle.

Only after several minutes, when he shifted in the seat did she say, "You're good with Warren. You're a good teacher."

"I had a good teacher myself."

"Yes, you did." Which was as good an introduction as any to what she wanted to explore. "You've asked me a couple times why I didn't leave Drago. Now it's my turn to ask. Why did you leave, Zeke?"

"You know why."

She found a parking spot not far from a side entrance to the park. They'd have a bit of a walk, but it was pleasant. They got out of the car, then fell into step as they climbed the three steps into the park.

"Humor me," she said. "Tell me again why you left. Why you couldn't wait to leave Drago."

"I wanted to do more."

"More than what?"

He sidestepped that. "I wanted to be respected."

She pursued it. "Your father was respected. As a kind and good man who worked hard and loved his family. As a man who loved this town and its people, and who was loved back."

The crushed-stone path took them through a tunnel lined by lilacs in full bloom. The individual scents peaked, blended and remixed, the olfactory equivalent of musical instruments in a symphony.

"I wanted to have influence on a wider scale, a bigger stage."

"Influence? That sounds like a nice way of saying power."

"Fine, say power then. I wanted power."

The path opened to the Coronation Garden. A ring of lilacs backed a grassy area that formed an elevated platform. Terraced below the platform was a wide fountain, like the orchestra pit in a theater, and then a wide, grassed allée with beds of tulips and lilacs down either side that formed a natural spot for spectators.

One more step, and they would be visible to participants gathering for the practice for tomorrow's coronation. She didn't take that step, though the voices of those already gathered were rising in contentious frustration.

"And do you have it?" she asked Zeke. "Do you have the power to be happy? To live a good life?"

"What about you, Darcie? Do you have the power to be happy?"

"Darcie!" the director called, having spotted her. "Finally!"

She didn't look away from Zeke. "Of course. I *am* happy."

"Are you? Not pursuing your dreams. Staying in Drago because you think you have to for your mother. Pushing me away with an ultimatum because you liked kissing me a little too much. Are you really happy?"

"Darcie, come," the director ordered with more authority than she'd heard from him all month. He took her arm and tugged her toward whatever the current crisis was, while she looked back at Zeke, who watched her with intensity.

"Brenda, I know you're not there," Zeke said briskly into the cell phone, glad to be doing something to keep his mind off the look of confusion he'd put in Darcie's eyes.

"But when you get back, first thing you do… No, second thing. First thing is give yourself two extra weeks of vacation.

"Next, I want Development to figure out the best way for farmers around Drago to get their product to the top-selling markets—that's getting it there fast, cheap and reliably. Then I want Programming to work up software to assess whether it's better to limit supply and sell high or increase production and sell low. Send me somebody to start talking to local farmers, to get the real data. Oh, and talk to Legal and find out how we can give the program to family-owned farms when it's completed. Don't let them bully you about how we can't give it away. What am I saying? Like you'd let them bully you.

"There might be more later. I want it all humming when I come—" The word *home* would not come. "Back. When I get back."

He disconnected the call and automatically looked for Darcie.

She and Jennifer were in a corner. Jennifer seemed both intent and amused. Darcie looked hunted.

He stilled an urge to stop whatever was making her look that way. Darcie wouldn't appreciate his butting in.

Besides, he was better off keeping a distance. He wasn't an idiot—not on this issue—Darcie had been angling to involve him in Drago all along. With Warren, she had a major success. Now, even though she didn't know about it, he'd done more. Get too close, and she'd pull him in completely.

Jennifer tsked. "I'm serious, Darcie. Zeke's nuts about you."

"Then you're seriously nuts. Zeke? The guy who could have won a Nobel Prize in high school if they'd had a category on Jennifer Truesdale?"

Although the tone sounded like her usual self, somehow the words sounded threadbare to Darcie's ears.

Pushing me away with an ultimatum because you liked kissing me just a little too much.

Had she done that? Was she doing that?

"High school is long gone. And there has never been that special light in Zeke's eyes when he looks at me that there is when he looks at you. Believe me, I know a little something about the light going out of a man's eyes."

Sometimes Darcie wished that rat bastard Eric had stayed in town long enough so that she could've gotten her hands on him.

"Don't Darcie," Jennifer said. Her smile was firm, "Don't let that soft heart of yours ache for me. I only brought it up to persuade you that I know what I'm talking about. You're the woman who matters to Zeke. I'd say the guy's head over heels in love with you."

In her deepest heart, it's what Darcie had always wanted. So why was she scared to death?

* * *

"'Morning."

"'Morning, Mr. Hooper."

The farmer huffed out an acknowledgement that Zeke had tracked down his name. Not that it had been a challenge. The name was painted on the mailbox. He'd made sure to go past it on his way to his usual spot this morning.

"Call me Everett."

"Zeke," Zeke replied, though he suspected Everett Hooper knew that.

In comfortable silence, they watched the sun rise together again.

"Well, that's another day started," the farmer said with satisfaction.

"Yup."

A couple weeks ago Zeke would have ignored that this day would include the coronation of the Lilac Queen—with the judges' meeting and vote along with all the other hoo-ha—or would have been doing his damnedest to think of a way to get out of it and stay in front of his computer. Now he could face the prospect with equanimity. And look forward to seeing Darcie.

But he had a lot to do before tonight.

"Everett, would you be willing to talk to somebody who works for me today?"

"What about?"

"Farming. And computers."

The man made a disparaging sound. "If I were half useful around this place I'd say no, but I suppose there's not much else I can do."

They set a time for Zeke and his employee Larry to come to the farmhouse. Then they settled in for a few more minutes of watching the sun.

"First time I rode out here," Zeke found himself telling

Everett, "it seemed like the biggest adventure I could possibly have. Seemed so far away when I was little, and not daylight yet and nobody around, but I needed to think and…"

He'd been maybe twelve. Wrestling with the problem of being different from his classmates. He'd had a growth spurt that summer that had his mother despairing about keeping him in pants from one Sunday's churchgoing to the next. The distance between his academic interests and the devotion of his one-time friends to sports had exploded. He'd felt lonely, but also defiant. Worst of all, he'd felt he couldn't talk to his parents about it.

Especially his father.

Fathers were supposed to know about baseball and football and basketball. His didn't. His father taught him about scientific method, about intellectual inquiry. How could he talk to his father about feeling different and isolated when his father was part of the cause?

"And your dad used to bring you out here when you were a kid," Everett concluded his long-dangling sentence.

Zeke faced him. "How'd you know that?"

"I got eyes. Besides, how'd you think Mischar knew to come out here?"

"You knew my father? Oh. Right. From his shop. Got your shoes repaired there."

"Yeah, I did. Also played chess with him most Thursday nights. Seventeen years we did that."

Forgetting the sunrise, Zeke stared at the man.

"What?" Everett demanded. "You don't think a farmer can play chess?"

"I—that isn't…" He sorted through the jumble of thoughts racing through his head. "You talked? With my father?"

"I can't say we carried on like those people on *Oprah* or

nothing, but seventeen years of sitting across a chess board, yeah, we talked. He was my friend."

Zeke jerked his head back around to face the sun, letting its brightness burn into his eyes.

After an interesting morning spent with Warren and a thought-provoking meeting with Everett and Larry, Zeke's day had shifted to Lilac Festival duties, and the pace picked up.

The votes were cast and the queen decided. In a couple hours Drago would crown its Lilac Queen.

"It's been a pleasure, Zeke," Mrs. Rivers said as he held the door for her at the library conference room where they'd met.

"Thank you, ma'am. I've enjoyed serving as a judge with you, too."

Her smile brightened. He hoped she gave his mother a good report.

He was more surprised when Warinke slowed, then stopped beside him.

"You know, I wasn't too sure about this whole deal with having you as Chief Judge, and all. When Darcie and Jennifer brought up the idea, I said right out that Zeke the Geek would think he was too big a deal for little ol' Drago these days. But it's turned out okay. We did a good job. Got a good queen. Our town can be proud."

Zeke looked at the man, really looked at him, without the memory of Ted's teenaged self superimposed for the first time.

He had thinning hair and his belt rode low to accommodate a rounding belly. His face showed no great intelligence, but no meanness, either.

In the nearly three weeks Zeke had been here, Ted had done nothing worse than shoot his mouth off and he'd actually had some sensible things to say, including in the just-concluded discussion among the judges before they voted for Lilac Queen.

"I think so, too," he said.

Ted grinned and extended his hand. "You're not such a geek after all."

"You're wrong, Ted. I am entirely a geek." Zeke shook the man's hand briefly.

The bands had played, the mayor had talked, the officials had taken a bow, the committees and judges had been thanked and the candidates had been presented. They were down to the climax of the coronation ceremony—announcing the queen.

Zeke had done his best to get out of that duty, but it was part of the package as Chief Judge.

Darcie wondered, as she watched his tall figure turn from the lectern to look at the five girls lined up, holding hands, if he realized he was smiling. She had to fight a grin herself. Zeke didn't know it, but he'd grown fond of these girls—or at least most of them—over these weeks. The old softy.

"The most important thing I can tell you about this Lilac Queen competition," Zeke told the crowd, "is that all five girls receive scholarship money to help them pursue higher education, with the four princesses each receiving two thousand dollars and the Queen three thousand.

"The second most important thing is who that Queen will be."

The crowd's reaction was wildly mixed—some applause, some chuckles, some groans of impatience.

"Okay, on to the second most important thing," Zeke said with a grin.

He held up the envelope, a bit of a flourish for someone who'd griped about the formality, since he (along with the other two judges) already knew the name of the queen. That rebellion had only been quelled when Darcie said, "Consider it a bit of theater and just do it, Zeke."

"And this year's Lilac Festival Queen is—"

Darcie saw Cristina's smile broaden and she seemed to take a half step forward.

"—Mandy Reynolds."

Nobody moved. Nobody said a word. But the mass intake of air should have stripped every petal off every lilac bush in the park.

Becky, the princess standing between Cristina and Mandy, came to life first. "Oh, my God! It's you, Mandy! It's you!"

She shoved the stunned queen forward, and Mandy stumbled. She might have pitched headlong into the fountain if Zeke hadn't lunged forward and caught her arm, spinning her back to safety.

That broke the freeze. Last year's queen glided up with the crown and sash and began outfitting Mandy with her accoutrements, while the crowd went wild. Darcie had never heard such a reaction to a queen selection.

The other princesses gathered around Mandy for hugs and tears. All except Cristina Wellton, who remained where she'd stood, smile still in place.

Even after Mandy made a brief, excited yet articulate acceptance statement, even after the formality on the coronation platform gave way to newspaper photographers, family members and milling officials and dignitaries, Cristina didn't move.

Ashley, standing nearby and wringing her hands, gave her mother an anguished look. Jennifer looked to Darcie, who sighed, but moved forward to meet Jennifer in front of the frozen girl.

"Cristina," Jennifer said softly, "let's go in the back now."

She took one arm and Darcie the other, and they guided

Cristina off the platform and into a sort of anteroom created by a horseshoe of lilac bushes.

There, to everyone's dismay, Cristina Wellton's numbness evaporated.

All it took was seeing her mother.

"Oh, baby," Yolanda said.

"You! This is all your fault. If I didn't have to take care of you all the time, I could make something of myself. I could get out of this town. I could go after my dreams! I could be somebody!"

"That's not fair, Cristina," Darcie heard herself saying.

And she should know, she thought, because hadn't she laid similar charges at her mother's door? Never in public. Never even out loud. But just as unfair.

"Fair? What do you know about it? What do you know about having to work in her stupid salon because she's having one of her *spells?* What do you know about having to feed a stupid brother all the time because she *just can't?* What do you know about your father walking out and ruining everything?"

Darcie's heart ached for the girl.

And if Cristina had stopped there, she and the others might have been well disposed toward her.

But Cristina quickly shifted into her more familiar mode, with a rant that she would have won if her mother had bought her the shoes she'd really wanted, that everybody was against her because she was so much more beautiful than anybody else and that not one of the other princesses had a clue of how to apply eyeliner, and didn't anyone *see* that Mandy hadn't had the sense to wear waterproof mascara?

Ashley, apparently feeling she was in more familiar territory now, went to Cristina's side and tried to calm her with sympathy and one hundred percent agreement.

Cristina rounded on the girl. "You think I don't know what you're doing? You think I don't see that you've been sucking up to me, trying to learn all my secrets so you can replace me? I'm not stupid, you know!" she wailed.

Ashley burst into tears and Jennifer swooped in and took her away.

At that moment, Zeke appeared at Darcie's side.

Zeke regarded Cristina, still ranting at Ashley's retreating form, with fascinated horror. "Is this a hissy fit?" he asked, without taking his eyes off Cristina.

"Oh, yeah, this is definitely a hissy fit."

Cristina spotted Zeke then and launched herself at him.

"It isn't fair…." She bleated. "How could you vote against me?"

"I didn't vote against you."

"You didn't?" Hope and calculation jumped back into her expression. "Oh, Zeke, I just *knew* you felt it, too. I don't care about this little Lilac Queen title—let Mandy have it—it was only because I thought you were fighting what's between us. That's the only reason your voting for me is important—"

"I'm not fighting, because there's nothing between us. And you know it, Cristina, so stop this stupid game."

Cristina stared back at his glare, like a snake mesmerized by a mongoose.

"Okay, but—"

Having that admission, Zeke charged ahead. "And I didn't vote for *or* against you. I voted *for* Mandy. Everybody did. It was unanimous."

"But you said—"

"I said I didn't vote against you. I didn't. I don't have anything against you. Except the way you keep hanging on me." He disengaged her hand. "And you wear too much makeup. You think the universe revolves around you. You don't think of other people's feelings. You're letting your mind turn to mush. And you only talk about clothes and that crap."

By the end Cristina was gaping at him, along with everyone else. She blinked fast three times, as if her eyes stung, and Darcie thought this time it might be real, especially because of the way the tip of her nose was turning red.

"You horrible, horrible man! How can you say those things to me?"

"If you're smart, you'll listen," Jennifer said, her arm still wrapped around a sobbing Ashley. "I wish someone had said them to me at your age. It would have saved me a lot of years of grief."

An hour later, Jennifer and Darcie sat in Jennifer's apartment, each with a glass of wine in hand.

Cristina had flounced off. Ashley had been put to bed and had fallen asleep, exhausted from crying. The rest of the court had been safely dispatched for a party at the mayor's house. Zeke had disappeared.

And Darcie and Jennifer had agreed that they would rather walk on nails than go to the party.

Darcie raised her glass in mocking toast. "Here's to our grand plan."

They clinked glasses.

"You really don't think Zeke will consider helping us set up a trust?" Jennifer asked after a sip.

"I really don't."

"What are we going to do?"

"The only thing we can do. Forget this silliness of looking to the future and instead look back on tonight and say, 'Well, that went well!'"

Jennifer stared at her a moment, then they both started to laugh until they cried.

* * *

The window of the narrow storefront was covered by plywood decorated with a painting of lilacs. A sign proclaimed the space available for lease.

Zeke cupped his hands to his face and looked through their tunnel, but the window in the door was too dirty, the space beyond it too dim to see anything of the interior.

He tried the handle. Locked.

He stepped back, looking at the brick building that must have been built about the time Mischar Zeekowsky had been born on the far side of the world.

No conscious decision directed Zeke's footsteps, but he knew where he was going once he started. Down the passageway—narrower than he remembered—between two buildings that opened to the alley—sooner than he expected.

He eyed the high double-hung window beside the padlocked door. It hadn't been replaced. A pair of crumbling concrete blocks stood ready to prop open the heavy door. He moved them into position. He felt around the wooden window frame, the paint flaking away. He found the spot on the right side, rapped the edge of his right hand against it sharply and the left side came toward him.

He grinned as he worked the frame free, carefully removing the entire window, and leaned it against the building.

In his youth he would have opened the door from the inside and replaced the frame immediately to cut the risk of anyone knowing he was inside. The padlocks made that impossible. But the odds of anyone coming back here at this time of night and seeing the missing window were nil.

He hoisted himself through the opening—the motion easier but the fit tighter than it used to be—then dropped to the floor inside.

He felt his way by memory to the door that led to the front of the shop, opening it without going in. The long customer counter remained, but nothing was left of his father's workbench.

The open door added a murky strip of light from the front door to the gray wedge from the back window, giving him enough light in this small storage area to find the second door. He opened it, seeing a windowless room lined with shelves and holding an old metal desk.

His heart thudded hard against his chest in conditioned response. To guard against anyone spotting a light inside the shop, he'd always stepped into the room and closed the door behind him before turning on lights. So there'd been a second of absolute darkness, of not knowing what was ahead, while his heart bammed away at the possibilities.

He didn't close himself in the room now, but found the switch.

No surprise, no electricity. But his eyes were adjusting. The shelves were empty, starting to crumble.

Nothing of his father here, either. As if Mischar Zeekowsky had never hunched over his workbench for hours stretching into days reaching into years, putting on new heels, replacing soles, repairing damage. Smiling for customers, trying to smooth over language differences with good cheer.

Had he loved this shop? Or had it been a prison for him?

To his son, it had been his father's prison, but his own route to the future. In the tiny, windowless room he'd taken apart a thousand electronic gadgets, experimented, tested his theories, read books and articles.

It had started when his mother found him reading in bed at 2 a.m. He was nine. Following that, reading was strictly forbidden after he'd been sent to bed. A growing boy needed his sleep, she'd said. But Zeke had needed even more to learn and know. He'd slipped out the next week, reading by flashlight under a tree. With cooler weather, he'd needed shelter—that's when he'd remembered his father saying how the whole window frame at the back of the shop could come out.

All those years, surely Zeke had slipped up sometimes by not clearing away every sign of his current project. And the articles his father would happen to produce when Zeke was working on something similar. Yes, Mischar had to have known. But he'd never said anything.

Zeke turned his back on the windowless room and looked again toward the front of the shop.

There was something…

He drew in the air, dusty, abandoned and stale. Yet, just on the edge, came the scent of leather.

Darcie's cell phone rang as she reached Old Cemetery in her run. She flipped the phone open, the dial glowing against the light of not-quite sunup. Who would be calling at this hour?

She was earlier than usual this morning because there'd been no point staying in bed when she could have qualified for the Olympic Toss and Turn after last night.

"Darcie? Oh, Darcie, I'm sorry if I woke you. It's Anton."

Darcie's heart lurched, then training set in. "What's wrong, Mrs. Z?"

"Is he there? With you? I know he is a grown man, but all night he is gone. When I visit in Virginia, he does that, but I know he is at his office. Here? I don't know. His machine is in his room, so he is not working. But if he is with you—"

"He's not with me."

"I know it is a modern thing to do, and I am not a busy mother. I would be happy if—"

"Mrs. Z, he isn't here. I don't know where he is."

"Oh." The older woman's tone changed on that single

syllable. Darcie would have said to this point Mrs. Z was a little worried and a lot a curious "busy mother." Now her voice held only worry. "He could be hurt. An accident or that car could be broken."

"I'm sure I would have heard if something had happened to him."

Clearly mollified, the older woman said, "You find him, Darcie. You bring him home. No matter what he thinks."

"Mrs. Z, I can't arrest a man because he didn't come home last night."

"I worry for him."

"I know you do." And not just this one night.

"You worry for him, too."

"He's a grown man, Mrs. Z."

"Yes, he is." She added a trace of slyness to that, as if she thought she knew something.

"Mrs. Z, I've gotta go. I'll let you know if I hear anything. And you call me when he comes in, okay?"

Rosa Zeekowsky accepted that. After a brief hesitation— it was awfully early—Darcie tried Zeke's cell. It went over to a message service immediately. It was off, or not working.

Darcie skipped her loop through the cemetery to reach home faster. In less than an hour she had showered, dressed and driven to the police station to check the few overnight reports.

Darcie called Mrs. Z, to reassure her Zeke hadn't been in an accident and wasn't in the hospital—at least not in Drago—and just in case she had forgotten her promise to let Darcie know when Zeke came in.

"No, he's not here," Mrs. Z said. She sounded calmer. "I remember something, Darcie. His father's shop. You know it? I think Anton goes there."

"But why? It's been empty for years."

"Not of memories."

Chapter Ten

The front door of the deserted shop had been locked. But as Darcie looked for Zeke's car, she picked up a single set of footprints—long footprints—in the dusty gap between buildings.

In the alley, she ran the beam of her flashlight over the back of Mischar Zeekowsky's shoe repair shop and saw the window in its frame leaning against the wall. Point of entry.

"Zeke?"

No answer.

She put the flashlight away, then, using the blocks already in place as a mount, she levered herself into the window opening. Zeke's extra inches of height would have helped him with this maneuver, but her training helped her complete the move with a minimum of noise.

Inside, she waited, letting her eyes adjust and listening. She heard nothing. The door to the front of the shop was open. Instinct might have pushed her to check that room out first.

But training reminded her that with the front door locked and the back door padlocked, she could be caught in a dead end.

There was one other door visible in this small area. She focused her flashlight on the floor leading to it, and saw footsteps. Standing to the side, she carefully eased open the door.

The room was empty. She didn't enter. Because the footsteps had barely advanced past the threshold. She changed her angle and shifted the flashlight. What could have kept Zeke standing there, looking into a windowless, featureless room?

She flicked off the flashlight and went to the front room.

He sat on the floor, with his back against the counter and his legs stretched out nearly across the entire width of the narrow shop.

"Zeke?"

"Hi, Darcie."

"This is getting to be a habit, Zeke, me finding you when someone's worried."

"No one could have seen a light in here. I don't have one."

"Your mother's worried you weren't at home last night."

"Ah." In that syllable, she heard regret that he'd worried his mother, but also what sounded like the echo of a decision. "Darcie, I want to ask you something."

She advanced into the room. "Okay."

"Have a seat." He gestured to the space beside him as he looked up, a half smile tilting his mouth. "It might take me a while to come up with the words. You know I'm not good at that."

She sat, more than a foot between them, with her knees pulled up. Light from the back area sketched out his face for her, and she supposed light from the window in the front door did the same for him with her face.

She wondered if the daylight growing outside would have much impact in here, or if they would remain rough outlines devoid of detail to each other.

Zeke drew in a breath, "Okay, I've been sitting here thinking. Thinking about a lot of things you said. A lot of things that have happened. These past few weeks and before, when we were kids."

As many times as she'd wished that Zeke would occasionally stop his relentless pursuit of the future, her stomach tightened at the prospect of hearing what conclusions he'd come to about the past—and the present.

"What I want to know about is your parents not believing in you."

"Zeke, why on earth—?"

"I want to know, Darcie. You can say it's none of my business, and the only reason I can give you is I want to know."

She laughed. It wasn't pretty, but it eased some of the tension in her throat. And it acknowledged that his reason was going to be enough for her.

"Mom's okay. She never really showed that she believed in me, at least not the way I wanted, but…" She didn't know exactly how to express the feeling that had been building in her lately. "Maybe she didn't know how, because she didn't believe in herself. Not then."

She became aware of Zeke watching her, shifted to her other hip and stretched out one leg.

"Your father?"

"Ah, dear old dad," she said with an attempt at flippancy. "That was another story."

"He didn't support your academics?"

She snorted. "Brains in girls were a waste according to Gordon. He would talk about how beautiful mom was, like a perfect porcelain figure, he'd say, and then he'd look at me and say what a shame I hadn't taken after her."

"So, you entered a career that requites brains and

strength—porcelain figures need not apply. But before you did that, you entered the Lilac Queen contest."

"That again?"

"Yes, that again," he said decisively, turning aside her scoffing. "You were a princess, didn't that tell you that other people saw that you'd be a great representative of Drago?"

"Other people, not my father. You probably don't remember, but he was a judge, right up until he died. Everyone in town knew Jennifer was unanimously voted Queen, so everyone knew my father didn't vote for me. But I'd heard him even before the court was announced telling Mom the other judges were idiots. *Can you believe it, Martha? They actually voted for Darcie.* He hadn't voted for me in the preliminaries. I was on the court despite him."

She shook her head. "I never would have entered if it were solely a beauty contest, because who can hold a candle to Jennifer? But it did hurt that my own father didn't think I could represent our town."

"Your father was an ass."

He said it with such calm certainty that it took Darcie an extra beat to recognize what he'd said, then she laughed. "You know, he really was."

She found herself telling him about Gordon's beloved collections that turned out to be mostly unwise purchases, and about the debts he'd left, and even a little of how she thought she might have had her eyes closed to how much her mother had blossomed since she'd become a widow.

By the end, she had her shoulder propped against the back of the counter, facing him, her knees drawn up, one nudging his thigh.

When she was quiet, Anton Zeekowsky astonished her by saying. "You stayed in Drago to prove you weren't what your father thought."

She looked into his dark, shadowed eyes.

"I think you're right, at least partly, Zeke."

He licked his lips, and spoke again. "I wasn't what my father thought I was, either."

She waited, her heart hammering with a kind of joy that he would talk to her and anxiety at the pain she heard in his voice.

"You said this town respected my father, but you were wrong, Darcie. Not everyone respected him." He looked away then, around the room, as if he could see it as it had been. "I used to help out here. Unloading supplies, doing cleanup, inventory—all that I didn't mind. But I hated waiting on customers." His mouth twisted. "That problem I have with people again. My father knew how I felt, so he mostly let me stay in back.

"But this one Saturday in November when I was a freshman, we were about to close when the bell over the front door rang telling us someone had come. I heard the voices, I knew who they were and I grabbed the garbage like it needed taking out right that instant and headed for the alley. He called my name to come take care of the customers and I ignored him. So he went out front.

"I heard them, Darcie, I heard them. Drunk and loud and full of themselves. I knew they were giving him a hard time, laughing at him, mocking him. He offered no resistance and I did nothing.

"I was ashamed. Of myself for being the coward who stayed in the alley. Who didn't rush in to protect his father. To fight for him. And I was ashamed of him. For not standing up to them. For being the strange man in town who they felt they could do that to."

She touched her fingertips to his fisted hand. His hand jerked. Her fingers slid to his leg. She left it there, feeling the tension in him, but also the strength and warmth.

"When I came in, he was straightening out the counter—they'd shoved everything on the floor. And the cash drawer was open. I could see money was missing. I said we had to call the cops, get them arrested. He just shook his head and said they must have needed the money more than we did.

"But I knew that wasn't true, because I knew who they were—Ted Warinke, Mark Truesdale and Eric Stenner. I realized that's why he didn't report them—not because they needed the money, but because their families had money. Because they were important—the school's two senior jocks and the budding jock.

"And that's when I knew what Drago was really like. That's when I knew that being that good and kind and generous man you keep talking about my father being wasn't enough in a place like this."

"Zeke, the actions that day of three drunk high school boys doesn't define a town, not any more than your actions that day define you. You have to forget that. And you have to forgive yourself."

His silence was as deep and unreadable as the shadows around them.

He'd closed off, shut down. Shut her out.

"I'm going, Zeke," she said quietly, pulling her stretched out legs under her and rising.

"Darcie."

She stood, waiting. Twice over, she decided he would say nothing more and she should leave him to his brooding alone, when he spoke.

"I thought about you, Darcie."

"What?"

"I thought you should know that. I didn't want you to think…I thought about you a lot. And it meant a lot to me…making love. Our first time."

Darcie's muscles jumped. Her right heel skidded on the worn flooring, and she sat down again, hard.

"I used to wake up," he said, "and know I'd dreamt about you again. I could still smell you. It was like the scent and taste of you were inside a box, and I could keep it locked when I was awake, but when I slept it came free."

He faced her in the gloom and she could see his desire so clearly. "I still dream of you."

Now she knew. Why she'd pushed him away with that ultimatum. Why she hadn't listened to Jennifer's certainty that Zeke had fallen for her. Why she'd been afraid.

Because this was real. Because this was not fantasy or safe or temporary. She wasn't a dreamy-eyed girl and Zeke wasn't leaving first thing in the morning.

That long ago night, she had made love with Zeke for their past together, and to have that one moment between them forever. She'd known there had been no chance for a future for them, and that's why it had been a chance she could take.

Making love with him now would be different. It would be about the present and, even more, about the future, that shining place Zeke was always speeding toward. Except the future for her could include a splintered heart that might never recover. Because, really, what were the chances things would work out between them?

She was a realist, she saw the problems. Not one of them had gone away since he'd arrived nearly three weeks ago.

But then—and even with that splintered heart—for the rest of her future, she would have this.

She would have loved Zeke, really loved him. And been loved by him.

She couldn't pass up the opportunity to fulfill that dream.

She kissed him.

Kiss. Such a simple, short word for something that encompassed past, present and future. That brought a man and a women together in one sensation. That expressed sweet tenderness and knife-edged need.

He tugged at her bottom lip, sucking it slowly.

Melting. She was melting. From the inside out. Until she had nothing holding her together except Zeke's touch.

He pulled back, enough to part their lips, then returned with a swift pressing of his lips against hers, his tongue touching her teeth.

She moaned, and with a deep-throated rumble, he followed the sound deeper inside her. The sensations of that touch and the sensations of the sounds he made and she made bolted through her.

Her hands found a sliver of space between them, barely enough to begin working on the buttons that kept his skin from hers.

"Darcie, wait."

Instead of being wrapped around her, drawing her closer, his arms held her away from him. His large hands cupped her shoulders, his elbows locked.

As if he had to fight her off. Holding her at bay.

She tried to scrabble back, but his grip didn't loosen.

"Darcie."

"I know, Zeke. I know. It's not... It's okay. Really. I won't... It's okay."

She brought her arms up sharp under his, breaking his hold.

"What are you doing? This isn't—"

"I know it isn't. You don't have to worry. I know. I really do." She was on her feet. "I have to go. Lots to do. The parade this afternoon and everything. All this—we'll forget about all this."

Zeke came half up to his knees, his eyes intent on her face.

Then he collapsed back against the counter wall with what almost sounded like a groan.

She said, "Goodbye, Zeke." But he might not have heard. She was moving pretty fast by then.

Zeke knocked on Darcie's door for a third time, loud enough to rouse a dog two yards over, who joined the extended hammering with a chorus of barks.

"Darcie, I'm not going away."

She was in there. Not only was her car in the driveway, but there were lights on in the apartment.

The door swung open. "Zeke?" she asked, as if she didn't know. "What are you doing here? What's wrong?"

"Nothing's wrong, except you wouldn't answer the door."

He walked past her, brushing against her hip in the narrow passageway. He caught a flash of vulnerability in her face before she resumed an expression of confused puzzlement.

"I was in the bathroom. Washing my face. I must not have heard you over the water."

Her face was damp, so maybe she had been washing her face. Her eyes were also red. Darcie crying. He hadn't known that just the thought of it could twist his gut like this.

"What's wrong?" she demanded again.

He came back to her, taking her face in his hands. "I won't have you crying over me, Darcie."

"I don't know what you're talking about."

"You think I don't want you? That was it, wasn't it? That's why you took off like a scalded rabbit from my father's shop."

"A scalded rabbit? I did not."

"Dammit, Darcie, shut up."

She gawked at him.

"I'm not the best with words and I'll never get it out right with you taking things the wrong way and rushing in trying to make it so I won't say what you don't want to hear."

Her eyes got big, but her chin went rock hard. "Fine. I won't stop you from saying whatever it is you want to say."

Even if it killed her. That was the subtext of that little speech.

"Do you know where I've been since you—" he wasn't going to refer to a scalded rabbit again, he was not self-destructive "—left?"

Her lips parted then she clamped them shut. She shook her head.

"I closed up the shop and I drove to Ma's. From the minute you walked out the door, I was coming after you, but I needed to tell Ma. To apologize for worrying her. And to let her know I wouldn't be back until later. Because this time we're going to be in a bed, Darcie. I was not going to make love to you on a deserted, dusty shop floor. A bed, Darcie. A bed and room and time and patience."

She swallowed, but said nothing.

"But not too much patience," he added, closing the space between them.

Her head tilted back to keep their gazes locked.

"Zeke."

That was it. Just his name. And patience was gone.

His hand cupped the back of her head as he kissed her hard, his other arm behind her waist providing support, enclosure. She wrapped her arms around him, holding on, too.

He was moving them as if he knew exactly where he was headed. Her bed, she realized, her slight surprise that he had known the direction swamped by her satisfaction at arriving at that destination.

He caught the hem of her sweater, pulling it up. Arms over her head, she watched him watching her, absorbing the intensity of his focus so deeply into her bones that she felt she would never be completely cold again.

She renewed her earlier assault on his shirt's buttons. She opened it, stroking her hands down his chest. He flung the shirt up and away. She had already started on the closure of his jeans. He yanked something from his pocket, reaching around her toward the nightstand, then his arms crossed hers as he unhooked and unzipped her jeans while she worked on his.

Faster. She wanted this faster. Taking off her own clothes and letting him strip his would certainly be more efficient. But the sacrifice of her hands on him, his hands on her, was far too much to ask. Then jeans and underwear were gone, leaving him naked and her covered only by the length of her T-shirt.

He caught her to him tight, drawing her up on her toes to press more fully against him, the slide of cotton between his body and hers, transferring heat and glide.

He dropped back to the bed, carrying her, surprising a gust of laughter from her that turned to a moan as he aligned their bodies so she straddled him just above where she most wanted to be.

"This has to go." He pulled her T-shirt up.

His mouth narrowed in concentration as he watched her hair release from the enclosure of the T-shirt's neckline. He discarded the shirt, his concentration becoming a smile that heated with even more desire as he smoothed her hair back, then continued the motion to cup her head once more and draw her to him for a kiss that both promised and fulfilled.

He released her only to reach to the nightstand for one of the condom packets he'd dropped there.

As much as she regretted the tiny separation that maneuver required, she enjoyed this moment as well. It gave her a chance to see him. See what she hadn't seen that first night—

had been too inexperienced to know, to look for, to understand. She stroked her hands across his pecs, down the valley at the center of his muscled rib cage and lower.

Sitting back, she slid down first one strap of her bra—not teasing, but not fast—then the other.

He sat up, his gaze on her mouth, his hands behind her, unhooking with deft, talented fingers.

He drew that last scrap of material off her, skimming his fingertips over her flesh. Then he bent his head and kissed the underside of first one breast then the other. Soft, warm kisses as he drew in slow, full breaths. She shuddered with the sensation, deep and shattering.

"Zeke. Please."

He looked into her eyes as his hands guided her, and brought her down on him. She felt the push, hot and hard and slow. But his hands on her hips only steadied, leaving the pace to her.

And then he was inside her.

He went still.

"Zeke, if you don't move, *now,* I'll...I'll do something."

One side of his mouth twitched, his eyes glinted. "Something with handcuffs?"

"Ahh!" Cry, laugh, groan—all together, it twisted her as she reached for him.

Laughing and moaning with her, he flipped them, holding his weight off her, yet thrusting deep and fast. She met that stroke. And the next. Matched him.

She pushed at his locked elbow, the one holding him safely off her.

"Darcie—"

She knocked it again, and all of him came against her, the friction and weight so exquisite she felt tears burn the corners of her eyes even as she smiled.

"No more patience, Zeke. No more."

Together they raced, pushing each other.

She cried out his name, quaking and shuddering as he went taut, then convulsed and collapsed, shifting his torso at the last moment to one side, but wrapping his arms around her, taking her with him.

Zeke strode into her kitchen stark naked and aroused. Darcie swallowed so hard she almost choked on the mouthful of water she'd just taken in.

"Where'd you go?" he growled.

She'd left her bed minutes ago, pulling on her running shorts and top.

"You were sleeping, and I didn't want to wake you. I left a note." Along with a mug of coffee, which he now put on the counter beside her. Something was different about it, but her peripheral vision hadn't pinned down what before it was out of sight. "I'm going to take a run, then I need to get to work. I'm on duty during the parade."

He growled again, then stunned her by grabbing her hips and lifting her to sit on the counter. She dropped the running shoes she'd planned to put on outside so she wouldn't wake him. He was definitely awake.

By instinct she grabbed his shoulders for balance. He took that opening to move in closer, nudging her knees apart and stepped between them.

"Zeke, what are you doing?"

He stroked his tongue into her mouth, deep and hot, an answer both eloquent and blatant. Then he skimmed his mouth over her jaw and down her throat.

He drew the scoop neck of her running tank lower, lower, stretching it down until her breasts held it in place, revealing the utilitarian fabric of her running bra. Then he started sliding that down.

"Zeke!"

She had no breath for more. Because with the tank and bra now bunched to the sides and beneath her breasts, acting like the best push-up bra ever, he had his mouth on one nipple and his thumb tormenting the other. She dug her fingers into his shoulders. Closer to climax faster than she had ever been before. With no way to stop it, or control it. All she had to do was let go, just let go.

He lifted his head, just an inch, only for a moment as he switched to stroke his tongue over the other nipple. But it gave her a breath, a chance to try to hold onto some shred in the midst of this man tornado.

"Okay, Zeke. I know what you're doing—you're melting my self-control. I'll rephrase—"

He looked up. "Really? Melting your self-control?"

How could he look like that—boy-genius-on-the-verge-of-discovery delight mixed with an entirely male satisfaction that had nothing to do with boys or genius?

Oh. Yes.

"Darcie, I want you to listen to something."

"Yes." Yes, to anything.

"It's important you know that your father was a complete idiot. Nobody could represent Drago better. Every resident of this town should be grateful to have you. And you are beautiful. A beauty so deep—"

"I can't believe this. You're saying this now? While I'm sitting half-naked on my kitchen counter?"

"You're right. I can't believe you're half-naked, either."

Zeke slid his big hands down her back, under the elastic of her loose running shorts and her briefs, then over the rounds of her buttocks. The fabric followed. He lifted her up, pulled at the clothes, tipped her back, and before she could suck in a breath, he'd stepped back to strip shorts and briefs off her legs, then came back between them, sliding her toward him at the same time, so they met, the tip of his penis probing at her.

"Zeke. Oh— Wait."

"I know. I know. Hold this." She heard the clank of the coffee cup on the counter, then felt a damp foil packet in her hand. He'd ripped it open and was putting on the condom before she connected the dots of her senses to realize he must have used the nearly drained coffee cup to hold the condom packets. "No pockets," he mumbled, confirming her supposition.

Then he wrapped one arm around her back, while his other hand guided himself into her. She slid off the edge of the counter and over the edge of reason, with only Zeke to hold on to.

When Zeke got home after lunch, Ma greeted him with a big smile and the news that "the boys" were in his bedroom, as if he were nine and some playmates had come over to see him.

Larry sat at Zeke's desk, working on the laptop, with Warren looking over his shoulder and practically drooling.

The third "boy" was on the bed, his back against the headboard and his legs stretched out, with no shoes. So either Peter Quincy, who was as good at reading people as Darcie, had taken Ma's measure or she'd already scolded him.

"When did you get in, Quince?"

"An hour ago or so."

"Would it be rude to ask what you're doing here?"

"Sure, but that's never stopped you before. Brenda sent me to check things out after that attempt on the laptop and with you issuing peculiar orders right and left." His bemused gaze went to Larry and Warren, then returned to Zeke. There was concern in his eyes. "So I'm delivering some news in person and checking how things are going here."

"You've got news for me?"

"Yeah, but first, how're you doing, Zeke?"

"Fine. Just fine." He touched the side of his neck, where Darcie had nipped at his skin. "Never better."

Quince's gaze had followed the gesture, and his eyes crinkled in a grin. "Well, I'll be damned."

"Probably," Zeke mumbled. "Now, what's the news?"

"The news is what you wanted." He leaned over the narrow space between the bed and the closet door and pulled an envelope out of his suit coat hanging on the knob. "There's a cover letter to you, then the one you asked for."

Zeke looked at the official seal on the envelope and grinned. "Thanks, Quince."

"You're welcome. Now, about this project you've got Larry on…"

"Yeah," Zeke said, turning to the man at the desk, "what'd Everett say about the projections we worked up, Larry?"

"He says no."

"No? Did you variable in the previous four years' weather?"

"Yeah. But he said beets still weren't the right choice for that field this year."

"I don't get it. I was sure we had it."

"Well, duh," Warren said. When Zeke and Larry turned to him he added in a world-weary tone, "You have to variable in the human factor for the software interface."

"Out of the mouths of babes," murmured Quince.

Zeke had learned enough about the human factor these past weeks to know Warren was aching to show off. "Right. Like you've figured out a way to do that?"

"Yeah. I have."

"How?" He might as well have said *prove it.*

"My mom griped about women at her salon not liking the color their hair turned out—they'd say it wasn't what they expected when she showed them the sample. So I set up a program to fill in variables like any dye or perm they'd had, how long ago and junk like that. Then I scanned in color samples and wrote a program. Mom snips a sample of their hair, fills in variables, picks a couple of dye colors, runs the program and it prints out what color their hair will be. As long as she doesn't mess up the calibration."

"I'd like to see that program," Larry said with professional interest.

"We should buy it," Zeke said crisply.

Quince gave him an exasperated glare, before saying, "We *might* be interested in licensing the program, *if* it tests out to do what you say it does."

Warren rose to that bait with an explanation that had Larry getting more and more excited.

"Anton!" Ma called from the kitchen. "Almost it's time for you to leave for the parade."

Zeke's mind had returned to farming. "That's it. That's what we need to give Everett—the same principle as Warren's program." And just as Darcie had said about the handheld. "We have to give the farmers options. Give them tools to make their own decisions instead of trying to hand them answers. Warren, work with Larry on how you did that."

"Hey, your guy said you'd license my program. That means money and—"

"You're still working off your crime. So you'll work with Larry for free on crop selection. And we aren't licensing your program, not yet, anyway, because Quince here will try to get it at a bargain. I'll set you up with people to give you advice, and then you take it to auction. Just remember the top bidder isn't always the best deal."

"An auction, Zeke?" Quince protested. "We could've had that thing for pennies."

"Now, Anton," Ma said from the doorway of his bedroom, hands on hips. "You change into your suit. And you, there is cake in the kitchen. Come eat."

"Yeah," Zeke said, as the males scrambled to obey, "but I know his mother, Quince. Worse, my mother knows his mother."

"You look natural sitting on the back of a convertible."

Zeke twisted around to find Darcie, in uniform, standing beyond the back bumper in the parade staging area, otherwise known as the D-Shop parking lot.

"So, you made it to work on time."

"Barely."

He grinned. "Barely is what almost made you late for work."

She blushed.

He wanted her out of that uniform and somewhere comfortable—or hell, it didn't have to be that comfortable. The trunk lid would do.

"Don't even think about it." She held up a cop's stop-sign hand.

"Oh, I'm thinking about it."

"I'm on duty. I'm leaving."

They looked at each other across the trunk of the car.

"You better go, Darce. You better go now."

She looked at him for three more long seconds, then pivoted and left. Just before she went behind a van, she looked back.

"Have fun, Zeke."

He was crazy about the woman, and he'd give a hell of a lot to have had time after their lovemaking to talk out everything they needed to talk out. A lot of possibilities, a lot of changes.

He might have handed her the envelope Quince had brought right here and now. But there was no time.

It would have to wait.

The parade started with his car, driven by Kurt, the rookie, right behind Sarge in the leadoff patrol car. He saw Ma, with Quince, Larry and Warren. Also Warren's mother. Mrs. Richards. Josh Kincannon from the high school with three kids who appeared to be his. Everett Hooper with an attractive, unsmiling young woman. Jennifer and Martha Barrett with the dignitaries at the review stand beside the Dairy Queen. Mildred Magnus. Loris from the café. A blur of people, hands waving, faces smiling, voices calling his name. People he knew, some he remembered, those he recognized and strangers he guessed were out-of-towners. He surprised himself by hoping they spent generously while they were in Drago.

He spotted Darcie, saw her turn from a hard-eyed teenaged boy she was talking to, and their eyes met for one heated moment before the parade carried him away.

It went by so fast. Before he knew it, he and Sarge were spectators, too, watching the rest of the parade come across the finish line. Until the final float, the one with the queen and her court, drawing cheers all along. Cristina's smile appeared rather brittle and Traci still looked nervous, but they were there. Mandy and the others were radiant. Vital and excited and bright.

He watched with a strange pressure growing in his chest that he finally realized was probably pride. They were good kids, even Cristina in her way. It took backbone to show up today, to sit not in the queen's spot where everyone had expected, but in a lower position. To sit and smile and wave.

Bringing up the rear was a whirring fire truck letting loose with occasional blares to the delight of the kids.

Behind it, it seemed half the crowd followed, becoming part of the parade, walking down Main Street, greeting friends, shouting hellos.

Ma and Quince found him, standing on the curb, chatting with Sarge. Quince's surprise showed. Ma smiled and said it was time to get ready for the Lilac Ball, and for Quince to stop arguing, of course he was staying with them and not at that motel clear out by the interstate.

Quince could have his narrow boyhood bed, Zeke thought, because he had every intention of spending the night in Darcie's bed.

Chapter Eleven

Darcie had no doubt that the person who had originated the official schedule for the final day of the Drago Lilac Festival, a schedule now fixed in tradition, had been a man. No woman would plan a parade to end in late afternoon, with a ball to start only a few hours later.

So the queen and her court all had to repair the wear and tear on clothes, hair and complexion in short order.

A cop who'd been on duty had the same concerns about hair and complexion, but at least she got a change of wardrobe after her quick shower. On the other hand she had less time, because as a member of the festival committee, she had to be at the country club early.

Darcie put her hair up in a French twist. Dangling gold earrings added to the look. Then there was the dress. From a deep cinnamon red at the top, it blended lighter tones in ombré satin that swirled at the bottom of the bias cut skirt. Wide set straps set off the sweetheart neckline—and her bust.

Zeke would love it.

She was thinking exactly how much—and how—he would love it when Chief Harnett intercepted her just inside the side entry of the country club.

"I want to talk to you, Barrett—Darcie."

"Yes, sir."

"This is unofficial. That's why I wanted to talk to you off-duty."

The only response that came to mind was *yes, sir* but that didn't seem to be what he wanted to hear.

"Marty—your mother—doesn't know I'm doing this, and you're not to blame her. She wants nothing but your good. She won't consider marriage until we've lived together for a full year."

Darcie heard the words, she understood each of them separately—*your mother, marriage, lived together*—but they wouldn't come together in her mind to form a coherent whole.

"I told her I'm not Gordon Barrett," the chief went on. "But I can't really blame her. She'd be a fool not to test out what I'm really about before she commits to me, because she's a woman who won't back away once she's committed herself.

"Otherwise she would have left that man years before he died. Idiot never saw what Marty had to offer. He made her stop seeing it, too. I never met him, but your father was a first-class sonuvabitch. Sorry."

"That's okay," she said automatically.

Hard to argue with the truth.

While her brain still struggled to put together her mother and the chief, the concept of her father's sonuvabitchness was one she'd chewed on for some time.

Idiot never saw what Marty had to offer. He made her stop seeing it, too.

Even after Gordon Barrett was dead, his influence had lived on, with his daughter looking at Martha—*Marty*—through Gordon's eyes.

"Yes, well." The chief looked toward the ceiling light, then down at the patterned carpet. "I wanted you to know, because I'm not going to let Marty say no to dancing in public this time, and I didn't want you to be taken by surprise."

Oh, no, she wouldn't want to be taken by surprise. "You—you're dating my mother?"

He blushed.

As if this conversation weren't weird enough, Chief Dutch Harnett blushed. He also stood straight and looked her in the eyes. "Yes, we are. And I intend we'll be doing a lot more. I love her. And she loves me."

From his first glimpse of Darcie in that amazing dress, Zeke wanted to get her out of it.

They were both showing the effects of little sleep last night and their energetic morning.

He was mellowed, relaxed.

He couldn't wait until this Lilac Ball was over, yet he was enjoying himself. Especially dancing with Darcie. The movement of the dance and having her in his arms was exquisite torture. Having her smile up at him was perfect.

She was wired, wound up.

About the ball, the end of the festival, her mother's obvious romance with the chief, and how people were reacting to the fact that the Guest of Honor danced almost every dance with their Darcie.

Most of the women smiled at them, from Ma's beam to Martha Barrett's more gentle smile to Jennifer's delighted grin. The men's responses were more varied. Chief Harnett gave him a look that in another century might have ended with the question, "What are your intentions, young man?" Sarge grinned from ear to ear. Ted Warinke clapped him on the back and said, "The geek comes through!"

Zeke let Quince have two dances with Darcie. After the second, the two friends stood by the windows, watching Darcie try to avoid Sarge's big feet on the far side of the dance floor.

"She's terrific, Zeke," Quince said. "A real natural with people."

"Glad you approve. But you are not going to use her for any sort of publicity. Understand?"

"She would be terrific, especially— Okay, okay." Quince raised his hands in surrender. "At least she'll keep you busy enough so I won't have quite as many products to promote. That'll make me her biggest fan."

"Get in line."

The music stopped. Darcie exchanged a few words with Sarge, then turned toward Zeke. Before he could start across the dance floor, though, Josh Kincannon approached her. When the band struck up a song, Kincannon swept her into a dance.

"Let's make the announcements now, Quince," Zeke said.

"Kind of early, don't you think?"

"No."

Quince scanned the dance floor, then grinned. "Zeke, you do know that's not an issue, don't you."

"Yeah." He liked the high school principal. Liked him a lot. He just didn't like seeing him with his arms around Darcie. Come to think of it, he hadn't been that wild about seeing Quince with his arms around her.

"Okay. Announcement time it is."

Quince led the way around the edge of the dance floor

to the bandstand. Zeke saw Darcie tracking him, and his blood sped up.

After Quince had a word with the band, they segued into a flourish, then fell silent.

Quince stepped forward with his usual ease, introducing himself, apologizing for interrupting the dance. He gestured for Zeke.

Zeke usually hated moments like this, giving speeches or talking to groups. He looked at Darcie, her eyes wide with questions, but no doubts. Then to his mother, and on to other people he knew. Friends, he realized. He looked back to Darcie, and the words came.

"Most of you know I grew up here. A few of you know that that process continued just these past three weeks." That drew chuckles. "Part of growing up is learning to change my mind when I've made a bad decision first time around. Josh, I'm changing my mind. Zeke-Tech will fund the program you outlined to me in my mother's kitchen a couple weeks ago, the program to give more of Drago's students and citizens computer training and access."

A grin creased Kincannon's face as he stepped forward to shake Zeke's hand.

"Quince here will get you started with the details," Zeke told him, passing the delighted high school principal on to his friend.

That left Zeke free to concentrate on Darcie, whose whole being seemed to beam at him.

After an immediate hush, the audience was applauding and whooping.

"One more thing." Zeke's words quieted the crowd. He never took his eyes from Darcie. He reached out a hand to her, when she took it, he drew her to him at the same time he held out the envelope. "I also have something for Darcie—"

"A ring!" gasped a voice from the middle of the crowd.

He looked around. *A ring?* He'd never considered a ring. Would Darcie be disappointed he wasn't giving her a ring?

He couldn't see her expression because her gaze had dropped to the envelope he still held.

"What is it?" she demanded.

He breathed again. She was curious, not disappointed.

"It's an invitation to be interviewed by one of the assistant directors of the FBI and to take the entry test. That's a formality—you'll definitely pass. There'd be training at Quantico—that's not far from where I am—and there's a good chance you'd be assigned to the area afterward."

He opened the envelope and handed her the official letter. She looked down, apparently reading it word for word.

From absolute silence, murmurs rose from the crowd. Subtle at first, then a few loud enough to make out the words. "Don't go, Darcie!" "We need you here, Darcie!" "What's the FBI got that we don't?" A few people tried to quiet the discontented sentiments—he caught murmurs about wanting the best for Darcie after all she'd done for Drago—but the unrest grew.

And all the time, he had no idea what Darcie thought. He had no way to read her reaction…until a tear hit the left margin of the letter and bled into the type.

He felt as if he should be bleeding, too—it was that kind of pain.

"Why are you crying?"

"Because…." It wobbled and she swallowed before she continued. "Because you did this for me."

He waited, his heart pounding against his chest like an angry fist on a door. Whatever followed next would tell him a lot, maybe everything. If it started with *And,* it would be good news, right? If *But* was the next word from her, though, then…he didn't know what then.

She didn't say *And,* she didn't say *But.* She pivoted away from him and sprinted along the edge of the room to the doors, disappearing before he thought to move.

The next thing he knew, his mother had his arm in a death grip, dragging him down so she could say directly in his ear.

"Go after her, Anton. Do not let our Darcie go away."

He found her trying to fit her key into her car door.

"I wasn't going to drive," she told him between gulps of sobs. "It's dangerous to drive when you're—" another sob hit her "—crying."

"I'll drive. Anywhere you want to go."

"Home."

At her apartment, he kept one arm around her as they climbed the stairs, then he led her to the couch, where he pulled her against his chest.

After a while, he took her shoulders and held her back from him until their eyes met. "You've got to tell me why you're crying, Darcie."

"Because you were thinking I'd be in Quantico and that's close to where you live." She pulled in a breath. Her chin wobbled. "Because I can't take this, Zeke. The FBI was a dream, the dream of a girl I no longer am."

She opened her hand and the crushed letter dropped onto her lap. Neither of them touched it.

"You've got to know you can do this. You'll be great in the FBI, you'd—"

"I already am great—at what I want to be doing, and where I want to be doing it. I'm sorry, Zeke. I've spent a long time being a coward and dishonest with myself—blaming circumstances and life and my mother for choices that I made. Hedging my bets, so anything that didn't turn out, any disappointments, I could say, Hey, it's not my fault. I wanted to leave and I'm only here because of—fill in the blank. And I misled you, letting you believe that's how it was, too. Because it's not true. I made the choices. I've stayed because I want to. Because this is the life I want, and this is where I want to live it. I love this town."

"Darcie—"

"I know, Zeke, I know." Her tears dripped down her cheeks, off her jaw. His arms tightened around her. "I know you wanted to give me a wonderful gift, but it's the one thing I don't want—a ticket out of Drago."

"We could be together in Virginia. We could make a life…"

She cried harder. His words stopped.

Because Zeke had given her so much. He'd helped her find her answers. He'd helped her know where she belonged. He'd even helped her town—their town—despite his very best efforts to resist it. And now she couldn't take the one thing he wanted to give her.

He held her for a long time, her head tucked under his chin, his hands stroking and soothing. Her crying ending, but still they sat like that.

"Do you want me to leave, Darcie?"

"No." She took his hand, stood and led him to her bed. "I love you, Zeke."

"Darcie." He closed his eyes, pain and pleasure drawing his face. "You know nothing has changed…"

He was telling her that loving him, that making love with him now would not keep him here. Because he couldn't give her the one thing she did want. Him, without the past constantly driving him.

Sixteen years ago, she had taken a chance because she thought it would be her only opportunity to love Zeke. Now she took a chance because she feared it would be her last opportunity to be loved by Zeke. Because he was wrong when he said nothing had changed—everything had changed.

"I don't want you to leave."

* * *

"Please stay, Zeke."

He straightened slowly, completely dressed except for his jacket. "I can't. I don't belong here."

She pulled the sheet up. She wouldn't get out of her bed—their bed—she wouldn't try to keep him that way. But she wouldn't let him leave without trying.

"Because you're afraid that if you stayed you would become your father. That's what you've always been afraid of. That's why you left."

He spun around to her. "What the hell are you talking about? I loved him. If I could be half the man..." He swallowed hard.

"Of course you loved him. That's part of why you are who you are, and why you've done what you've done. But you can love your father so much you're afraid you'll let the love make you give up who you are and just be a shadow version of an original. So you fight it—both the wanting to please him and the love. You fight so hard you go in the opposite direction.

"You don't think I've read the articles? All the interviews? All the profiles? Do you know how many of them mention your father? Quote you talking about your father? All of them Zeke. Every last one of them."

"He was a great man."

"Yes, He was. But not because of his mind. He was great because of his heart. You keep thinking he was a failure because—"

"I do not."

"The hell you don't! You've always thought he was a failure because he sacrificed the acclaim and intellectual status you thought he deserved. You took on that guilt and you determined to achieve success for him. You know in all those articles, all those articles where you talk about your father, you never once talk about the success of your company. Never talk about what you've achieved financially—"

"That's Quince and Vanessa's doing. Not mine."

She nodded. "That's right. Because you don't care about that kind of success. Only about achieving, creating intellectually—the way your father could have if he and your mom hadn't left that behind and emigrated here. For you."

The final two words were hammer blows. She could see that. But a hammer, a sledgehammer, was the only way to get through to him.

"But you've got it wrong, Zeke. Your father achieved great things. He created a loving marriage, a home, a family. He created a respected position in his community, where he was looked to for common sense and uncommon kindness. Those are goals for you aspire to. Those are accomplishments that would make your father proud of you. They would make him happy."

Silence held the moment. A thin band of hope squeezed around her heart, making it hard to breathe.

Then he bent and picked up his suit coat from the floor. He didn't look at her.

She bit her lower lip between her teeth to keep from crying out. She wouldn't do that. No even when he reached the door.

He stilled, his hand on the knob, and looked back.

"I do love you, Darcie."

"You let him go?"

Darcie didn't turn as Jennifer came to sit beside her on the stone bench with the best view of the fountain and Coronation Garden.

"No one lets Zeke do anything."

Darcie had successfully avoided everyone this long Sunday by locking her apartment door and turning off her phones.

When her mother knocked on her door for a third time, saying, "Just let me know you're okay," she'd called out in a rusty voice, "I'm okay. I need some time alone."

As sunset neared, though, she'd found herself restless, yet too fatigued to go for a run. She'd driven to the park, nearly empty now as a spring afternoon gave way to a blustery evening that bowed tulips on their stems and rocked the lilacs.

"Here," Jennifer said, wrapping a fleece blanket around her shoulders. "Why didn't you go with him? He did everything he could to show you he wanted you to go with him. I know you love him, Darcie."

"I think I've loved him since I was sixteen years old and looked across a Bunsen burner into those eyes for the first time."

"You could go after him."

She shook her head. "It's always been me going after Zeke. Dragging him out of his isolation when we were kids, dragging him into social situations, dragging him back here for the festival. While he was here, too. Going after him for his mother or for the town or for myself... Not this time. It wouldn't—" she sucked in a breath to keep from sobbing "—work."

"But you love him, and he loves you. Real love." She said it with an anguish that reminded Darcie that Jennifer carried the scars of something else masquerading as love. "Why—?"

"*Because* I love him. Because he won't be happy until he figures out what he really wants. If I went back there with him, he still wouldn't know, and I'd be there, all mixed in with his not knowing, and then I'd be part of his unhappiness. That would be worst of all."

Jennifer studied her. "But you know, don't you, Darcie? You know what you want."

"Yes, I do." She smiled, despite the pain. "I'm glad, even though I know I'm not going to get it. Not all of it."

Jennifer put her arms around Darcie's shoulders. "If anybody does get it all, it'll be you, Darcie. It just has to be."

Monday morning, Chief Dutch Harnett strode up to Darcie's car as she emerged from it in the parking lot behind Village Hall.

"You're not on duty yet. I want to talk to you. Unofficially."

She wasn't sure she could take the shock of another unofficial talk with the chief. "Sir?"

"I hear Zeke's left town."

"Yes, sir, he has."

"That's, uh, permanent?"

"Yes. But I want to assure you that the interview with the FBI— I'm not resigning, Chief."

"I'm sorry."

She froze. He was sorry she wasn't resigning? She knew they'd never been the best of buddies, but he wanted to get rid of her?

A welling of something sharp clawed at her throat. Chief Harnett swore. And Darcie realized a tear had escaped. A few weeks ago she would have been mortified. Right now, in the hierarchy of things, it was nothing.

"Maybe you better take the day off, Darcie. You worked a lot of overtime during the winter and—"

"If it's all right, sir, I'd rather work. Only… You want me to leave?"

"Leave? Who the hell said anything about— Oh. Damn. I didn't— No, I don't want you to leave. I consider you a fine officer. If I've been hard on you, it's because I see what you're capable of. And—" he rubbed a hand over his jaw "—if I'm honest, probably because I didn't want anybody thinking I favored you when it came out about me and your mother."

His erect stance went even straighter. "When I said sorry,

I meant about you and Zeke. And I am. For the two of you, and selfishly, too. I hoped you'd get together and then Marty would be satisfied you were settled enough that she'd move in with me."

Darcie rocked back on her heels, then took one step backward. Before she got back in her car, though, she did get out a couple sentences.

"If you'll excuse me, Chief, I'm going to take you up on that day off after all. I need to talk to somebody."

Her mother was hanging up the phone as Darcie walked in the kitchen.

"That was Dutch—the chief," she said, looking at Darcie warily.

Darcie nodded as she took a chair at the table and gestured her mother to another. "Mom, come sit down. I have an apology to make to you."

Her mother paused, her blue eyes wide. "To me?"

"Yes. I worked all this out in my head recently, but I never said it to you. And you're the one person who needs to hear it. I was using you as an excuse for coming back to Drago. Not taking responsibility for my own decisions. I could have left a long time ago. You don't need my rent and you don't need me to keep the place going. You do fine on your own."

Martha sat down, hard, with none of her usual grace.

"Oh, Darcie." She gulped in air. Her words came out trembling between a laugh and a sob. "I do need you, but not… Oh, God. You stayed because you thought I needed your help?"

"Yeah, initially. Or you would have lost the house."

"*I* would have lost the house? I only wanted the damned thing to give you a sense of security. I tried to protect you, to keep you from finding out those collections of Gordon's were worthless, but I couldn't stop you, I just couldn't stop you."

Darcie opened, then closed her mouth. Her brain was too busy chewing over *the damned thing* to produce words.

Her own words to Zeke about his gifts to his mother sounded in her ears as if the Fates were laughing at her.

This isn't about what you need to give, it's what she needs to get.

She'd been lecturing him, but she'd made the same mistake—only on a much more grandiose scale. What an idiot!

"Oh, God," her mother repeated, sobbing. "Dutch says I need to learn to say what I'm thinking, what I'm feeling, and he's so right. I've kept you chained here because I didn't have the courage—"

"No! Mom, that's what I'm saying. Yeah, I came back and lived here so we could pay off the house. But these past years it wasn't because of the house or because you—" Better not to spell out her earlier views on her mother's lack of competence when she was trying to apologize. "I stayed because I made that decision. Because I wanted to stay. For a long time I wasn't grown up enough to admit that. I blamed you instead of taking responsibility for my decisions. I apologize for that."

Her mother smiled, and gulped in a sob. "You have nothing to apologize to me for, Darcie. There are so many things I wish I'd— No." She shook her head. "No. We're not going to do that. We're going to look ahead. We each did the best we could at the time. I thank God our best is better now than it was."

"Amen!" Darcie said with irreverent enthusiasm.

Her mother giggled. Then they were both laughing.

Ribs aching from laughter and cheeks stained from tears, they finally came up for air.

"Darcie, I know the timing on this is awful, what with Zeke…"

The last bubble of laughter in Darcie's lungs evaporated like a drop of water on a skillet "He's gone, and he's going to stay gone, Mom. I can't live my life waiting for that to change." Or waiting for the hurting to stop.

She had a feeling she'd waste a lot of time if she waited for that.

Her mother laid her hand over Darcie's on the table. "I don't know how I came to have such a strong and courageous woman for a daughter, but I am so grateful I have you, Darcie Ann." She straightened and hesitated before she continued. "So, what would you think if we sold the house? Because I want to move in with Dutch."

The box had fallen apart. The box he'd told Darcie about where he kept memories of her. Splintered, shattered, turned to dust. *Poof.*

He'd accepted the box might need to be larger—a lot larger—after these weeks with her, after making love with her again and again. But he'd thought he could contain them. Eventually.

It used to be they were neatly contained during his waking hours, spilling out only in the weakness of dreams. He'd thought he could return to that when he left Drago. He'd thought that not getting much sleep would mean he'd be free from Darcie.

Except the box had fallen apart and now those memories and thoughts and feelings haunted him all the time.

There were the insidious Drago thoughts. Catching a weather map on TV and knowing Mrs. Richards should be warm enough. Hearing a reference to soybean futures and wondering how Everett's niece-in-law was doing with the farm. Seeing a prototype for a game and thinking Warren would like it.

But those weren't nearly as powerful as the other moments. A glint of sun on brown hair, the echo of a laugh that almost sounded like her. For God's sake, last night he'd seen a cop car and he'd had to pull into a parking lot and sit there, waiting for the wash of reaction to ease until he could finish driving to a dark house that seemed utterly unfamiliar.

Darcie could have been here with him, if she'd wanted. It wasn't him running away. It was her refusing to leave.

"Zeke." Brenda was at his office door.

He snapped, "Knock, dammit," without looking up.

"You'd tell me to stay out. Again."

He growled. "I'm working on something."

"You're working on bringing your company down."

He slowly raised his head. Vanessa, Quince and Brenda stood shoulder to shoulder in front of his desk.

"Ever since you came back from Illinois," said Vanessa, "you've been possessed. It can't go on like this."

"I'm okay."

"You haven't left this complex in a week, Zeke," she said.

"Bull. I drove home last night. I saw a— I drove home last night."

"That was last week."

Zeke started to scoff, then his gaze connected with Brenda's grim expression. "Five days ago," she said.

"You're looking worse and worse, you blew off the board meeting last week, you've got Wall Street nervous, you're not producing anything," Vanessa said, with the assurance she always spoke with when citing facts, "and you're driving everyone crazy."

Brenda leaned forward. "Here are today's resignations." She slapped papers on Zeke's desk facing him so he could read them. The top one said, "I resign, effective immediately," signed by the VP for Development. "That brings the total to thirty-seven, Zeke."

"Who needs them?"

Holding his gaze, Brenda added another sheet to the pile. "And mine."

"What? You can't—"

"I can. I do. I quit."

"You ungrateful—"

"Ungrateful, my ass. I have worked ten times harder for you than you noticed. And five times more than you pay me for. I haven't minded because of the break you gave me at the start. And because you were a good guy at heart. Good, but lost. Now you're only lost. I am not going to sit outside that door and watch you tear your company, your life and yourself apart."

She had tears in her eyes. Brenda Truman had tears in her eyes. The shock reached right through his fog and grabbed him around the throat.

"This has got to stop," Vanessa said, "for the sake of Zeke-Tech. If you don't stop it, I will take over the company, Zeke, and force you out. I'd hate to see you lose your company, but I'd hate even more to see you kill it."

Zeke looked from her to Brenda, and finally to Quince. His college roommate. His oldest friend.

Except for a girl from chem lab, now a cop in Drago, Illinois, who wasn't willing to leave her hometown for him.

"Quince?"

"You're like a brother, Zeke. If you need to crash on my couch indefinitely, get drunk, talk, I'm there. But I won't see Zeke-Tech go down. If you don't snap out of this as far as the company's concerned, I'll back Vanessa's takeover. If it doesn't succeed, my resignation will be in that pile."

Vanessa didn't give Zeke time to respond. "The news conference for Z-Zap that you've had Quince postpone four times is the day after tomorrow, Zeke. You will go home, get some decent food, sleep for twenty-four hours, shower and shave and return for a meeting of all employees at which you will assure them that Werewolf Zeke is gone for good. Then you will go home for more decent food and regular sleep before putting on your slickest suit and you will wow them at the news conference. This is not negotiable. You have twenty minutes to leave this office."

She sounded cool and crisp and certain, but he saw her hand shake as she reached across the desk and touched his. "Take care of yourself and take care of this company, Zeke."

Then she turned and left.

Quince came around the desk and rested his hand on Zeke's shoulder. "We had to do this, buddy. You're in a tailspin. Another few days and you'd crash and burn. You want anything—anything—you call me."

Then Quince, too, left.

Brenda remained, looking him over. "I don't know all that happened out in Illinois, but I know enough to know you screwed up, Zeke. Now you're punishing yourself and everyone around you. I won't watch it any longer."

She pivoted, heading for the door.

"Brenda."

She stilled, but he didn't know how to start. Or was it that he didn't know how to stop. How to stop doing what he'd done all his life. Driving. Achieving. Pushing.

Living for two people's dreams, even when one had never asked him to do anything but live for his own dreams.

He created a loving marriage, a home, a family…. He was looked to for common sense and uncommon kindness. Those are goals for you aspire to. Those are accomplishments that would make your father proud of you.

"What, Zeke?" Brenda demanded.

He met her eyes and said the only thing that came to mind. "Please."

* * *

Zeke looked terrible.

That's all Darcie could think as she watched the business network's coverage of the release of Zeke-Tech's spam killer on the café TV usually tuned to sports or soap operas.

"Look at that Zeke," said Loris. "He puts the rest of them to shame."

"Bet that suit's Armani," added Mildred Magnus knowingly.

Darcie felt glances dart her way, but she kept her eyes on the screen.

Oh, he was dressed great, in a suit that slid across broad shoulders like a lover's hands. His face was as arresting as ever. But his eyes were…gone.

Except nobody but her seemed to see it.

Everyone in Drago was thrilled at their hometown boy doing it again, especially with the stock recovering just as everybody was getting nervous about its recent slide. It had jumped up yesterday, with analysts citing some hush-hush meeting at Zeke-Tech that they said had restored confidence in Zeke and his company. As if anyone with a brain would doubt Zeke.

But Darcie could only watch and ache. For him, and for herself.

He looked terrible. And miserable. It would break her heart if his time in Drago had done this to him permanently.

C'mon, Zeke. See the good side of people. Be curious about them. Solve the problem of who they are, and they'll be putty in your hands.

Just the way she was any time he touched her.

No. No more morose wallowing.

She concentrated on the screen—making herself focus on the bigger picture, watch the interplay, and not solely on Zeke's face.

You can do this, Zeke. You can do this.

* * *

What was the guy on the other side of the microphone grinning about?

Oh, yeah. Spam killer software. Zeke blinked, trying to remember how he'd come up with the idea. Thank God, Quince stepped in.

Who cared how he'd come up with it? He'd moved on to other problems.

After Quince, Vanessa and Brenda's ultimatum in his office, he'd gone home, eaten the balanced meals Brenda had had delivered and slept. The next morning, he'd read all the resignation letters, talked to each of those employees, then to the assembled staff.

Before Brenda sent him back home for more sleep, he'd managed to e-mail to his home account copies of what he'd been working on since he'd returned from Drago. The projects he'd been driving his staff nuts about.

And nuts was the operative word. As in—was he nuts?

Pure junk, he saw after a second night's sleep. No wonder they'd rebelled.

This morning, though, he'd awakened with a new idea. Two, actually.

One was to check on Larry's project to make the market work better for farmers around Drago. Interesting that Larry was the one employee who'd been perfectly happy these past weeks. Darcie would love that.

His smile and pleasure faded. Darcie wasn't here to share it with him. She'd made that decision.

Of course, decisions could be unmade.

Like his decision this morning to carefully study his second new idea, to think it through, to run it by Vanessa, Quince, Brenda and others.

Yeah, that decision definitely could be unmade. Because, dammit, when a move was right, it was right.

"...wraps up our presentation," Quince was saying. "We hope you—"

"Not quite yet, Quince," Zeke said, stepping to the microphones. "I want to tell you we'll be making another major announcement. In three days in my hometown of Drago, Illinois."

Zeke was back in town.

Even before Mrs. Richards flagged her down in front of the library at ten in the morning and breathlessly informed Darcie that Zeke had been seen, she had sensed him. Like a vibration traveling through the air and pounding against her nerves.

The vibration was so strong it threatened to knock her knees together as she stood at the front of the Community Center, keeping an eye on things outside as most of the citizens of Drago streamed inside.

Zeke was back. But he hadn't come to see her. He hadn't called. He hadn't even let her catch sight of him.

That had to be deliberate. Didn't it? There were only so many places to be in Drago and he hadn't been in any of the obvious ones. Because she'd looked.

Strictly within her regular duties.

Of course, she'd known he'd be back. Ever since he'd made that mysterious announcement at the end of his news conference—when he'd called Drago his hometown—the town had been buzzing with it.

Zeke-Tech had rented the Community Center to hold a news conference and the media had poured in. Soon, according to the schedule Chief Harnett had given the department this morning, Zeke would arrive at the back entrance and be escorted inside by the chief and other dignitaries. Darcie would remain at her assigned station out front and never see him.

So, before she'd come to the Community Center, Darcie had made a detour. The only sop to her pride was she hadn't slowed blatantly as she drove past Mrs. Z's house and saw an unfamiliar dark sedan with dark-tinted windows parked there. The kind of car driven by a man who didn't want anyone to see inside.

She had dared to look inside him anyway. That had driven him away.

So why was he back?"

"Darcie." Chief Harnett called on the radio. "Change of plans. They want me on stage, so I want you at the back of the room."

"But—"

"Benny's going to take your position."

"Yes, sir." She didn't know whether she wanted to laugh or cry.

The news conference started like most as far as Darcie could tell from her limited experience with news conferences.

The PR guy—Zeke's friend, Quince—said there would be two announcements, then he introduced Zeke. With a grin that twisted her insides, Zeke said, "I discovered some intriguing challenges when I was in Drago recently, and Zeke-Tech is going to take on those challenges. For one, we've working on helping farmers pinpoint their best markets."

Zeke scanned the audience. Darcie managed to both do her job of keeping an eye on the crowd and to not be picked up by that Zeekowsky radar by shifting discreetly behind cameras and other equipment set up by the media. Sometimes, as now, by standing behind a big person.

Someone from the audience said, "You don't usually reveal what you have in development for fear of a rival getting ahead of you. Why tell us this?"

"It's not fear of them getting ahead of us," Zeke said. "It's not wanting to be slowed down by them grabbing onto our coattails."

That drew a laugh, and Darcie felt her heart expand. *That's the way to win them, Zeke.*

"Besides, this time I'd like to challenge Zeke-Tech's competitors to also help farmers. We've got a lot of projects to tell you about—"

"Zeke," Quince warned from beside him.

"—Later," Zeke concluded, earning more chuckles. "In the meantime, there's something else I got interested in while I was here in Drago."

Darcie's breathing hitched for an irrational second, then smoothed as he continued.

"Zeke-Tech is going to bring out a new product we've licensed from a talented young man whom I'd like you all to meet, Warren Wellton."

With a flourish, he brought Warren on stage to applause from the Dragoites and surprise from the out-of-towners. Oh, yes, and one Drago native who also looked more than surprised. Ashley Stenner gaped at Warren as if he'd just been revealed as the prince who'd been masquerading as a pauper.

"It's a kid!" said the cameraman Darcie was standing behind.

Darcie moved from behind that cameraman to another. As she reached him, he sat down and she had to sidestep, then scrunch up to get behind a short skinny reporter from a Chicago radio station.

The media bombarded Warren and Zeke with questions. Darcie admired the way Quince took the pressure off them both, but especially Warren, with a comment or joke or rephrasing of the question, allowing them to come up with an answer. As the questioning went on, it almost seemed that Warren grew taller before her eyes. Amazing what self-esteem could do for posture.

Abruptly aware that she was as bent over as a troll, Darcie straightened.

At that moment the radio reporter asked a question. She was all for the First Amendment, but his timing stunk.

"The economy in this area is struggling. And while this licensing agreement will certainly help the boy's family, what about the rest of the area? Will this mean more jobs for Drago? Or is this—"

"Excuse me. Sorry to interrupt," Quince said pleasantly. "But that brings us to the second half of this news conference. So if you'll allow us to fill in some background, we'll answer your question in a moment."

At that instant, Zeke's roving gaze slammed into her.

Heat and cold hit Darcie simultaneously, like ice cubes amid a sauna. She wanted to sink behind the reporter. She wanted to run. She wanted to cry. She stood straight and looked back at Zeke.

"By way of background—" Quince started.

Without taking his eyes off her, Zeke stepped in front of his VP. "Screw background." Then, louder, he said, with no embellishments. "We're bringing a division of Zeke-Tech here to Drago. It'll mean more money coming in, more jobs for Drago—for my hometown. It's a start."

The last words were washed over by a gasp from the crowd.

Darcie still hadn't looked anywhere but at Zeke, but she didn't have to see to know that her fellow Dragoites' mouths had dropped open, and they were vainly trying to suck in oxygen to replace what had whooshed out of them at the shock of joy. She knew, because that's what she was doing.

Only her shock was wider, her joy deeper.

Anton Zeekowsky had truly claimed Drago as his hometown.

The corners of his mouth twitched, and she knew she must look like an idiot, but she didn't care, because the intensity in his eyes held her.

The crowd started to cheer, but Zeke talked over them—talked right to her. "I'm moving back to Drago, Darcie. I'm coming home."

"Oh, Zeke."

She wasn't sure if her mouth formed the words or if any sound came out, but she knew he received the message.

He tore the microphone off his lapel and strode past the town dignitaries and the Zeke-Tech representatives onstage, jogged down the steps and strode to the center aisle, heading straight for her.

Darcie saw hands reaching out to pat him on the back, touch his sleeve. She knew people had to be speaking to him, asking him questions, trying to get his attention, but the intense beam of intelligence and heart that was Zeke was trained solely on her.

She might burn up like tissue paper in a laser beam—but what a way to go.

He picked her up.

Right there in front of all of Drago and a good part of the business media, he picked her up. Scooped one arm under her knees and the other behind her back and picked her up like she was a skinny thing.

She put her arms around his neck and hung on.

"What the hell! That's a cop! Are you getting this?"

"Get the camera on this! Turn the camera! You're going to miss it!"

"Wait a minute! Zeke! Zeke! Turn this way! Over here!"

"What does this mean? Who is she? What's her name?"

At the main door, Zeke shifted her in order to grab the handle, giving the maneuver enough of his attention to avoid them getting whacked with the heavy door. Outside, he looked at her again and smiled.

"Welcome home, Zeke," she said, just before his mouth came down on hers.

Epilogue

The wedding had been beautiful.

Her mother and Mrs. Z had planned it with an attention to detail that would have done an invading army proud. Yet they had respected Darcie and Zeke's wishes to keep it modest. Best of all, they had stuck to the deadline, so they were married the first weekend of October.

The most difficult decision had been where to hold it. In the end, they had been married in the backyard of their home on a sparkling fall day.

Sure, the house was still being renovated, but that didn't bother them.

Where better to have the wedding than in the present Zeke gave her not long after he'd carried her out of the Community Center.

She'd been so out of it, clamped to his side as he drove the sedan with the dark-tinted windows—which were quite cozy with two people on this side of them—through the deserted streets of Drago that she hadn't even noticed where they were going until he pulled up in front of her childhood home.

"Oh, Zeke, I don't live here anymore. I have an apartment over on—"

"I know. We're here because I bought it."

He got out of the car and tugged her to follow him. She clambered out with her head spinning.

"You bought it!"

"For you." He kept her moving, around the car and onto the front walk. "When I found out it was for sale, I figured you and your mother must have hit a rough spot, so I had a lawyer contact Jennifer and offer top price. She didn't know who the buyer was. That way—"

"You *bought* it! *You* bought it?"

"You keep saying that, Darcie. Is something wrong?"

"Did you notice we've already moved out?"

His face cleared. "Oh, yeah. After I bought it, it took me a while to know what I wanted to do. Brenda—my assistant, Brenda—has it all arranged."

"All what arranged?"

"The people to come in to paint and clean and do anything else you want done before they move you and your mother back in. They should be here in an hour or so."

"I don't think so."

He checked his watch. "Yes, an hour."

"I meant about moving back in. Mom's moved in with Dutch and it's about time I have my own place, don't you think?"

"But…" His gaze never left her face. He wasn't looking off to the horizon, he was looking into her. So deep and so concentrated, she might just stop breathing. 'No."

"No?" Not a complicated word, but darned if she could

make sense of it or of the man standing in front of her—who most definitely was complicated.

"No, it's not time for you to find your own place. It's time for you to live with me. No— I mean here. I'm really moving back to Drago. It seems someone taught me that I *can* go home again. Especially since it turns out everything I need is here. And the only person I want."

How could she not kiss the man after that? But when they emerged from the kiss, which hadn't become more only because they were standing on the front sidewalk in broad daylight, she had to give him another chance.

"Zeke, Zeke, are you sure?"

"I better be, or my staff is going to shoot me for all the arrangements we've made in three days. Headquarters will stay in Virginia, but I asked who might be interested in moving to Drago and so many said *yes,* I'll have to turn some down. At least until we get up and running. Can you believe it? All those people want to bring their families to a small town surrounded by cornfields. Said they're looking for a simpler life."

"You're going to hire local people, too, aren't you? You're—"

He stopped her with another kiss. "Yes, we'll do local hiring. Quince is probably explaining that right now. Local hiring will increase once the training program we're starting takes hold. Internships, stuff like that. It's all set." He stared past her. "All set except one thing. A place to live—a home for us."

He looked at her, then returned his stare to the same spot.

She turned, and there sat her childhood home, solid and settled.

"Your apartment would make a great office, and I do already own the place," Zeke was saying. "We could do whatever you wanted to it. You made over Drago for me, I could make over your old house for you."

"Yeah? Don't think I didn't notice what you put first, Zeke—an office."

"That's because I know it best. Although, I admit," he added in that accuracy-is-vital voice, "you'd do most of the deciding about where to put things and paint and stuff like that. But I could help."

Her effort to be stern melted. "You've already helped Zeke. You came home to me."

In the end, he'd helped with the house, too. Primarily by telling her, whenever costs gave her a case of the nerves, to do it the way she really wanted to do it. He'd also insisted on planting several bushes of a lilac called Tinkerbelle, though she never could get a straight answer from him on why. In the meantime, her old apartment served as their home.

For the wedding, they'd halted work for two weeks, blocking off the unfinished kitchen but otherwise leaving it open to the wedding guests—more open than it used to be with several walls already knocked down. Mrs. Z and Martha Barrett draped fabric over unfinished surfaces, rented bistro tables and chairs for throughout the house and had candles everywhere.

Darcie's smooth dress had suited her perfectly. She hadn't even been tempted to try to find a dress that would make her matron of honor, Jennifer, look dumpy. Quince was Zeke's best man. The chief gave Darcie away. In a break with tradition, the mothers sat together, happily crying.

Darcie let out a contented sigh.

"What was that for?" asked Zeke. Since he sat behind her on their hotel room's window seat, his chest as her backrest and his arms crossed at her ribs, he had absorbed the motion of her sigh as if it had been his own.

"Bliss. About everything. The wedding, all our friends, getting to know your friends, our mothers and being here with you. Because, I admit it, you were right—Paris is a better place for a honeymoon than Drago."

Zeke laughed. It rumbled through her with a pleasure as intense in its own way as what they had brought each other an hour ago in the big bed behind them. "And here I was thinking we might as well have stayed in Drago, because who wants to leave the room?"

She turned in his arms and kissed him.

"Good point."

* * * * *

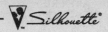

SPECIAL EDITION™

BABY BONDS

A new miniseries by
Karen Rose Smith coming this May

THE SERIES BEGINS WITH
CUSTODY FOR TWO

Shaye Bartholomew had always wanted a child,
and now she was guardian for her friend's
newborn. Then the infant's uncle showed up,
declaring Timmy belonged with him.

Could one adorable baby forge a
family bond between them?

*And don't miss
THE BABY TRAIL,
available in July.*

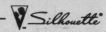

SPECIAL EDITION™

*Luke Tucker knew he
shouldn't get involved.*

"Mary J. Forbes is an author who really knows how
to tug on the heartstrings of her readers."
—*USA TODAY* bestselling author Susan Mallery

TWICE HER HUSBAND
by *Mary J. Forbes*

What he and Ginny Tucker Franklin had
shared was over, had been for ten years.
But when she returned to town, needing
his help, years fell away. All the loneliness of
the past decade vanished.

He wanted her as his wife again.

Available May 2006 wherever books are sold.

If you enjoyed what you just read,
then we've got an offer you can't resist!

Take 2 bestselling love stories FREE!

Plus get a FREE surprise gift!

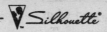

SPECIAL EDITION™

WHAT SHOULD HAVE BEEN

by *Helen R. Myers*

May 2006

A grave injury had erased Delta Force soldier Mead Regan's memory—until a chance encounter with first love Devan Anderson, now widowed and raising a daughter, brought everything back. Could they stake a new claim on life together, or would Mead's meddling mother make this a short-lived reunion?

Look for WHAT SHOULD HAVE BEEN wherever Silhouette Books are sold.

COMING NEXT MONTH

SSECNM0406